CHRISTINA

AN HOUR OF LOVE (

A NIGHT OF PASSION CAN BE BLISS . . .

BUT JUST TEN MINUTES WITH CHRISTINA
IS A LIFETIME OF HEAVEN ON EARTH . . .

Christina does all right for herself in the
sophisticated world of cosmopolitan wealth
and glamour—where her obvious talents and
accomplishments have always been so
enthusiastically received. But what happens
when you take the girl off of the private jet
plane and put her in the jungle? Tycoons and
titled millionaires are one thing—bandits,
rebels and hard-bitten ranchers something
else. Still, Christina is a woman who has
made love as lusciously in a broom closet as
in a luxury yacht. Surely a few flying bullets
and a few isolated mountains won't cramp
her style as long as they come with a few
rugged men. After all, isn't it meant to be
torrid in the tropics?

Also in Arrow by
Blakely St James

Christina's Challenge
Christina's Confessions
Christina's Need
Christina's Paradise

CHRISTINA'S PARADISE

Blakely St James

ARROW BOOKS

Arrow Books Limited
62-65 Chandos Place, London WC2N 4NW

An imprint of Century Hutchinson Ltd

London Melbourne Sydney Auckland
Johannesburg and agencies throughout
the world

First published in Great Britain
by Arrow 1984
Reprinted 1985

Printed and bound in Great Britain by
Anchor Brendon Limited, Tiptree, Essex

ISBN 0 09 936460 3

CHAPTER ONE

Making love in a broom closet is not the most comfortable pastime in the world, but like almost any other way of making love, it is definitely worth the trouble.

The sharp edge of the dustpan jabbing me rather painfully in the back did nothing to detract from the pleasure of what Jack was jabbing into me from the front. It was a pretty small broom closet, so we had to stand up, and I was forced to lean back against that damned dustpan with one of my legs raised high to wrap around Jack's waist. He had both his hands under my buttocks and was hoisting my loins against his. Both his feet were braced solidly on the creaking floor so that he could get the leverage to ram his hips repeatedly upward and forward. We were both panting loudly from exertion as well as passion. "Oh, God, Jack . . . keep it up," I moaned, my fingernails digging into his broad shoulders as his penis dug into my vagina. "More . . . more . . . more . . ."

Then I realized I'd already had all he could give as I felt his cock swell inside me and begin spouting its hot, wet discharge up into my body. "Ah!" I cried out sharply as my own orgasm began. We clutched one another desperately, our bodies writhing so hard that the dustpan was knocked from its peg and clattered loudly to the floor. That made us both giggle as we began to decompress from the intensity of our shared orgasms. Becoming serious, Jack asked, "I wonder if anybody heard that?"

1

"Who cares?" I replied flippantly, glowing from head to foot. "Nobody's going to bother the boss lady at her favorite sport."

"Then how come we're fucking in this goddamned vertical coffin?" Jack growled, letting his softening prick slip from my thoroughly drenched vagina.

That one made me think. Indeed, why *was* the notoriously independent and supposedly shameless Christina van Bell, fabulously wealthy heiress and magazine tycoon, hiding in a broom closet in the headquarters of her own magazine while she took her pleasure? I am not usually so shy. Many times I've made love quite openly in my office, usually on the huge couch that is there mainly for that purpose, but sometimes on top of my desk, too, scattering papers, knocking over old awards and trophies, and never, never caring whether or not the staff in the outer office might hear my joyful cries of passion and the often bull-like bellows of my partner of the moment.

So why this time? For the fun of it, partly, but also because of practicality. The entire suite of offices that houses the headquarters of *World* magazine was overflowing with people, most of them drunk and all of them celebrating. Jack and I *had* started into my office, but discovered my secretary already on the aforementioned couch, half undressed and in the company of an equally *déshabillé* young man, so Jack and I had backed out the door, and since the offices were full of some pretty stuffy and important people, and a modicum of libidinal propriety was called for, the idea of the janitor's handy little broom closet had come to me, and, voilà, there we were, bouncing each other and dustpans off the narrow walls.

If this apparent chaos sounds to you like a poor way to run a magazine as important as *World*, I hasten to assure you that this is not our normal operating procedure. Today was an exception. A celebration. For the past several weeks *World* had been waging a violent editorial war against a corrupt but powerful politician, who, after we had publicly called into question the propriety of some of his legislative and legal activities, had promised to "get" us. Well, *we* had gotten *him*. Weeks of unending digging, of brilliant reportorial work, had unmasked the last of this slippery senator's machinations and now he was about to be expelled from the U.S. Senate. Meanwhile, the accumulated tensions of our long battle, combined with the euphoria of winning, had burst forth in the *World* offices in a wild orgy of celebration. With my—the boss lady's— blessing. I knew that today's excesses would result in improved efficiency among the staff. All work and no play does indeed make Jack—and Jill too—into very dull people, and dull people do not make a great magazine.

Jack, my broom closet companion, was Jack Hallinan, a free-lance writer whom I had hired to infiltrate the senator's political machine. In the end it was his work which had broken the story wide open. How natural, then, that Jack and I would want to celebrate together. And inevitable, too, given my proclivities. For weeks Jack and I had been eyeing one another during our clandestine meetings to discuss the progress of the investigation into the senator's machine. Jack is a big, good-looking man, quite well built, and the sinewy size of his hands and feet always made me wonder about the possible size of another of his extremities, but in the interests of morale and professionalism I had kept my curiosity under control. Jack had behaved quite gentlemanly, too, although more than once I had caught him casting speculative glances in the direction of my breasts and crotch.

Now in the broom closet, as I listened to the sibilant whisper of Jack's ascending zipper I knew that both our curiosities had been at least temporarily satisfied. Jack's genital proportions matched my expectations, and the way his fingers had dug into the sensitive flesh of my breasts before, during, and after our brief copulation, had left no doubt that I had not been found wanting either. Not that I ever am.

I cautiously opened the door of the broom closet and peered out. "Oops," I said, spying Malcolm Gold, the Editorial Director of *World*. He was leaning against a wall a few yards away, looking at the broom closet and at me with poorly disguised disapproval. Not that Malcolm disapproves of sex, or of me making love, but he often feels that I overstep the bounds of propriety. Actually, I suspect that Malcolm is a little in love with me, but faced with the knowledge that he could never have me all to himself, he prefers to have none of me at all. I prefer it that way myself. As much as I care for dear sweet Malcolm, and I do think that in my own way I love him too, I insist that our relationship be first and foremost a business relationship. On the one hand, there is Christina the executive, and on the other is Christina the bonne vivante. I only mix the two when it's to my advantage.

"Hi," I said brightly to Malcolm.

"Harrumph," he grumped back, but then he began to smile. I suppose I must have looked a sight, my blond hair disheveled, the skirt of my neat business suit rucked to the side, my blouse spilling out of my jacket, barely covering my still-tingling breasts. I was managing to smile back when Jack, tousled and with a piece of shirttail protruding from his imperfectly zipped fly, also appeared from the closet. Both Malcolm and I began to laugh. "Doing a little more undercover work?" Malcolm asked, forcing his face back into a deadpan expression.

"Just checking up on the cleaning supplies," I replied, equally as deadpan. "After all, cleanliness is next to godliness, right?"

"Right," he answered. "And what did you find?"

"We need a new dustpan. A plastic one. With rounded corners."

That left Malcolm a little puzzled. He was still scratching his head as I started off with Jack. "Wait," he said, running after me. "Congressman Franklin's been looking all over the place for you."

"Oh, no," I moaned, remembering all the times short, fat Franklin had tried to paw me. "The world's original dirty old man."

I am usually very generous with my body. Once given, it may be reclaimed again and again, but only as long as it is *freely* given. Frankly, Congressman Franklin's damp, pudgy little hands gave me the creeps. Usually, power in a man acts on me like an aphrodisiac. But sex with Franklin? I shuddered at the thought. "You handle him, Malcolm," I said. "Tell him . . . Oh, hell, tell him I was called out of town to my ailing mother's bedside."

"But you haven't *got* a mother," Malcolm protested.

"Well, then, *improvise*. Edit it, Malcolm, edit it. But handle it without me."

I wanted to get out of the office, away from *World* magazine, where I'd been cooped up, under incredible tension, for what seemed like years. "Zip up your fly," I told Jack. "We're going out on the town."

CHAPTER TWO

I realized I was getting very drunk, but I didn't care. Self-indulgence is such a wonderful antidote for overwork. Champagne was my drink of the night, laced with an occasional snort of the finest cocaine whenever I felt myself sliding down a muzzy trail of champagne bubbles into incoherency.

Jack and I were no longer alone. We'd necked all the way uptown in the taxi, with the driver's goggle eyes staring at us, huge in the rear-view mirror, probably because Jack had his hand up my skirt and his fingers up me while my own fingers were busy teasing my bare nipples. I've been told that Christina in full heat is an eye-catching spectacle.

We began bar-hopping, but only to the best and most glamorous places; "21", Sardi's, Elaine's. Along the way we had picked up quite a party of people all of whom were eager to celebrate the reportorial triumph of Christina and *World* magazine. Well, almost everybody. There were some old enemies of mine present, too, like Claudine Perier, the French actress, who, like the sly cat that she is, seemed to be waiting to pounce should I make a drunken social gaffe. So far, to her annoyance, that had not happened, so she changed her tactics, going after Jack, who she knew was my escort for the night.

That in itself didn't bother me. Jack and I had already *had* one another tonight; we were already old history, and

6

I'd begun to let John Tolliver, the Shakespearean actor, stroke my bare thighs under the table. He had such knowing hands. No, what bothered me was that it was *Claudine* who was trying to monopolize Jack, and with considerable success. Not that I can blame Jack. As much as I dislike Claudine, I must admit she is a considerable woman, who fairly oozes hot, dripping sensuality. At the moment, she was sitting next to Jack, on the other side of the table from me; she was half-turned toward him and her hand was probably on his knee—I couldn't actually see her hand because it was underneath the table, but I doubted if she had progressed beyond Jack's knee. Poor dazzled boy, to have two of the world's most beautiful women paying attention to him tonight! Anyhow, he was staring, mesmerized, down Claudine's incredible cleavage, which in her vulgar style extended all the way down to her nipples, when I said sweetly to the bitch, "Careful, Claudine, your tits are going to fall into the soup."

Claudine turned toward me, her sensuous but over-made-up lip curling disdainfully. "You're drunk, Christina. It's an ashtray, not a soup bowl, and my tits don't fall."

"A testimony to the miracles of modern science," I murmured, but loudly enough for everyone to hear.

That was a low blow because while many people suspect that Claudine's phenomenal breasts are a result of silicone injections, no one really knows for sure. There was a moment's tense silence at our table, with Claudine glaring at me and breathing so heavily that it seemed for a moment as if her tits might indeed fall into the soup. Oops, ashtray.

"The only reason yours stay up," she hissed, "is because they're too damned small for gravity to even bother with."

It was Hugh Johnson, the paper mill king, who saved the day. "We seem to have the makings of a contest here,'' he said gaily, which some say he is—gay, I mean, although I know better from firsthand experience. ''Which lovely lady has the most beautiful breasts?''

''Here, here. Contest, contest,'' John Tolliver slurred, tipping over his glass as he comically bulged his eyes, staring first at Claudine's chest and then mine.

''Tit for tat,'' someone else added. ''Let's see 'em.''

''All right,'' I replied, smiling. Fumbling only once or twice, I quickly unbuttoned my blouse and bared my breasts, letting them jut triumphantly in Claudine's direction. She hesitated only a moment, and then simply shrugged her low-cut bodice lower yet, which had the effect of shrugging it right off her large nipples and down around her waist. She and I sat there, tits aimed at each other like rounded sleek weapons, our mutual challenge open.

''Mon dieu,'' I heard someone whisper; it was the only sound during the long moment's silence. Then a low murmur grew around us as everyone within range of our table became aware that four of the most beautiful breasts in the world were on temporary display.

I have to admit Claudine's breasts are indeed magnificently formed, and of enormous size, but I have been told that mine, while admittedly smaller than her enormous globes, are the most perfectly shaped breasts anyone has ever seen. And they are by no means small—only smaller than my rival's. Still, I could not help admiring the haughty way Claudine's tits swelled out from her body, the nipples broad and perfectly centered. If she only weren't such a bitch!

I turned toward Hugh, who had proposed this contest. ''Well?'' I demanded. ''Who wins?''

He smiled. ''It's like comparing apples and oranges,'' he finally said. ''Each perfect in itself, each with its own special characteristics.'' A corner of his mouth twitched upward in the beginnings of a leer, which he quickly suppressed. "Visually," he said, "I find it impossible to make a decision. Perhaps tactilely . . ." and quite boldly he reached out and cupped his hands first around my breasts, then around Claudine's. A gasp went up from neighboring tables, but not from our table of hardened libertines.

"Well?" Claudine demanded as Hugh's hands left her tits. I noticed that her nipples were beginning to pucker a little, as were mine. At least her breasts seemed to be commendably sensitive.

"I . . . just can't seem to choose between them," Hugh said with a dramatic shake of his handsome head.

"Careful," I warned. "You remember what happened to Paris when he couldn't make up his mind as to who was the loveliest of those three goddesses."

"Yeah," Jack muttered. "He got Helen of Troy, the greatest piece of ass in the world."

That brought a general laugh which relieved some of the tension. Then John Tolliver spoke up, enunciating much more soberly now. "If I may suggest," he said, addressing Hugh as his eyes flicked back and forth between my and Claudine's naked torsos. "If you can't decide visually, and if it's a dead heat tactilely, then, getting back to the metaphor of apples and oranges, perhaps you could decide by *taste*."

"Yes," someone else, I don't remember who, chimed in. "Let's make it like a wine-tasting, with everyone joining in, and then all of us deciding by secret ballot."

The general libido around the table was beginning to simmer as everyone tried to visualize the new rules, which would call for them to lean down and lick and suck our nipples. I liked the idea myself, and my nipples were rapidly growing harder and harder in anticipation, to everyone's obvious interest.

"Just a moment," a cultured voice said from another

table. "Pardon my interference in what appears to be a private matter, albeit in a rather public place, but it seems to me that, while laudably lovely, the scope of your contest is too narrow. I propose—"

"And who are you, sir?" I asked coolly, although I felt far from cool. The man who had spoken appeared to be in his late forties or early fifties, very urbane, very well dressed, and very, very handsome. I wondered if all the attention that had been paid to my breasts, which were tingling pleasantly, was causing my appreciation of the newcomer's looks. I later decided this wasn't the case. He had about him a perfect melding of aristocratic purity and decadent depravity that I'm sure will still be with him if he lives to be a hundred. In certain ways he was my kind of man, appealing to the virgin-whorishness inside my own persona.

The stranger nodded without standing up, but it had the effect of a most elegant bow. "Jean de Plessy," he said. "Comte de Braban."

"And what, my dear Count," I asked, "is this change in the rules that you propose?"

"Simply that you are looking only at the part and not the whole," he replied. "The contest should include all of the loveliness that I'm positive resides in the body of each of you charming ladies."

"He wants to see her hole," someone sniggered drunkenly. "No . . . the *whole* of her," someone else corrected with that great seriousness often displayed by the nobly smashed.

"And," I added, "would this broadening of the scope of our contest include not only the visual, but also the touch and taste tests?"

His cool but somewhat hooded eyes moved slowly up and down what he could see of my body. "Whatever the lady desires," he said in a voice so loaded with well-bred innuendo that I nearly had an orgasm just sitting there.

"The lady wants it all," I murmured.

I don't know what might have happened next, but the proprietor of whatever establishment we were in—frankly I can't really remember who or where it was—came bustling up nervously, wringing his hands as his shocked gaze flicked back and forth between me and Claudine. "What is this . . . what is this?" he kept repeating nervously. "What is going on here? My God. My God, this is a public place. What if someone calls the police?"

"Perhaps the police could decide who wins," someone drawled.

"No, it would take a judge," someone else contributed.

"Good, let's all go to jail," John Tolliver hiccupped, his moment's sobriety slowly sinking once again beneath a sea of champagne bubbles.

It was Jean de Plessy, Comte de Braban, our aristocratic neighbor, who had the most sensible suggestion. "If I may venture the use of my place," he said, "for the conclusion of this most interesting and worthwhile contest. It's very private."

"And just where the hell *is* your place?" Claudine snapped, apparently annoyed because she'd been left out of the conversation for the past few minutes.

"My château—in Luxembourg," de Plessy said coolly.

"Oh God, what a blast," Jack said impulsively. Of course he'd already seen, touched, and tasted as much of me as the broom closet had allowed. But Claudine was unplowed ground as far as he was concerned.

The Count stood up. "I have my plane waiting at the airport," he said matter-of-factly. "If you are ready . . ."

"How many of us can you take?" Jack asked nervously, perhaps suspecting that the Count was about to run off alone with both me and Claudine.

The Count, looking slightly amused, cast an appraising glance at the dozen or so of us seated around the table:

Hugh and Claudine and I, John Tolliver and Jack, and two other men I didn't know, as well as the half-dozen starlets who had so far been too dazed to offer a word. "Why," he said nonchalantly, "all of you, of course. My plane is rather large."

CHAPTER THREE

I love arrogant understatement, and I laughed joyously when I saw de Plessy's private plane. It was a Boeing 707, painted the most lovely purple and gold.

Now, here was a man who was decidedly in my league, I thought, as I looked at de Plessy with increased interest.

The plane was beautifully appointed inside, and was broken up into a main lounge and several small suites. Since de Plessy had phoned ahead, the engines were already warmed up, and the group of us immediately buckled up in our seats for the takeoff. Bending FAA rules slightly, we sipped from champagne-filled glasses as the plane thundered down the runway and soared into the air.

By the time we unbuckled and began to move around the cabin, some of the sexual intensity from the restaurant had dissipated. However, it was still there, lurking just below our gay, chattering surfaces as we circulated around the lounge, imbibing more bubbly. The starlets were the first to become bolder. One redheaded minx, hoping to steal the thunder from Claudine and me, pulled off her blouse and began parading around half naked. Laughing, John Tolliver lurched unsteadily over to her and began caressing her gorgeous breasts. "Look," he howled with glee. "I've found a new contestant."

No class, I thought, watching the girl sway sensuously while John mauled her big tits. Just plain sex. None of the intensity Claudine and I had shown.

As the mood spread, more and more of the girls took off their blouses. One stripped completely naked, revealing a thick ruff of auburn pussy hair. I remember thinking she looked like a lion standing on its head. The outnumbered men were, of course, in heaven. John and Jack and Hugh were laughing, and began to dribble champagne on naked breasts, licking it off and sliding their hands up and down sleek thighs. The girls were indeed acting like starlets, advertising their only assets and even offering to sell them, although the orgiastic mood in the plane was accelerating so much that some of them would undoubtedly begin giving it away.

The only man not participating in the general foreplay was Jean de Plessy. "I see that interest in the contest has been considerably diluted," he said, coming up to stand suavely next to me, champagne glass in hand.

"Yes," I agreed. "I think the contest you suggested is now moot."

"On the contrary, my dear," he said, looking at me meaningfully. I looked straight back at him, then glanced over at Hugh, who was kissing the auburn-haired starlet on the mouth, his left hand cupped around one of her breasts, his right hand shoved half out of sight up between her naked thighs. I could see his hand pumping and caught a glimpse of a shiny finger stub moving in and out of the girl's vagina. She was kissing him back fiercely, her hips grinding hard against his hand.

"Now there's a good idea," I said, turning back to Jean de Plessy, my body heating up as I tried to imagine his finger sliding up into me. I wondered what he would look like naked, what he would *feel* like.

Claudine had been standing just a couple of feet away. "Ah, no," she insisted. "No private contests. We must finish this thing between us, chérie. Or are you afraid your puny little body won't be able to match up to mine?" she added scornfully.

"Why, you fat, leather-titted, cow-cunted sow," I burst out angrily, losing my usual cool. "The only place you'd win a tit contest is in a dairy herd. You—"

"Bitch!" Claudine shrieked. "You're afraid of a real woman!"

"Hah!" I said, getting ready to add something *really* nasty, but de Plessy quickly stepped between us—a brave man, indeed.

"Miss Perier is right," he said. "The contest must go on, but not here, not in the plane. It will wait until we reach Luxembourg, and there we will do it with the correct style and grace."

I nodded. "Agreed," I said. I looked around the lounge. Hugh was now on his knees in front of Miss Lion Ruff, noisily smacking his lips against the pink meat underneath all that fur. The girl was desperately clutching his head, her face turned to one side, her eyes closed in ecstasy. Now, that was something I could relate to. "In the meantime," I said to the Count, "perhaps it's time for a little warm-up." I looked meaningfully at his crotch, which showed an interesting fullness.

"But that would affect the contest," he insisted. When I shook my head scornfully, he added, "Can't you see? The taste test. Parts of you would be carrying additional flavors, a maleness . . ."

"You mean I'd have cum running out of my twat," I said.

"Exactly," de Plessy agreed with a cool smile.

"Crude American savage," Claudine interjected maliciously, but I could see that she too was staring at the Count's crotch.

"I *like* cum running out of my twat," I said stubbornly. I was getting mad. I was getting horny. I was also drunk out of my mind. I might have gone straight over to one of the men and asked him to fuck me if Claudine hadn't aimed her braying laughter in my direction.

"You have no panache, chérie. A defect clear to anyone willing to compare the two of us."

The white heat of my anger cooled to a slow burn. "Okay, watermelon-tits," I hissed. "The contest is still on. I'll play against you, any rules, any time. And I'll win hands down."

"No . . . pants down," she corrected with a phony tinkly laugh. "And *I* will win."

"Bullshit," I shot back. But de Plessy now had us both by the arms and was leading us down a corridor toward the back of the plane. "Where are you taking us?" I demanded.

"To a place where you can rest for the demanding contest to come." He opened a door to one of the little cabins. I caught a glimpse of a small bed and a wash basin. He ushered Claudine inside, and she went in a little hesitantly. He smiled and closed the door after her. I noticed there was a latch on the outside, and I savagely slammed it into place, locking Claudine inside.

Then it was my turn. But as I stood just inside the door to my little cubicle, de Plessy smiled and I was suddenly kissing him. I don't know just how it happened. I supposed I pulled him toward me, or perhaps he made the first move, but we ended up locked together, mouth to mouth, breast to breast, groin to groin, his thigh pressing up between my legs, my hips shuddering forward. "If he can kiss this way," I thought muzzily as tremors of passion pulsed through my body, "I wonder how he fucks?"

Then suddenly I was alone in the little room. The door closed solidly behind me. I heard the sound of the latch falling into place. I was as locked in as Claudine.

Unsteady on my feet, I sat down on the bed. Had de Plessy kissed me just so he could lock me up without a fuss? What the hell did it matter? What a kiss! I vowed that I would eventually get a lot more than a kiss from Jean de Plessy, Comte de Braban.

For the moment, all I wanted was to sleep. The champagne, the long night in addition to the weeks of tense work—everything was catching up with me. I lay back on the bunk, about to close my eyes when I heard noise in the corridor. It sounded like two people, and they were laughing and talking drunkenly and literally bouncing off the corridor walls. "Good. Here's an empty one," I heard a man say. It was Jack's voice.

A girl giggled. One of the starlets? "I wonder why the other two are locked?" she asked.

"Maybe somebody doesn't want to be disturbed," Jack grunted. I heard the door close as they entered the adjoining cubicle.

"But, locked from the *outside*!" the girl queried. Even through the wall she sounded very drunk and not too smart.

"Don't worry. We'll lock ours from the inside," Jack said. I heard a click of metal.

"Good," she giggled coyly. "I . . . really don't like doing it in front of a lot of people."

"I don't know why not," Jack muttered. "You've sure as hell got a lovely body."

I heard a rustle of clothing. "Jesus! What a gorgeous set of tits!" Jack burst out.

More giggling. I wondered which one this bubble-headed girl was. "Do you think *I* could win the contest?" she asked coyly. "Are my breasts as nice as Christina's?"

"Oh, yeah . . . sure," Jack mumbled. The treacherous bastard. Then his mumble turned into a wet smacking sound.

"Ooohhhhh yessssss," the girl whimpered. "Suck my nipples . . . hard . . . harder."

Louder smacking. Then a quick gasp from the girl. "Ah! Your finger's so *strong*! Oooohhhhhh . . . open me up . . ."

There were more wet noises coming from the other side of the thin partition separating the two cabins. I tried to visualize Jack's finger sluicing in and out of the starlet's twat, his mouth greedily engulfing as much of her tit as possible. Jack could really suck. I knew.

I heard the creak of springs, heavy panting. Something hit the floor. It sounded like the buckle of a man's belt. "Oh God . . . God . . . it's big!" the starlet yelped happily. I ground my teeth. I *knew* it was big. I thought of all those rock-hard inches of Jack's cock ramming their way up into the girl's pussy. My own pussy suddenly felt horribly lonely. I wanted to run out of the cabin and rape the first man I met, but I knew I was locked in, and I had too much pride to bang on the door.

So I did the only thing I could. I lay down on my little bed and spreading my legs, I hiked the skirt of my thoroughly rumpled suit up around my waist and stared down at my naked cunt. As usual, I was not wearing underwear. I saw how my inner juices, flowing strongly, had already darkened my blond pussy hair. "It's okay," I whispered to my throbbing twat. "You're going to have company."

Slowly, lovingly, I inserted my index finger up inside my vagina. "Aaaahhhhhh," I sighed in relief. I began to move my finger in and out, searching for all the right places, the ones that felt best. That might have satisfied me, but by now a furious bumping and moaning was coming from the cabin next to me. I tried to visualize Jack's cock flashing in and out of the girl's box. It didn't help. I still felt deprived.

I shoved another finger in beside the first, then added a third. I started finger-fucking myself hard, timing my thrusts to coincide with the rhythmic thumping next door. While my thumb pressed down against my clitoris, I dipped the fingers of my other hand into my blouse and found my passion-swollen nipples.

I timed it so that I came with Jack and the girl. As soon as I heard her first sharp cries and Jack's loud moan, I bucked my hips upward, and writhing helplessly, let it all go. To my surprise, I heard ecstatic moaning from the cabin on the other side of me, the one occupied by Claudine. For one terrible second I imagined that the Count must be in there making love to my rival, but then I realized that Claudine, obviously as horny as I, had adopted the same remedy I had. I was laughing as the last of my orgasm rippled through my cunt, and for the moment I almost felt a kinship with big-titted Claudine.

I let my weary fingers slip wetly from my still-throbbing pussy. Feeling very relaxed, very sure, I fell asleep.

CHAPTER FOUR

The Grand Duchy of Luxembourg is a small, fairy-story principality sandwiched in between Belgium, France, and Germany. Called Luxemburg in German and le Grand Duché de Luxembourg in French, its two official languages, it is indeed ruled by a Grand Duke, its hereditary prince.

Like many other tiny independent national entities, Luxembourg's economy centers on banking, providing financial secrecy for the citizens of other, larger and more repressive, countries and allowing them to evade the taxes of their home lands. I'm all for that, although in Luxembourg this money-centered mentality tends to foster a noticeable amount of monetary greed among the natives.

Physically, Luxembourg is a beautiful little place, and it takes less than an hour to traverse the entire country from north to south by car. The capital city, Luxembourg, is situated near the southern end, and it is all one would expect, with part of the old city wall still in place, propping up the mass of medieval and baroque buildings which are packed together near the main square. Lovely parks and bridges and crags and green canyons surround the town.

Luxembourg is quite mountainous, and on top of a particularly handsome crag about a half-mile from La Ville de Luxembourg, as the city is called, was the château of the Count de Brabein, our host. It rose from its rocky base, looking very much like something Disney might have designed, all soaring towers, lacy battlements, and high walls.

The count pointed all this out to us from the plane as we circled for a landing at Luxembourg's small international airport. I had awakened earlier, refreshed from a very nice sleep. Finding my door unlocked, I joined the others just before we landed. Because of the time difference between New York and Europe—six hours—it was late afternoon before the Count's 707 finally touched down. A small fleet of limousines met us as we deplaned and I found myself sharing the back seat of one with Jack.

"Jesus Christ, this is some setup," he exclaimed. "And to think that only yesterday I was plain Jack Hallinan, boy reporter. Now, thanks to you, boss lady . . ."

He reached over and tried to caress my tits through my blouse. I firmly disengaged his hand. "Mustn't bruise the merchandise," I said.

"Merchandise?"

"My assets . . . for the contest," I reminded him. "My winning hand, or should I say chest. Unless you still think that eager bit player you were with last night has a better chance."

Jack colored. "How did you know—?" he started to say.

"I was locked in the cabin next door."

"Oh." There was a short silence. "Is that weird contest still on?" Jack finally asked.

"You bet your lecherous ass, typewriter-pounder," I said vehemently. "I'm going to plow Claudine right into the ground."

"But why are you so set on it?" Jack insisted.

"Because I want the prize."

"Which is . . .?"

"Can't you guess?"

"The loser's tits mounted as a wall trophy?" he asked with a smile.

"Uh-uh. The Count."

"Ah," he sighed, enlightened. He smiled wryly at me. "You know, Christina, as the old saying goes, you're really something else."

"I know," I said matter-of-factly. "Now shut up for a while. I want to watch the scenery."

Our caravan of cars skirted the town, but I caught a magnificent view of it as we started up the mountain slope toward the Count's castle. For a moment I could see no modern buildings below at all, just a tightly packed, turreted old city from hundreds of years in the past.

Then the Count's stronghold loomed above us. "Jesus Christ . . . where's the drawbridge?" Jack muttered. There had probably been one at one time, but now we drove up a ramp and in between two massive gray towers that flanked the main entrance—a huge wooden and iron gate standing wide open. An enormous stone courtyard lay within. As the last car pulled to a stop there, the huge gates swung ponderously shut behind us. The crash as they met reverberated from the surrounding stonework with a sound of finality.

A throng of servants met us at the outside door that led to the main hall. The Count guided us inside. After the grim stonework of the courtyard, I expected a dim, damp interior but was pleasantly surprised by the light and luxury within. Huge clerestory windows rising almost all the way to the high, vaulted ceiling let in floods of late afternoon sun. Gorgeous tapestries and hangings softened the golden yellow stone of the walls. Priceless carpets covered the flagged flooring. There were magnificent works of art everywhere.

The Count came up to me, two pretty young women in servants' livery trailing a few paces behind him. "Christina," he said, "these are Greta and Marie, your maids. They will take you to your room so that you may prepare for dinner."

As he said nothing about the contest, I was tempted to

ask if he had forgotten, but decided it would be in bad form. I smiled in agreement, then followed the two girls up the huge curving staircase that led from the main hall to the living quarters above.

My room was a delight: a huge chamber with tall windows giving a view of the valley leading down toward Luxembourg. The furniture was ornate eighteenth century, the bed a canopied marvel. Best of all was the bathroom, an enormous tiled enclosure with a huge sunken tub and gold fittings. I decided I liked it here.

I liked it even more as I luxuriated in the huge tub, buoyed up on a sea of soothing bubbles. Greta and Marie expertly bathed me. I thought for a moment of trying to seduce them—they were certainly lovely enough and each exuded an air of light-hearted sensuality that I thought thoroughly in keeping with the Count's libertine manner—but I decided against it. There would be time for fun and games later, and at the moment all I could really think of was food. I was starving.

Of course having come to Luxembourg direct from a New York restaurant, I had no wardrobe with me—only my poor tired business suit. I was very pleased, then, when the two smiling servant girls dressed me in a loose, flowing, and admirably low cut velvet gown. The color was a rich burgundy, which always goes well with my blond hair and ivory coloring. I did indeed feel like a countess as I regally descended the vast staircase, to join the Count and his other guests. As usual, I accepted as my due the hum of admiration from the others as I entered the grand dining room where we were all to eat. The only thing that marred my pleasure was that Claudine Perier, dressed in flowing red, her huge breasts once again bare nearly to the nipples, got just as admiring a reception as my own. I smiled icily in her direction. Her answering grimace was equally as frigid.

We were all seated at an enormously long oaken table,

Claudine and I at either end, the Count in the center. As I
have said, I was starving, but there was no food in sight.
The Count, as if reading my mind, got to his feet and
announced, "My friends, we are all famished, of course,
but I think it only fitting that we proceed in a civilized
manner and partake of the appropriate sacraments before-
hand."

I wondered for a moment if I had misread the Count's
character and he was going to dumbfound us all by saying
grace. However, to our general relief, he merely produced
several small golden boxes and had the servants circulate
them up and down the length of the table. "For the
sharpening of *all* our various appetites," the Count
explained.

The golden boxes, as I soon found out, contained beautifully rolled marijuana cigarettes, each box with a different
variety. There was the best Colombian, the finest Hum-
boldt County sinsemilla, Hawaiian Maui wowie, aromatic
Thai sticks, and a box of the tiniest joints I had ever seen,
each one about the size of a small matchstick. The Count
saw me puzzling over one of these. "From Southern
California," he explained. "Hand grown by a dedicated
horticulturist, using the seeds of *cannabis indica* rather
than the more common and less effective *cannabis sativa*."

"But why so incredibly small?" I asked.

"Try it and see," he replied, smiling. "But no more
than two or three hits."

I shrugged and lit the tiny joint. It was so thin that it
was difficult to draw air through it, but I managed a couple
of pretty good hits. Nothing much happened at first, except that the smoke I inhaled was particularly aromatic,
and then, wham!, a tidal wave of sensation washed over
me. I sat perfectly still, holding desperately onto the edge
of the table while my soul tried to leave my body. After a
short, intense struggle, I won out, but as I refocused on the

world around me, I realized how incredibly stoned I was. "See?" the Count said, still smiling.

Then the food and the wine and the liquor came. Stoned out of my mind on the finest grass I had ever smoked, I reveled in the feast laid out before me. My high was intensely physical, leaving my mind clear and sharp. When I picked up my glass of champagne, I was intensely aware of the coldness of the glass against my hand. I could *feel* the bubbles rising and bursting in the liquid, and when I drank, they continued to rise, floating right through the top of my mouth and into my brain.

I gorged like a pig. Never had food tasted so good. Halfway through the meal I smoked some more but I immediately regretted it, because I knew I would not be able to get up from the table by myself. Yet my mind was still clear. The only problem was that it was no longer associated with my body. So all I could do was sit like a statue and observe. I noticed how stoned everyone else was, all except the Count, who seemed perfectly in control of himself, as impervious to the intoxicating enticements of hell as Mephistopheles himself, I thought in a moment of stoned revelation.

I noticed other things as well. At first the food and drink had been served by good-looking young men and women quite decorously dressed in the Count's usual livery, so it was with a pleasant shock that I realized that the girl now pouring more wine into my glass was wearing an odd costume from which holes had been neatly cut over the breasts and genitals, leaving a pair of pert young breasts jutting nakedly out at the world, while lower down, the soft material of her tight costume framed a neat vee of pubic hair.

The male servitors wore equally revealing costumes, with their penises and testicles protruding in a most bizarre and intriguing manner. The meal had indeed taken a turn toward lasciviousness.

Now, little silver boxes made the rounds of the table. This time it was cocaine.

"To overcome the rather numbing effects of our previous ingestions," the Count explained. Nothing loath, I let one of the servants lay me out a set of glittery white crystalline lines, which I snorted as decorously as I could. The effect was immediate. A wave of scintillating energy now superimposed itself on the reflective high of the marijuana. I was floating at 40,000 feet over a sea of deep blue velvet. I had energy unlimited. I could feel my nerve pathways vibrating with an intolerably powerful surge of strength that would either have to find an outlet or burn me out.

Everyone else seemed to be reacting the same way. The obscenely dressed servants, both male and female, naturally channeled all this abundantly flaring energy in a sexual direction. The girl seated on my right, one of the starlets, began to stroke the protruding cock of the waiter who was pouring her wine. He coolly continued filling her glass, but his cock reacted visibly, quickly lengthening and hardening. Further down the table, John Tolliver, drunk as usual, turned and began licking the bare breast of the waitress closest to him. Others followed suit, and in a moment most of the dinner guests were paying more attention to the servants than to what was left of the meal. The starlet on my right was vigorously masturbating her compliant waiter, who was no longer reacting so coolly. Standing beside her, he held tightly to the back of her chair with one hand as her clenched fingers raced up and down the length of his now enormously swollen cock. She had greased her fingers with butter, to make them slide more easily. The shaft of the man's prick glistened, the veins standing out, the bulbous head massively swollen. He suddenly groaned loudly, and a moment later thick gouts of semen jetted from the tip of his prick and shot all over the table in front of the starlet. She laughed hysterically. "Thank God. At last, a decent white sauce."

She was answered by a general roar of laughter. Any sexual inhibitions the guests might have had had been exorcised by the dope and the wine and the cocaine and by the power of the Count's strange personality. By now everyone but Claudine and myself had a finger in or a handful or a mouthful of whatever part of their personal waiter they desired. Claudine and I just sat and stared at one another across the length of the table, while more semen spouted, women moaned, nipples grew swollen and wet with saliva, and the rich smell of aroused femininity filled the room.

Then the Count clapped his hands loudly and the servants immediately withdrew. This was followed by a murmur of complaint from the guests. Meanwhile, I saw Jack wiping the wet and aromatic first and second fingers of his right hand on a napkin. But before there could be a general revolt and a wholesale pursuit of the retiring servants, the Count stood up once again and spoke.

"I know you may be disappointed at the moment," he said, "but let me remind you of the reason we all came here."

"The contest," Claudine said in a rather hard voice that went poorly with her voluptuous figure.

"Yes, the contest," the Count replied, and the cry immediately went up around the table: "Contest . . . contest . . .""

The Count motioned to me and to Claudine. We both stood up. Anyway, I think I stood up. I was suddenly on my feet, with no memory of how it had happened. My body throbbed, wavered, floated as a result of all the drugs I had put into it. Then I found myself hand in hand with the Count. He was leading me somewhere. I looked past him and saw that Claudine was attached to his other hand. We seemed to float along, or at least I did, feeling as if I were sinking a hundred feet into the floor with each step, which was strange, because the hallway had a wooden floor. Still, its polished surface seemed miles deep, reaching all the way to the center of the earth.

And then I stumbled as my feet encountered genuine softness. We had entered a large room whose floor was padded with thick, soft carpets and fabrics. Low couches lay along the walls and in the very center of the room was a sunken area filled with more carpets and cushions. The Count led both Claudine and me into this central area and the others gathered around us.

"And now," the Count said, "we shall take up where we left off in New York."

With his own hands the Count slid down the top of Claudine's gown. The material caught against her nipples, then slipped past, leaving Claudine's huge breasts completely bare and still jiggling a little. There was a hiss of appreciation from the onlookers.

Then it was my turn. I felt the cool material of my dress sliding down my breasts. The various drugs I had imbibed had made my nipples amazingly sensitive. I gasped as they sprang free into a cool wash of open air. The crowd gasped, too.

"I'd forgotten how beautiful they were," Hugh Johnson murmured.

People crowded around. Hands reached out to touch my breasts. They were so sensitive it was almost more than I could stand. I bit into my lower lip while fingertips plucked at my throbbing nipples. Looking to my right, I could see that the same thing was happening to Claudine, and I could also see that her nipples were beginning to swell. They were very big and very long. "Jesus, both of their breasts are like velvet," John Tolliver said. "So hard to make a decision . . ."

One of the starlets was standing right in front of me. The dope and the alcohol had made her bold. She looked up at me like a cat looking at a bird, and then looked back down at my naked tits. "We've looked . . . we've touched," she said. "Now let's taste."

I watched in fascination as her lips approached my swollen nipples. "Oh, God . . . no!" I burst out as I felt heat and wetness surround those taut mounds of supersensitive tissue. "Stop . . . I . . . I'll come . . ."

"What's the matter with that?" someone demanded.

"But . . . I can't stand up any longer," I whimpered, and began to fall. Many hands took hold of me, helping me down, at the same time stripping me of the rest of my clothing. I found myself on my back, lying on a soft surface completely naked. I felt hands pulling my unresisting thighs apart. "My God!" someone said. "That's the most beautiful cunt I've ever seen!"

"You ought to see the one over here," someone else said from Claudine's general direction.

"Hey, I thought this was supposed to be a tit contest," a man said.

"Everyone to their own tastes," a woman's voice answered. "And speaking of taste . . ."

I looked down and met the sly, hungry eyes of the same girl who had sucked my nipples. She was kneeling between my outstretched thighs, her fingertips peeling back the soft, sensitive petals of my labia. "It's so pink," she said, as she mashed her mouth against my cunt. "Aaaaahhhhhh!" I moaned loudly, my body reacting with an immediate orgasm as I felt her tongue dart into my slit and unerringly locate the swollen knob of my clitoris.

I was suddenly buried in an avalanche of bodies, both male and female. As fingers pried, tongues licked, and lips sucked, I writhed helplessly while orgasm after orgasm ripped through my drug-sensitized body. I could hear moans and only gradually realized they were my own mixed with someone else's. Another woman's. I turned my head and saw that Claudine was experiencing pretty much the same thing, being serviced by numerous panting, licking, sucking supplicants.

My mind seemed to be working on two levels. While I was fully aware of the ecstasy flooding through my body, I was also able to fully observe what was happening to Claudine. I watched greedy lips pull at her amazingly long nipples, saw Tolliver's shaggy head buried between her lush thighs. But what amazed me most was the look of complete rapture on Claudine's normally haughty face. I saw her stomach suck in powerfully as she began to have an orgasm. It amazed me that normally frigid Claudine could be experiencing all the delights that I, Christina, was experiencing.

Perhaps it was the drugs, perhaps it was our shared predicament, but I suddenly felt an enormous sense of kinship to Claudine. I reached out a hand in her direction, but she was too far away. I wanted to touch her, to move closer, but the weight of bodies was holding me down.

I noticed then that everyone else was as naked as Claudine and I. Contest had turned into orgy. I watched as Hugh Johnson crawled into place behind the kneeling girl who was eating my snatch. I caught a glimpse of swollen cock jutting from his lean loins before the girl's body blotted it out. Hugh fumbled for a moment underneath the girl's ass, and I saw her eyes fly wide open in pleased shock, then grow hot with passion as Hugh flexed his loins forward, burying his swollen member up inside the girl's vagina.

By about the tenth stroke, Hugh's cock was giving the girl so much pleasure that she began to forget about my cunt. Her head rose, her face shiny with my internal juices, and she began to fuck back, slamming her hips against Hugh's, eager for more and more of his pistoning cock. For just a moment I was free. I rolled quickly toward the side, toward Claudine. "Get out of the way," I said, pushing John Tolliver aside. I knelt on my heels, looking down at Claudine. Her chest was heaving, making her remarkable breasts rise and fall most enticingly. Her legs were parted far enough for me to see the shiny pink glow of cunt meat beneath her neat triangle of pubic hair. Her eyes were still unfocused with passion, but she slowly became aware of me. "What . . .?" she started to say.

"The only way we're going to settle this thing," I told her, "is to duel woman to woman."

Sharp, hard awareness returned to her eyes. "And just how do you propose we handle that?" she asked craftily.

"Sixty-nine," I rapped out. "Just you and me. The first one who stops sucking loses."

"You're on," Claudine snapped back at me. "What position do you want? Top or bottom?"

"Makes no difference to me."

"I'll flip a coin," Jack said, somehow producing a coin from the crowd of naked people that had gathered about us again. Jack himself was mother-naked, and as the coin soared upward, I called out "Heads."

"Heads it is," Jack reported. Someone else sniggered, "It'll be heads *and* tails in any case."

"I choose the bottom," I said. I figured Claudine would have to do more of the work that way. "Come on," I said to her jeeringly as I lay down on my back, spreading my legs.

"Okay, you asked for it, chérie," she replied, clambering into position above me, her loins right over my face, her own face poised above my crotch.

"Who'll say go?" I demanded. Claudine's pussy hung right above my mouth. I had to admit it was a really nice snatch, tight and clean. The thick outer lips were swollen enough by now so that they more or less folded back out of the way, baring the glistening pink valley in between. Her inner labia were so engorged that they were almost purple. Further up I could see, past its protective prepuce, the taut little nubbin of her clit hanging down like a miniature punching bag. This is going to be fun, I thought.

"Ready . . . go!" I heard someone shout, so I reached up and jerked Claudine's loins down toward my face, pressing the hot wet flesh of her cunt tightly against my mouth. My tongue shot out and buried itself in that simmering little valley. I felt Claudine's entire body jerk, and I started to smile, but then her tongue was in my slit, too, and I found I could no longer concentrate.

It's hard to summon up memories of the early part of that fantastic duel. I quickly discovered that Claudine had a tongue at least as clever as mine. Time and again she literally sucked orgasms from my shuddering pussy. I moaned, I twisted, I whimpered, but I still managed to keep my own tongue busy inside Claudine's gushing slit. I began to regret having chosen the bottom position. Claudine's cunt was pouring out so much lubrication that I was in danger of drowning, and of course she was able to press down against my face so hard that both my tongue and mouth were buried in the soft, hot wet flesh of her box. Breathing was terribly difficult.

We were having quite an effect on the onlookers. "Jesus Christ, look at them go!" Jack cried out.

"A fitting illustration for the book *Women in Love*," John Tolliver drawled, but there was lust in his drawl.

"More like *Women in Heat*," Hugh Johnson added much more excitedly.

It was all very funny, but I was unable to laugh. Half drowning in slippery pussy flesh, unable to breathe, with my own cunt being devilishly tormented by Claudine's agile tongue-work, I was slowly becoming aware that I might lose this contest, and I hate to lose. I had just about given it up, although I had my tongue at least two inches up into Claudine's gratifyingly spasming cunt, when good old Jack rather unknowingly came to the rescue.

He wasn't trying to help me, not directly. It was simple

male lust. I suppose he must have been staring too long at Claudine's luscious ass thrust back toward him, with a clear view of my tongue slithering the length of her slit. Anyhow, the first I knew of what he intended to do was when I saw the light above me partially blocked out. I blinked, and looked up to see an enormous set of cock and balls swaying just above my amazed eyes. The cock was fully erect and headed straight toward Claudine's pussy hole. It was Jack's cock, of course. I saw his fingers slip up into Claudine's slit just above my eyes and spread her pussy lips. A moment later the bulbous tip of his cock followed, pushing soft wet flesh aside as it ground up into Claudine's body.

She gave a huge lurch, and frantically burbled something into my cunt. She almost jerked her mouth away, which would have cost her the contest, but with an obvious effort she kept on licking and sucking. She tried to twitch her nether regions out of the way of Jack's encroaching prick, but I had a pretty good hammerlock on her hips and thighs and easily held her in place, aided by Jack's powerful hands.

And then Claudine quit struggling. A low hum of ecstasy vibrated from her mouth into my cunt as inch after inch of rock-hard cock flesh lanced up into her vagina. When I say rock hard, I know from firsthand experience, because all those inches of cock had to rub against my nose and forehead as they went in. I had the most spectacular ringside seat as Jack fucked Claudine from behind. I watched his thick shaft pucker her hole inward on the in-stroke, then, as it slid out again, I could see little pink tendrils of Claudine's inner pussy flesh clinging lovingly to Jack's withdrawing organ. Then, wham!, in again, the tempo gradually picking up until Jack's cock was a slippery blur flashing past my eyes, his balls slapping hard against my forehead.

Claudine was fucking back madly, grunting loudly into my cunt, her sweat-slippery body sliding against mine. I could feel her huge breasts pressing hotly against my stomach, the nipples digging into my skin. How she managed to keep sucking my twat through all this, I don't know. I hated to admit it, but Claudine was a real champion.

But it couldn't last forever. Jack's cock slamming into her cunt was just too much stimulation to allow Claudine to maintain control. I watched things develop close up. Jack's cock began to swell larger and larger. I caught glimpses of the huge head as it slipped partly out of Claudine's gaping, hungry hole, and then I rather maliciously speeded things up by alternately licking Claudine's clit, just below where Jack's cock rammed up into her vagina, and sucking Jack's balls.

That did it. Jack began to groan loudly. I saw the thick tube on the underside of his cock begin to pulse, and I knew he was coming. Thick gouts of semen began creaming back out Claudine's pussy hole, dripping down onto my face. Claudine, with that enormous rod pouring its hot load into her, couldn't control herself any longer. Her head jerked up and back and she began to howl wildly, "Oh, God . . . stick it to me, you son-of-a-bitch! Come in me . . . Come in me . . . I'm coming tooooooooooooo!"

So much for cool, controlled Claudine. I felt her body shuddering above mine as her climax took control of her body. I laughed, not only because all this was so funny, but also because I had obviously won the contest. Claudine was no longer licking my twat!

It was a hell of a struggle to roll out from under all that rutting flesh above me. The fact that I was so slippery with sweat and cum helped. I got to my feet, triumphantly crying out in victory. That woke Claudine from her orgasmic trance. "What?" she shrieked, suddenly lurching to her feet. I saw Jack wince as her cunt tore away from his still deeply imbedded cock. "I call foul!" Claudine shouted. "If that son-of-a-whore hadn't started fucking me . . ."

"I didn't hear you complaining," I said sweetly. "And how does that old saying go? All's fair in love and war?"

Everyone was beginning to laugh, everyone except Claudine, who was adding to the crowd's delight by jumping up and down so wildly that her huge tits were threatening to get completely out of control.

"She's going to give herself a black eye if she doesn't watch it," Hugh snickered.

The Count stepped in, cool and controlled. "I think," he said, "that it would be best to call it a draw, considering the circumstances."

"Nothing doing," Claudine and I said simultaneously.

The Count shrugged. "Well, if you want to start it all over again . . ."

That sobered the two of us. The spell had been broken. Claudine was no longer a lovely, passionate woman to me. She was once again my old enemy. It would be very difficult to force myself to crawl between those thighs again and bury my tongue in her slit. I could see the same emotions on Claudine's face. "Well . . ." we both murmured.

The Count, smooth as ever, said, "Let us call it a draw, then. Who, after all, would be able to choose between two such lovely women?"

Loud cheers came from the onlookers, some of whom obviously wanted to get involved in contests of their own. I nodded at Claudine and she nodded back at me. Better peace between us than a piece of each other we didn't want.

I turned when I felt a hand on my arm. It was the Count. "Would you like your prize now?" he asked quietly.

"Prize?" I asked. "Wouldn't I have to share it with Claudine?"

The Count pointed to Jack's dripping cock, still shiny

with Claudine's pussy juices. "She's already had her reward," he said, his voice much more intense. "Now I'd like to give you yours."

Well, I thought, the bastard is getting around to it at last. I had begun to wonder about him. Unlike the others, who were in full rut, the Count had not even undressed; he was as immaculately groomed as ever. "Your place?" I asked with a lift of my eyebrows. "Or mine?" and I indicated the pile of cushions from which I had just arisen.

"I would prefer this to be a little more private," he said, and taking my arm, led me across the big room and around the piles of naked, writhing bodies. Since I like orgies, one part of me hated to leave, but I was interested in seeing what the Count had in mind, what kinds of things turned him on.

We went down a hall and entered a somewhat smaller room, the center of which was dominated by a large, low couch. I, of course, was still mother-naked. I lay down on the couch, partially propping myself up on one elbow, adopting a relaxed but provocative pose. The Count stood looking down at me for a moment. I could not read his face, but I thought he looked interested. I was a little surprised then when he turned away from me. But it was only to cross the room to remove something from a cupboard. As he turned and came back toward me, I saw that he held in his hand another of those tiny but megaton joints. "To heighten our pleasure," the Count said to me.

He put the joint in my mouth, then lit it with a beautiful gold lighter. I looked over the flame and the wreathing smoke, staring straight into his enigmatic eyes. They were rather cold, but, oh, so interesting. The dope hit me more quickly this time. While the Count was taking his hit a soft explosion went off inside my skull, then radiated throughout my entire body. Just the feel of the soft bed covering as it rubbed against my skin nearly gave me an orgasm. I looked up at the Count. He looked thoughtfully down at the glowing tip of the joint, then carefully flicked out the flame with his fingertip. "Aren't you going to take off your clothes?" I asked him.

He put the joint down. "All in good time," he said and reached out to pull twice on a bell rope that hung next to the couch. "What's that for?" I asked somewhat muzzily. The dope was making it hard for me to concentrate.

"I'm calling Hugo," he replied.

"Hugo? Who's Hugo?" I demanded. "What do we need anybody else for?"

"*I* don't need him, my dear girl," he assured me. "You do."

My stoned mind was still wrestling with his cryptic statement when the door opened and a man walked in. He was quite naked, but I became confused as I looked at him. In a way he was beautiful, with big gorgeous muscles, shaggy hair, and a rugged face. But at the same time there was something brutish about him, a coarseness of feature, an animal power about his body, and the most brutish part of him was the enormous cock that dangled between his muscular thighs. Even though it was still soft, it was already one of the biggest I'd ever seen.

My cunt gave a little lurch, half of fear, half of lust, as I stared at that mammoth cock. I tried to imagine it reaching up inside me, spreading my pussy lips, stuffing my vagina. I liked the images my mind was conjuring up. Maybe the Count was right, maybe I did need Hugo. But where did the Count come in? Did he simply get his kicks as a voyeur?

That was all right with me. The dope I had smoked gathered all my attention into one intense little bundle and focused it on Hugo's cock as he began to walk toward me and his cock swayed loosely back and forth, slapping gently against his inner thighs. Then I noticed that Hugo was looking at me as intently as I was looking at him. I saw his eyes flick over my body, assessing my breasts, staring up between my thighs, devouring what I have been told is the most beautiful cunt in the world, and with each step Hugo took toward me, his cock hardened a little, jerking upward inch by inch until it was no longer slapping against his thighs. By the time he stopped next to the couch, his prick was angling tautly up toward his hard flat stomach. His tool was so hard I could see it pulsing each time Hugo's heart beat . . . and it was so long . . . so thick . . .

I gave a little whinny of anticipation as Hugo climbed up onto the couch and rather unceremoniously pried my thighs apart. Ah, I thought, the strong direct type—not that I was putting up much resistance. After my cunnilingual battle with Claudine, my pussy ached to be filled with something besides tongue. "Ah!" I cried out as Hugo suddenly rammed what felt like the handle of a baseball bat part way up into my vagina. It hurt and my body automatically flinched, but Hugo continued to drive into me.

Thank God my cunt was already dripping wet because Hugo was merciless. I whimpered and writhed as inch after inch of his mammoth organ ground its way up into my vagina. Finally I felt his pubic bone meet mine. He was in all the way. I was thankful there was no more of him; I already felt like I had cock up to my throat. I lay below Hugo, feeling quite helpless, almost afraid to move, afraid that his huge prick would split me wide open.

But I really had nothing to fear. If politicians were as accommodating as the average vagina, we would never again have to worry about war. Once my twat had fully measured the dimensions of Hugo's intruding member, it began to expand hungrily.

"Come on," I urged Hugo, sinking my fingers into the hard-muscled flesh of his ass. "Get your motor going, King Kong."

During all this time Hugo had neither spoken nor smiled. Now, looking me straight in the face with a fierce intensity, he began to fuck, sliding his well-greased cock in and out of my eager hole. I think it was as much this wild, animal-like intensity as the size of his cock that turned me on. "Oh, Jesus Christ!" I wailed, and had the first of what was to be many memorable orgasms.

During all this time I had forgotten about the Count. Now he stepped back into my field of vision, coming up next to the couch. While his creature fucked me, the Count looked down at me thoughtfully and began caressing my breasts. It was all rather dispassionate, and I was thinking that I had been right—the Count was only a voyeur. But how wrong I was.

At the moment though, I was busy being fucked by Hugo, who humped over me like some primordial machine, his huge cock reaching a little further up inside me with each stroke. I was only vaguely aware that the Count was undressing. He's probably going to jack off while he watches, I was thinking when he was suddenly right next to me again, naked at last, hand-feeding his cock into my mouth. Okay, I thought, and began licking and sucking. It was a nice cock, not as big as Hugo's, thank God. I felt it growing hard inside my mouth, and wondered if he was going to come down my throat. It was a nice enough sensation, a cock in my mouth, another in my cunt.

But the Count suddenly pulled his cock from between my obediently sucking lips. He had a very nice looking erection, and I was thinking that it would feel good up inside my cunt after Hugo had shot his load, but the Count had other ideas.

"Now, Hugo," he said sharply. Hugo gave a grunt of acknowledgment, and before I knew what was happening, he suddenly rolled over, taking me with him, so that he ended up on the bottom with me sitting astride him, his cock still buried inside my snatch.

"Wh-what's going on?" I gasped.

"I'm joining the two of you, my dear," the Count said.

"But how . . .?" I blurted before the breath was pressed from my lungs as Hugo's powerful arms wrapped around my upper body and pulled me down tightly against his chest. I felt my breasts flattening against the hard maleness of his torso as his cock thoroughly anchored me in place lower down.

Then, as the Count knelt on the couch just behind my rather obscenely upthrusting ass, I realized what the Count had meant when he said he was going to join us.

"Oh, no!" I wailed. "Not in the ass! Not while Hugo still has that fucking tree stump up my twat!"

"Shush, child," the Count said with great gentleness. "All will go well." His hands glided caressingly over my naked ass.

"But it'll *hurt*!" I insisted.

"How would we know where pleasure begins if we had no pain to measure it against?" the Count said as his fingertip began to probe at the fear-puckered opening of my rectum. "Hold her in place," the Count sharply commanded Hugo. I was struggling wildly, trying to twist out of the way, but it was no use. Hugo had me tightly pinned, and now the Count's hands were steadying my ass.

"No! Don't!" I begged as I felt the tip of the Count's cock pressing against my rectum. I squirmed wildly as he tried to shove his cock up my ass, at the same time frantically tightening my sphincter muscles. For a while it worked, but then the Count suddenly slapped me stingingly on the ass. The unexpected sharp pain was such a surprise that I forgot for a second to fight the anal impalement the Count was forcing on me. Muscles loosened. The tip of his cock popped up inside the entrance to my anal passage.

"Aaaauuuggghhhhh!" I wailed. "It hurts! It hurts!"

The Count's voice was soothing as he worked his cock

deeper and deeper into my asshole. "Don't fight it, Christina, and you'll be amazed by how good it feels." As if I didn't know. I've been fucked in the ass before and I've liked it. What made this different was Hugo's massive rod inside my cunt. I was just too full of cock.

Maybe it was the dope making me reflective in the midst of all this activity but I began to think that I was acting like a fool. If I *really* hadn't wanted the Count to do this to me, I could have stopped him. I'd have found some way. How exciting, really, I began to think, having two cocks in one's nether regions at once.

"Ooohhhhh?" I whimpered tentatively, trying to concentrate on what it *really* felt like to have these two cocks inside me. Not bad, in fact, and then as my muscles began to relax, actually quite good. "Uuunnnggghhhh," I moaned, settling down against Hugo's broad chest. By now the Count's cock was all the way up inside my asshole. He stopped moving for a moment, as if gathering his energies. "Now, Hugo," he said once again, but this time his voice was thick with passion. Hugo grunted something, and then the Count and Hugo began fucking their cocks in and out of me in unison, matching each other's rhythms. "Mmmnnnnn . . . God . . ." I sighed. I had never been so totally filled with cock in my life. My lower body throbbed and glowed. I felt myself stretching inside with each double stroke, then partially emptying, and now I wanted more . . . more . . . My whole body was a receptacle yearning for cock.

Hugo was beginning to groan, too. I heard the Count panting behind me. "An incredible feeling," he gasped. "I can feel Hugo's cock inside you . . . right next to my own. There's only a thin membrane separating him and me . . ."

"You're telling *me*!" I panted. "Oh, God . . . Oh, God . . . I'm going to come . . . going to . . . AAAAAA-HHHHHHHHHH!"

An incredible orgasm ripped through my body. It was all Hugo and the Count could do to hold me down while at the same time keeping their cocks busily at work up inside my flailing, writhing body. My spasming cunt was too much for Hugo. With a loud moan, he began coming, his cock ramming far inside me.

The Count, losing his cool, controlled manner at last, went wild. "I can feel it!" he shouted. "I can feel the semen shooting through Hugo's cock . . . right next to mine. I . . ."

And then the Count was coming, too, shouting and moaning in some language I didn't know. I felt a wet heat spreading through my bowels as he shot his load deep into my ass. The three of us clutched tightly to one another, panting and gasping while our orgasms ran their course. Finally, we collapsed together in a pyramid of sated flesh.

After a few minutes I felt the Count's shrinking cock slip from my throbbing asshole. Sighing tiredly, I rolled from Hugo's body, wincing a little as his still-huge prick was jerked from my sensitized vagina. I lay on my back, looking up at the Count.

My emotions were still confused. He had been right; I had enjoyed what he and Hugo had done to me, but at the same time I was annoyed that the Count had not asked my permission first. I do not like to be used, although I was beginning to suspect that perhaps the only way the Count could get it off was to do something kinky, to use trickery and deceit. He was a thoroughly jaded libertine.

He must have sensed my thoughts and began trying to buy me off. "What is your heart's desire?" he suddenly asked me. "Let me know and I'll see that you have it."

My eyes narrowed. "Anything?" I asked.

"Yes . . . of course." I knew what he was thinking—anything money could buy.

I smiled at him. "I want to go to the beach," I said,

knowing full well there were no beaches anywhere near Luxembourg, and also knowing this was not the kind of request he expected. Jewels, furs, yes. But the beach?

I triumphantly watched as a look of puzzlement passed over the Count's face. I had the son-of-a-bitch. He shouldn't fuck around with rich girls like me, I thought. But then he quickly turned the tables by suddenly smiling and saying, "But of course, my dear. We will all go to the beach tomorrow."

CHAPTER FIVE

The beach was hotter than I'd expected; it must have been the reflective power of all that white sand around me. The sun beat down on my naked body, heating my skin and relaxing my tired muscles, cooking the tension out of my drug-jangled nerves. The soft susurration of the small waves was wonderfully soothing.

The Count, true to his word, had arranged for all of us to go to the beach—at Scheveningen on the North Sea, which was just outside The Hague, in Holland. This time the trip was by car rather than plane, even though it was a five hour drive. "Because it's such a nice day," the Count had explained.

We went in several cars, drawn from the Count's considerable motor pool. I drew a red Ferrari convertible, which I shared with Jack. It was a nice drive from Luxembourg to Holland. The first part, passing through mountainous Luxembourg, was very scenic, and the Ferrari was a ball to drive. Jack hung on, white-knuckled as I screamed around hairpin turns past Diekirch and Clervaux. We raced into Belgium, and once past Liége the road debouched onto the North European Plain. Here the scenery was not as interesting but the roads ran straight and I could let the Ferrari race flat out. At 140 miles an hour the roar of the wind past us was horrifyingly wonderful.

We made the trip in a little under four hours, near the end skirting Antwerp, then Breda in Holland. Along the way, I even managed to stop and do a little shopping, filling out the wardrobe the Count had lent me. At Scheveningen, we checked into the Steigenberger Kurhaus hotel, one of my usual five-star stops. There was beach right in front of the hotel, but Jack and I headed further up, toward one of the nude beaches. "Oh, God," I sighed as I shucked off my clothes and sank down onto the soft towel protecting us from the hot sand. "The simple pleasures of life . . ."

"Yeah," Jack agreed, lying down next to me. "The simple pleasures . . . drugs, sex, booze, gambling."

"Jack," I murmured drowsily, "You've got real taste."

I reached out and patted Jack's naked cock. I laughed when I felt it lurch half-erect. "For God's sake, Jack," I said. "After the way you were using that thing last night, I'd expect it to be in splints."

"The only splint it needs, baby, is your hot little fingers," he growled. He looked up and down the beach. "I know Holland is really a liberal place," he said, "but do you think they'd mind if we fucked on the beach?"

I idly fingered his prick, which was now almost fully erect. "I don't know if they'd mind," I said. "But I might. I had enough last night to last me for . . . for . . ."

"For an hour or two," Jack finished for me. "Come on, don't try and tell me Christina van Bell is all fucked out."

"Not fucked out," I replied. "Coked out. The Count is a real pharmaceutical wizard. He must have every pleasure drug known to man. My brain has forgotten where my body is located. I—oh damn, here comes Tolliver."

John Tolliver was meandering down the beach in our direction. He was more than naked, if you know what I mean. John has thin legs and a rather round belly and looks better with his clothes on, and besides, he can be a real bore at times. I wanted time to rest, or at the very least, to have a nice quiet fuck on the beach with Jack.

But John had spotted us. He came shambling over in our direction. He wasn't walking very well. As I wondered about that, I noticed that he was wearing a small shoulder bag and from time to time would reach into it and then raise his hand to his face. As he got closer, I saw a slight haze of white powder floating about his head and shoulders. I was staring, Jack was staring. "Can he really be . . .?" Jack started to say.

John plumped heavily down onto the corner of my beach blanket. "Anybody want a little toot?" he asked, dipping his hand into the bag again. His hand came up partly filled with a crystalline white powder. I noticed then how manic John's usually drawling voice was. I also noticed a strange wild light in his cocker spaniel eyes. "For Christ's sake, John," I said. "Is that bag really full of what I think it is?"

"Cocaine?" Jack added in awe.

"Naw," John said with a giggle. "It's only sugar." He raised his hand to his nose and snorted noisily. I watched his eyes unfocus and roll madly. When he was able to look at me again his eyes were nearly bulging out of his head.

Jack grabbed the bag and looked inside. He dipped in a finger and tasted some of the white powder. "Too fucking *much*!" Jack burst out in his quaint way. "There must be a couple of hundred thousand bucks worth of cocaine in here!"

"Where did you get it, John?" I demanded in a severe voice. John hung his head. "It was in the front seat of the Count's Aston Martin," he replied. "He had so many other bags of so many other things, I thought he wouldn't miss this one."

I thought about that for a moment. "Well," I finally said, "maybe he won't after all." By now John's hand was right underneath my nose, once again full of glittery crystals. Why not? I thought. I was still numb from jet lag, and the long night, and all the dope I had ingested in the last couple of days, so I lowered my head and snorted up a snootfull of pure uncut cocaine crystals. "Wow!" I burst out, leaping to my feet as a rolling wave of energy coursed through my suddenly supercharged body. "Damn . . . I want to *do* something . . . not just lay here in the sun like some creepy reptile. I wonder what kind of action there is around here?"

"We could fuck." Jack said hopefully, while he dipped his hand into the bag and then got his proboscis full.

"Sure . . . but later," I said vaguely. "I want to do something I haven't done for a while, something that really winds you up."

"You sound pretty wound up already," Jack giggled. The coke had hit him by now.

I had a sudden recollection. "Hey!" I said somewhat overbrightly, I'm afraid. My brain was racing madly. "What was it you said before that you like to do? You know, about drugs and sex and booze, and . . . and . . ."

"Gambling?"

"Yes! That's it! Gambling . . . I want to gamble. And you know what, Jack, you corrupter of innocent youth? There's a casino right here at Scheveningen!"

"No shit?" Jack blurted out enthusiastically. He was on his second handful of coke. Tolliver was sitting quietly on the blanket, staring at something a million miles away, obviously temporarily O.D.'d. He put up no resistance when I took the little shoulder bag of coke away from him. "Come on," I said to Jack. "Let's go play games."

Jack came running after me, probably just as much because I was carrying the bag of coke as because of me. "Wait a minute, Christina," he warned. "Shouldn't you take your clothes?"

That one stopped me. "Oh, yeah," I said, then went running back to scoop up my towel and clothes. I was in such a hurry to leave the beach that I tried to dress as I walked, but the shoulder bag got in the way, and when I tried to pull up the zipper on my very tight shorts I got annoyed and gave it up as a bad job, and I also didn't think it worth buttoning my shirt, so I ended up heading for the hotel with the upper half of my blond pussy fur sprouting above the crotch of my shorts and the breeze occasionally flipping my shirt aside to bare first one breast then the other. I looked back once to see Jack hopping up and down madly trying to get his pants on. "Come *on*," I said crossly, then continued on my way.

As I walked through the restaurant area of the hotel on my way to the lobby, I heard a couple of glasses crash to the floor. I was vaguely aware that every male eye in the place was on me, and some of the female eyes, too, but it didn't matter. I was halfway across the lobby to the elevator when I ran into Hugh Johnson, the Count, Claudine, and a couple of the girls. "My, Christina," Claudine said with a snicker. "You're sticking out of your clothes. What's the matter, gaining weight?"

"I'll let you answer that one, honey," I replied. "You're the authority on weight." Then ignoring Claudine, I turned to the others. "I'm going to the casino," I said. "The way I feel now I know I'm going to break the bank."

The Count looked at me closely. "You must have run across Tolliver," he said. "Thank you," and he reached out to take the bag away from me, but I danced beyond reach. "Uh-uh," I said. "Finders keepers."

I must say, the Count was quite gracious about it. He shrugged as if it were merely a bag full of old Kleenex I was carrying. "As you wish, my dear," he said. I liked him for that even if he *had* pulled that little trick on me last night, with him and Hugo making me the meat in a sexual sandwich, and even if he was paying an inordinate amount of attention to that bovine creature, Claudine Perier. "If you want it," I said, "you can come and get it in the casino. Now I'm going up to change."

When I came back down to the lobby, I was wearing an

evening gown I had purchased the day before, which was split so far up one side you could see my hip almost to the belt line. I was also wearing the little shoulder bag. I knew the others would appreciate the latter when we got to the casino.

Several of our group were waiting for me in the lobby—Hugh and Jack and the Count and Claudine and a couple of the girls. I imagined Tolliver still sitting in the same place on the beach, staring vacantly at whatever presented itself in front of him.

I'd been into the coke again while I was dressing, and I was more eager to get moving than ever. "Let's move around some money," I said, and we were off.

We made quite a stir when we walked into the casino. The Count seemed to be a familiar figure there, and Claudine's vapid but admittedly striking face has been seen by millions on the silver screen, and I myself am not exactly unknown. Eagerly rubbing his hands, a member of the casino establishment met us at the door. In his formal black attire he reminded me of an undertaker. "Ah," he said to the Count, "no doubt your party will want the use of the more private gaming rooms."

We agreed, a little raucously because we were all smashed incredibly high on our bagful of snow, which, by the way, the Count had extracted from me in a moment of inattention. I felt better without it, though. The bag hanging from my shoulder ruined the line of my gown.

We all bought chips, the Count and Hugh acquiring some for the starlets. I wrote a check for $10,000, enough to give me a good start at the tables. I don't know what arrangements Claudine made—she probably managed to sell her favors to the manager—but she came away with quite a handful of chips.

The private rooms were not really private; it was simply that only high rollers were permitted here. No gawking tourist peasants allowed with their ten guilder bets. We fanned out for a while, some of us trying the roulette wheel, others vingt-et-un, a few poker, but eventually most of us began to drift toward the craps table. There was very heavy play going on with large amounts of money being waved around.

With my load of coke aboard, I felt that I could handle anything. I pushed my way right up to the table. "Well, well," a loud, somewhat slurred voice boomed. "Make room for the li'l lady."

I turned coolly in the direction of the voice and saw the most stereotypically vulgar Texan I had ever encountered— ten-gallon hat, darted shirt with fancy buttons, tight pants, high, hand-tooled boots, and a face of such mindless arrogance that it made me gasp in admiration. Actually, he was not a bad looking man—he was quite broad in the shoulders and slim hipped, and his face, which was also long and lean, might have been handsome if it hadn't reflected such boundless ignorance.

However, I was fascinated by his vulgarity. I noticed the others edging away from him in distaste, and since I am at heart a rebel, and also because of the current state of my brain, I decided to have a little interaction with this primitive. "Well well," I drawled. "If it isn't Hopalong Cassidy."

He looked puzzled for a moment, then brayed with laughter. "And who we-all got hee-ur?" he roared. "Belle Starr? Whoo-eeeh! Looka that dress! If'n it was split up any higher, honey, yore armpit's be showin'."

"Are you playing or talking?" I asked coldly, and threw a hundred dollar bill down on the table. Wherever I am, I always like to gamble with dollars. I like them and they like me.

A glint appeared in the Texan's somewhat bloodshot eyes. I imagined he had quite a load on. He threw a hundred dollar bill down beside mine, and the play commenced. Of course there were others playing, but the real contest was between him and me as we bet against one another.

For a while I was way ahead; I'd taken several thousand dollars from him, and he accepted his bad luck jovially. But then my luck changed. Bit by bit he whittled down my lead until it was the Texan who was ahead. I accepted the situation in a somewhat different way than he had when I was winning. It was turning me on. Physically. Not just the fact that this genuine Dixie savage was tall and rather hard looking; it was the play itself, the money changing hands back and forth. To me, money is power, and as I've previously mentioned, power acts on me like an aphrodisiac. Each time I won or lost, it didn't matter which, I felt a little more heat build up between my nearly naked thighs, until my little honey-pit was seething.

A crowd had formed around us. It was made up mostly of our original group, but a few others had joined in too. Everyone gets excited when there are big winners and losers and that was the case now, with everybody a little bit out of their heads.

I was the big loser. I wagered my last $500 and saw it swept away. Someone else threw and lost, and then the dice were mine. I stood holding them in my hand, wondering what to do. I knew that if I broke the momentum by getting more chips, the magic of the moment would be lost. But I had nothing to bet!

The Texan noticed this too. "Whatsa matter, li'l honey?" he said. "Run outa chips? Never mind. I'll lend ya some. I love to watch what your dress does when you bend over to roll 'em."

I looked him straight in the eye. "I don't need charity, buster," I said, "but you've given me an idea. So you like my ass? Tell you what—I'm tired of playing for these funny pieces of green paper. What say we make the stakes a little more personal?"

His eyes narrowed, and he sounded a lot more sober when he asked, "Like what?"

"Since you like it so much, why don't we just play for my ass?" I said. "Or a piece of it."

"You name the terms, honey," he drawled.

"If I win this roll, I take my stake back from you, doubled. If I lose . . . you get me."

"Yore puttin' a mighty high value on that purty rear end of yours," the Texan growled.

"It's worth it," I said simply.

"Amen," someone else said from the other side of the table. I think it was Jack, but I was busy meeting the Texan's hard blue eyes. He suddenly nodded. "It's a bet," he snapped.

I smiled at him, then turned to face the table, slipping the dice into the dice cup. I rattled them around slowly at first, then more violently. "Come on, you little white bastards," I murmured, "and save Momma's pretty pussy from the big bad man."

Maybe I shouldn't have put it that way. Maybe I didn't really want to save my pussy from what everybody could see growing in the Texan's pants as he watched me bend over the table, and my skirt slid to the side to bare half of one buttock. I shook the dice one last time . . . and threw a double one.

"Snake eyes," someone said. "The shooter loses," the house man intoned. A deep silence followed, with everyone around the table waiting breathlessly to see what would happen next. I was still staring down at my double zero when I sensed the Texan move right alongside me. "Where do I collect my winnings?" he asked coolly.

Still partly bent over the table, I turned only my head toward him. The bulge in the front of his pants was huge. "Why not right here?" I asked in a sultry voice, bending a little further forward and thrusting my ass back toward him. The skirt of my gown slid a little further, baring more of my buttock.

"Think I'll take you up on that," the Texan drawled, although I noticed his voice was getting a little unsteady and thick. "You know, lady," he added, "you got balls."

"You'd better hope not," I said, then my breath caught a little as I heard the sound of a zipper behind me. I wanted to turn and look at what was happening, how much cock was erupting from the Texan's tight pants, but why bother? I'd find out soon enough.

A hand roughly jerked my gown completely out of the way, baring my lower body to the waist. "Wowee," the Texan murmured. "What an ass. But my granny warned me about people who don't wear no underwear."

"What'd she tell you, cowboy?" I asked, although I was having a little trouble with my voice. All my biological systems were set on sex, with nothing much left over for anything else.

"Don't matter what she told me," he muttered. "But since then I found out they're my kinda people."

The others at the table had formed a rough circle around us, which was good, I suppose, because it screened us off from the other tables and from intervention. The house man started to protest, but someone shoved a hundred dollar bill into his hand, and he shut up. I was staring down at the table, my hands braced against the raised edges, my barely covered tits hanging in space. I felt one of his big hands on my left buttock, the other up between my slightly spread thighs. There was something in that hand and it was hot and pointed and hard, and it was heading straight for my cunt. "My God!" someone murmured. "He's actually going to do it to her!"

And he *did* do it to me. I felt my pussy lips being parted by the head of a good-sized prick. I tightened my grip on the table edges. Just in time. With no real preliminaries, the Texan rammed his cock all the way up into my vagina, one big pounding invasion that forced the air from my lungs in a rather unladylike grunt. Then, holding onto my ass cheeks for support, he began to fuck me hard. For the first few strokes I kept silent, but I'm a noisy lover, and as the Texan's big organ continued to stroke in and out of me, I began to vocalize. "Ah . . . ah . . . ah . . ." I sang out each time his plunging cock slammed in the entire length of my vagina. Then I got louder: "Oh! Oh! Oh!"

I was hanging onto the table for dear life now, bending down so low that my nipples were scraping the tabletop. I could hear the Texan panting with effort behind me; his loins were slapping noisily against my ass cheeks. Somebody a little braver than the rest reached down and slipped a hand inside the top of my dress and began fondling my breasts. That did it. "Oooohhhhhhh," I moaned loudly. "Going to come . . . coming . . . cooooommmmmiiiiinnnnggg!"

"Aaaarrgghhhh!" the Texan groaned behind me, and then he was coming, too, his cock swollen huge inside my twat, filling me with that wonderful slippery hot stuff. He kept it hard for a long time, stroke after stroke, more and more of his semen gushing into me, until I could feel the overflow sliding down the insides of my thighs. He finally finished, and with one last hearty hand-squeeze of my naked ass, abruptly withdrew, leaving me gasping and helpless, half-hanging into the pit of the craps table.

Someone was kind enough to help me up, and I turned on shaky legs to face the Texan. "Gotta hand it to you, lady," he said. "You ain't no welsher. And I cain't say I ever had a better night shootin' craps."

I was still a little breathless from my orgasm. "The pleasure was all mine, cowboy," I said. Then I laughed. Jesus, this was beginning to sound like a grade-B Western. I looked around the casino. It was a nice enough casino, but my head was reeling from drugs, from excitement, from sex, and despite all that I'd experienced in the past couple of days, I wanted more. Lots more. Suddenly this somewhat sedate North Sea resort was not enough for me. I turned to the Count, who had his hand in the top of Claudine's dress. "As long as we're doing the casino scene," I said to him, "why don't we do it right?"

"And what is your version of right?" he asked, calmly shifting his hand to Claudine's other tit.

"Let's go to the casino of casinos," I said. "Let's go to Monte Carlo."

The Count smiled. "I'd already thought of that. I had my plane moved to Schiphol airport, in Amsterdam. The engines are already warming up."

CHAPTER SIX

The trip to Monte Carlo on the Count's plane was pretty much a repeat of the last couple of days, with a surfeit of drugs and alcohol. The natural high that had been supporting me began to collapse, but in my totally stoned and exhausted state a new clarity began to shine through. I know I was probably acting the same as I'd been the last few days, but inside, my head was different. It was as if I were dreaming and were watching myself dreaming. Some separate part of my being was able to observe the laughing, joking, coke-snorting, champagne-swilling me with perfect calm. This separate part of me was also somehow aware that something momentous was about to happen.

The usual queue of limousines met us at Nice airport, and we were whisked away to the tiny principality of Monaco just a few miles down the Grande Corniche. The sun was setting over the Mediterranean, its last amber rays warming the enormous, garishly colored high-rises that now dominate Monte Carlo. The old Monte Carlo of soft pink villas was gone forever, alas, along with its fairy-tale Princess.

The limousines let us out in the little park in front of the Victorian façade of the Casino. We were made especially welcome, of course, and were ushered immediately into the plusher parts of the establishment. I followed along with the others in my strange stoned-yet-perceptive mood. I played a few turns of the roulette wheel, but I was not

56

really paying much attention to what I was doing. That inner part of me was waiting, watching, while Hugh and John and Jack and the Count—who was quite openly courting Claudine, to the literal peril of her ass—as well as our diminishing contingent of starlets laughed and chattered and drank and played the tables.

Then I saw him—a tall and elegant man who was literally the tall, dark, handsome stranger standing at a nearby roulette table. He was beautifully dressed, so calm and yet so strong-looking and was playing the table with a glorious insouciance. Something drew me toward him like a magnet. When I got closer I saw that the pile of chips he had pushed out in front of him represented an impressive sum of money. It was all on the red.

"*Mesdames . . . messieurs,*" the croupier intoned ritualistically, "*faites vos jeux.*"

Then the wheel was spinning round and round, the little ivory ball descending, finally clicking madly in the numbered slots. The number it finally came to rest in was a red one. The stranger had won. Now there was a *very* lot of money in front of him, a lot even by my standards.

He made a motion indicating it was all to remain on the red. The wheel spun again, and again a red number won. And once again *he*—that's how I was thinking of him even then—signaled that his winnings were to ride again on red.

And again the winning cycle was repeated. There was now an astronomical amount stacked on the table in front of the stranger. This time when he indicated it was all to ride on the next turn of the wheel, the croupier began to sweat. He must have signaled in some way, because a head croupier suddenly showed up. There was a hurried whispered conversation between the two casino employees, and then another showed up, this one obviously very high in the pecking order. He frowned when he saw how much money was on the table; clearly a win would hurt the house. But then when he saw who was playing, his manner became instantly obsequious and ingratiating. "Of course," he said. "The señor may play as he wishes."

The señor, *He*, merely nodded politely and indicated that the play was to continue. Again the wheel spun, but this time when the ball came to rest, it was the black that had won. With an audible sigh of relief, the croupier raked in the fortune stacked on the table in front of the stranger. He betrayed no emotion as his winnings vanished instantly. There were no grandiose gestures at all; he didn't even shrug. However, I do think I saw a tiny smile tug at the corners of his well-shaped mouth as he turned away from the table.

His movement brought him face to face with me. He stopped. I didn't move. We looked into one another's faces for a long moment, and in that moment, something happened, something that had the feel of permanency, something of staggering importance. At least, that's the way it felt at the time, though later events were to make me question the ultimate meaning of these feelings.

"Madame?" he said to me in a soft, slightly accented, beautifully modulated voice.

"Mademoiselle," I corrected.

"You are not playing," he said.

"I have had enough of playing," I replied, vaguely aware that the words had a far larger significance than their surface meaning.

"So have I," he said. He took my arm and we walked out of the casino together into the balmy Mediterranean night. Neither of us spoke as a chauffeured limousine took us to the harbor and let us out on a dock next to a large and very beautiful yacht.

"Yours?" I asked.

"I think so," he replied. "I would have to ask my lawyer. In any case, I use it."

Once again I was struck by this man's attitude toward wealth and belongings. This magnificent boat was only something he used, like the money he had so serenely watched vanish at the roulette table.

He led me to a kind of small promenade deck, where we watched as men cast off the lines mooring the yacht to the dock. "Are we leaving?" I asked.

"It is a beautiful night to be upon the sea," was his only answer. I accepted it. Drinks were brought to us. The alcohol seemed to have no effect on me; I suppose I was beyond that point, although not from being sloppily drunk. It was that strange clarity, which was still with me. I was my own main character in a vivid, waking dream.

At first we watched the glittering lights of Monaco dwindle behind us as the yacht raced out to sea. Then the stranger turned to me. "We will go below now," he said. He stated it as a simple fact, neither an invitation nor an order. I nodded and let him guide me down a descending passageway into the heart of the ship. He opened a brass-handled mahogany door and stood aside for me to enter.

"Oh, how beautiful!" I said as I looked around me. We were in an enormous master stateroom, very beautifully furnished, with rare woods and precious objects everywhere and with a huge bed taking up fully a quarter of the available space. We both looked at the bed, then turned to look at one another. There was a moment of silent communion, a mutual offer, a mutual acceptance, and then as I continued standing, he began gently to take off my clothes. He was no longer so inscrutable. As each new part of me appeared, he would exclaim with a kind of childish joy, "How beautiful," or "You are perfect." And as each new part of me came into the open, he would spend a little time getting to know it. When my gown was down around my waist, he caressed my tingling breasts, his thumbs lightly brushing over my nipples, bringing them to a quick, throbbing hardness. He bent down to kiss their sensitive tips, which made me gasp with pleasure.

Then my gown was around my ankles. I kicked it away

as he trailed warm, soft kisses down over my naked belly, pausing for a few seconds to dip his tongue into my navel. I gasped again. Now he was kneeling before me, still fully dressed, his mouth muzzling the delta of my pubic hair. His hands slipped up between my thighs, but there was no sudden attack of finger against tender flesh. Instead, he stroked my upper thighs, glided wonderfully knowing and sensitive fingertips over the swelling contours of my buttocks. I felt his fingers pressing my pubic lips together, which was both oddly soothing and wonderfully exciting. His tongue made one brief, teasing foray up into my slit. "Aaahhhh!" I whimpered sharply, my hips jerking involuntarily toward his face.

He seemed to know just when to stop. He stood, leaving me trembling in front of him. I began taking off his clothes. "Please . . . let me," I begged, my shaking fingers fumbling with buttons and belts and all the other ridiculousnesses of our modern body coverings. Now it was my turn to exclaim over each new revelation—his lean-muscled torso, the perfection of his nearly hairless skin, the slenderness of his hips and the strength of his thighs. At the very last I fell onto my knees in front of him and took his naked cock in my right hand. It was half erect. I began to lick its tapering, rubbery tip, feeling the entire shaft slowly swelling in the gentle circle of my fingers.

It was not an enormously huge cock, not like Hugo's, but it was a lovely one, straight and hard and smooth-skinned and eminently qualified to fill a pussy. I had one in mind for it to fill, but I quickly discovered there were many more preliminaries ahead. My stranger suddenly scooped me up and bore me toward the big bed. "Oh!" I exclaimed in decent maidenly fashion, because I did feel maidenlike as strong arms laid me down on the luxurious coverlet. Then my lover-to-be was lying next to me and for an eternity I was aware only of the incredibly beautiful sensations that were kissed, licked, stroked, and rubbed into my receptive body. Warm, strong lips closed around my nipples, fingertips found their way into my most secret and sensitive places. We discovered I had erogenous zones I had never before known about. None of this tired me but only served to make me come more alive. I had a few orgasms. I remember one when his tongue tip was lightly flicking my clitoris back and forth. And each orgasm served only to heighten my sensitivity. His arousal, meanwhile, stayed constant. Part of the time I had my fingers either lightly stroking or tightly clutching the reassuringly hard shaft of his cock. It seemed to be always there, available.

Then that cock began to pay more attention to the achingly ready pit of my throbbing pussy. My lover ended up lying crossways below my body, with me lying on my back and both my legs trailing over his hips. The tip of his cock was pointed in the direction of my vagina, but was not quite there. I wanted it to come into me. I strained my hips in his direction, but he artfully avoided any direct genital contact. Instead, his fingers began playing a tune up and down the length of my gushing slit and on top of my almost painfully swollen clit. Somewhere during this time, a time of mini-orgasms and delirious sighing, I became aware of the tip of his cock sliding slowly up and down my inner slit, while his fingertips were up inside my vagina. Several times the two nearly swapped places, with the tip of his cock prodding lightly at my eager opening. But then the fingers would return, eventually to be replaced by the cock again until I was thoroughly confused and lay panting and moaning wildly.

I was not aware of just when his cock went inside me, but there came a moment when I realized my vagina was very full and that something longer and thicker than a finger was pushing inside. "Oooohhhhhhh . . . yesssssss,"

I sighed. "I want it. I want it inside me. I don't want it to ever leave."

I was aware of him changing position, moving above me without letting his cock leave my body. I adjusted my legs, then looked up at him. He was hovering above me, his arms braced, holding still for the moment, his expression very serious.

Then he began to fuck me. "Ah!" I cried out as his cock slid all the way up to the far end of my vagina. My body arched, my hips lurching mindlessly up toward his.

The rest is a wonderful, sensuous blur in my memory. I remember his cock lancing deeper and deeper into my cunt. I remember his hands on my breasts, then his mouth. I remember my legs rising to circle behind him, my heels greedily jerking his buttocks closer to my spasming cunt. His earlier lovemaking, the teasing and stroking and licking, had left me incredibly orgasmic. Now climax after climax ripped through my body, each one stronger than the last, each one lifting me to a higher plateau of sensitivity. The culmination came when he did, when I saw his face stiffen, when I felt his cock begin spewing its milky load into my body. I may have passed out then from the intensity of my final orgasm. All I remember is flashing colors and the whole world shaking, and then someone was pressing on my ribs and when I looked up it was him. "You stopped breathing for a moment," he explained.

"That happens sometimes," I managed to gasp. "When the pleasure is particularly intense."

He was still in me. I could feel his cock shrinking. I didn't want it to leave my body, not yet. We both rolled to the side, still locked together. It was in this position that we finally began to talk to, and about each other, and about ourselves. "Let me introduce myself," I said, clasping my pussy muscles around his cock in the way of a handshake. "I'm Christina van Bell."

I waited to see if his expression showed he had heard of

me. Most people have, but his face showed nothing in the way of recognition. He continued looking at me for several seconds. "Do you really want names?" he asked.

"Yes."

"Very well," he said, as if it were the end of something. "I am Javier Torralba Bienvia. Now, do you know anything more about what I am than you did a few seconds ago?"

"Well . . . no," I admitted. "Only that I like your name. Are you Spanish?"

"Colombian," he said with great pride. "My father's family was almost pure Spanish, my mother's family mostly Indian."

"Ah, yes," I said, noticing how his skin shone slightly golden against mine. "A son of the Incas."

"No," he said. "Not of the Incas. We have our own Indians. Their culture was quite distinct."

"I have never been to Colombia."

"It is very beautiful."

There was a long silence after that during which we changed our position and his penis finally slid out of me. I gave a little shudder of loss, which he eased by starting to gently stroke my body, not so much sexually as affectionately. It was then that I told him all about myself, how I had grown up very simply in Vermont, how I had inherited sixteen million dollars out of the blue, how I had used this money to buy *World* magazine, how I had fought to make it a great publication, and also how I had played just as hard, how the tabloids had a field day with "Christina van Bell, International Playgirl."

"Ah, yes," he said. "Perhaps I did see your name once in a magazine."

"Once? God, I wish *I* had only seen it once in those rags. But if you spend time at places like Monte Carlo, the Côte d'Azur . . ."

"I am almost never in those places," he said. "I rarely leave my home."

"In Colombia?"

"Yes. At my *latifundio*. I think you would call it a ranch. I am a simple *ganadero*, a cattleman."

Not so simple as you sound, I thought. No one who throws away such a huge fortune at roulette, obviously just to see what it feels like; no one who can command the services of a yacht like this one, is only a simple cattleman. Aloud, I said, "So you prefer living on the land?"

"There is no other life," he said fervently. "Everything else is only an imitation of life. The land is everything— living with the elements and sometimes fighting against them when they try to break you, fighting for the life of brute animals and then later taking that life so the animal may be food for others, matching wits with the sun, and with the rains, with other men, bad men. What other life could there be?"

For a moment he looked around the ornate quarters we were in with something approaching disdain. Now I understood that little smile that had tugged at his lips in the casino. None of it had had any real meaning for him. He had just told me where his reality lay. For a moment my mind toyed with a few clever ripostes; after all, he was putting down the world I lived in, the world of the cities, of sophisticated conversation where one could meet the thrust of other clever minds. But something in the purity of his convictions held me back. I sensed I would only end up showing myself to be in some way gauche. Certainly more gauche than this self-described "simple cattleman." I saw in him a depth of sophistication that far outstripped the sophistication of any of my so-called worldly friends.

The conversation began to lag. Javier's gentle stroking was beginning to have a far from soothing effect on my body. Within minutes we were once again making love, this time in a slower, deeper, more complete way.

Afterwards, I slept a little. Then hours, or minutes, later, I couldn't tell which, we were making love again. Sometime during a period of half-sleep, someone brought in food. We ate, then made love again.

All these days of too many drugs and too much alcohol and too little sleep were beginning to catch up with me. I slipped into a state of sensuous half-consciousness. I vaguely remember the yacht docking somewhere. I remember being half carried up a long winding walk in the dark and then into an enormous house. A big bed waited. I remember sinking down into its softness, Javier beside me, making dreamlike love, and then blackness.

When I woke, sunlight was streaming in through a high arched window. I was in quite a beautiful room, if a rather hard one. Everything was stone—the floor, the walls, even the tiles on the ceiling. Very Spanish. I was wondering if Javier had whisked me to his home in Colombia. I turned to ask him, but, alas, there was no Javier sleeping next to me. Only an empty bed. "Javier?" I called out, rising from the bed. I'd only gone a few steps toward the heavy wooden door when it opened and an old woman came in, obviously a servant. "The señorita wants something?" she asked in Spanish.

"Yes," I said. "I want Javier. Will you call him for me?"

"No está, señorita," she replied.

"He's not here?" I asked. "When will he be back?"

"No sé." It was the maddeningly flat Spanish "I don't know," which can also mean "I don't want to know," or "I don't want *you* to know." A statement of total ignorance. I knew I would have to find out for myself. I started toward the door, remembering at the last moment to snatch up a robe and wrap it around my naked body. I left the room and for a while wandered through the labyrinthine passageways of an enormous house. I eventually found my way outside. I was definitely in Spain. I recognized the

rockiness of the landscape, the ancient, gnarled olive trees, the blueness of the sea only a few hundred yards away.

The *empty* sea. A path led down to a dock. I remembered that path. I had walked up it from the boat. But there was now no boat at the dock. The old woman was right behind me. I twisted around toward her and asked fiercely, "Where is Javier?"

"Gone, señorita," was the uninflected reply.

"Gone *where*?"

"*No sé.*" That flat wall of not knowing. I begged, I threatened, I pleaded, I cursed. I ranged the house and the grounds, and everyone I met had the same answer. "*No sé.*"

I eventually had to concede that Javier had gone and left no forwarding address. At least not for me. Why, why, why? I wondered. Surely our being together must have been as wonderful for him as it had been for me. God damn it, the son-of-a-bitch had abandoned me!

I was doing a slow simmer as I prepared to leave. When the servants realized I wanted to go, they became much more cooperative. They produced clothing, an overnight case, and a car to the airport. We hadn't driven far from the house before I realized I was on the island of Mallorca, familiar scenery to me, although I had never before seen the house I'd awakened in. It was quite far, about a two hour drive from the airport. I was glad of that. It gave me time to think.

In the first place, I was angry. I don't like being dumped. I toyed with the idea of tracking down Señor Javier Torralba Bienvia and giving him a good swift kick in the balls. In front of lots of people.

Then my mood began to change. Javier did not seem like the kind of jerk I should kick in the balls. There had been a depth to him, a realness that he could not have faked. There had also been a depth to our lovemaking, to the way we were drawn to one another that would be possible but difficult to fake. No, I knew something powerful had taken place between us. But why, then, had the bastard left me?

Suddenly a memory surfaced in my mind. It was a memory of something Javier had said. I struggled for the words—I had been half asleep at the time, floating in a limbo of postorgasmic bliss, but Javier had seemed very much awake. The words . . . Ah yes . . . "We are from different worlds, Christina." Something like that. "Worlds that are at war. Worlds that do not recognize one another. I doubt either of us could ever leave their world for the world of the other."

Tears stung my eyes. That was why he had left—to avoid the degrading spectacle of our love being buried under the million petty annoyances of conflicting lifestyles. His leaving had been an act of love. But you can't get away from me that easily, you noble bastard, I said fiercely to myself. We have the possibility of beauty between us. It's worth a try, God damn it. It's worth a try!

CHAPTER SEVEN

At the airport, I felt free to go anywhere in the world I wanted. I thought for a moment of going to Colombia but knew I would be intruding in Javier's world, so instead I opted for New York, home base, where I had the resources to implement the plan that was beginning to form in my mind.

"Christina!" Malcolm bellowed when I walked into the offices of *World* that afternoon. "Where the hell have you been? Jesus Christ, you left the whole place hanging. We've been trying to decide—"

"Be quiet, Malcolm," I said pleasantly. "And don't think I'm back. I'm only a temporary apparition and I'll be gone again before you know it."

"But you can't just—"

"Oh yes I can. That's why you're here, Malcolm, to run this place when irresponsible little Christina goes flying off into the wild blue yonder."

Malcolm was beginning to swell up and turn purple. "If you think—" he began, and I knew it was time for a little honey.

"Malcolm," I said soothingly, "you know how I count on you. Who else in the world could I trust the way I trust you?"

Malcolm looked at me shrewdly. "Don't give me all that crap," he said. "Are you in some kind of trouble?"

"Well . . . I suppose you could put it that way."

His eyes opened wide in amazement. "Dammit! You're in love, aren't you?"

"Well, I—"

"You, Christina van Bell, champion heartbreaker of the world, and now it's your turn. Hah! Maybe there is some justice, after all."

"Malcolm . . . that's not kind!"

He saw that I was really upset and came over and put his arm around me. "Hey, honey," he said fondly. "You just tell me what you want me to do for you, and I'll do it. Okay?"

"Oh, Malcolm," I replied, laying my head on his shoulder. "Why are you so good to me when I'm such a bitch to you? It's just that this time I . . ."

He put his hand over my mouth. "Uh-uh. No details. You might start me crying. Just tell me the necessaries."

I felt both relieved and guilty. Was I using this nice man? Probably no more than he wanted to be used. Some people simply have endless amounts to give. "I'll probably be away for quite a while," I said. 'I'll need money and I'll need not to worry about the magazine. Knowing you're here, there won't be any need to. I'll be around for a few more days. We can set up operating procedures, and later I'll do my best to keep in touch."

There were a few more hugs and pats and we both felt better. I knew my back was protected now, and Malcolm felt good because he truly loves running *World* magazine. We exchanged a father-daughter-type kiss and then I went into my office and rummaged through my desk drawer for my master address book. I found the name I was looking for, Alfonso Gonzalez, with a string of numbers listed after it. I picked up the phone and dialed the New York number. I was lucky.

" 'Allo," a deep voice replied.

"Alfonso," I said, delighted. "You're in town."

A moment's hesitation, then recognition. "Christina!

How delighted I am that you have remembered my humble self. To what do I owe the honor of this call?''

"I'd like to come over and see you. May I?"

"You have to ask? When?"

"Right now, if it's all right. Say in about twenty minutes."

"*Bueno*. I'll see you then."

Alfonso is an old friend . . . and lover. We do not see each other very much; I don't know why. Whenever I do see him I have a wonderful time. Some people are just not fated to be close to one another, I guess. And now as I took a cab toward Alfonso's apartment, I knew I was going to use him a little, just as I had used Malcolm. I thought of Javier. "You bastard," I murmured, "the things I'm doing for you."

Alfonso kissed me as I went in the door of his apartment. It was a somewhat tentative kiss, not too brief, but not assuming too much, either. "You are as beautiful as ever," he said, stepping back to admire me.

"That's enough of that Latin charm," I said, laughing. "But I *am* glad you were in New York when I called."

"You Anglo-Saxons," he snorted. "You have no sense of romance, of the delightful games men and women can play. But, Christina, I've been in New York for weeks. You could have called before."

"I never know when you'll be here, Alfonso," I explained. Then as I looked around at the obviously expensive apartment, I jokingly added, "You probably spend most of your time running dope up from Colombia."

I knew I had goofed when I saw him wince. "Everyone thinks that all Colombians smuggle cocaine," he said. "If you only knew what the damned dope trade has done to my country."

"Oh, I didn't know. I'm sorry, Alfonso."

He waved his hand deprecatingly, but I had unplugged a torrent. "That's okay," he said. "The world thinks it's a clever comment to make just because we—the country as a whole—makes so much money on the dope trade. But the results are disastrous. In the first place, the trade is in the hands of our local Indian Mafia, a vicious bunch of bastards, if there ever was one. And all that damned money—usually cash—flowing around has caused the most terrible inflation and of course has fueled corruption. Then it entails terrible violence when different Mafia people fight among themselves, or try to terrorize people who have something they want. They have power, these Mafia, but they're so fresh from the gutter that they have no knowledge of how to use it.''

"That bad?" I said sympathetically.

"Oh, yes. Colombia has a history of violence anyway. The situation was beginning to improve when there was that terrible episode when one of our generals seized power. What a monster! His troops used to cruise through the streets in their jeeps and trucks, testing their new automatic weapons on passersby. You know, we used to have that very Latin custom in Colombia, the *paseo*, where people would promenade in the late afternoon and early evening just to see and be seen. Thousands in the streets. A wonderful social thing, but all those terrible experiences changed the minds of my countrymen to think that the streets are unsafe. And they are. They're full of thieves, killers, the police and military. Then after that monster was overthrown there was another twenty-year struggle for power. *La violencia*, we call it. The violence. Tens of thousands were killed. Neighbors would murder the entire family next door. That finally ended, but now we have that ugliness replaced by the ugliness of the drug trade, and we have a society which believes that it is all right to get money any way you can, even if it's another person's money.''

I was fascinated. I was getting a capsule insight into the social customs and conditions of Javier's country. I wondered how he would respond to what Alfonso had just said. Would he talk about the purity of the land? Maybe Javier's idealism was some kind of response to the other, negative conditions in his country.

"But forgive me, lovely lady," Alfonso said, abruptly lightening the mood. "You did not come here to talk politics and history. You came here to see me, right? I can only ask, how could you stand it to not see me for so long?"

I had to laugh at the sheer, lighthearted arrogance of Alfonso's manner. I knew what he was leading up to. As I have said, Alfonso and I are sometimes lovers. I had not come here for that purpose, but I was not completely averse to the idea, either. Alfonso is one of the finest lovers I have ever met. I suspect part of the reason for that is that he does not have a very big cock. Many well-endowed men become lazy. They rely on the size of their cock to please a woman. Not Alfonso. He knew dozens of different ways to please, and he was an expert in each of them.

Although I was in search of someone whom I was beginning to think of as my true love, it never occurred to me to use that as a reason not to make love to Alfonso. To me, love is something infinite. You can't use it up. You don't diminish it by spending some here, some there. There is always an infinite supply left over. Besides, I was horny.

I let Alfonso lead me into his bedroom. There was the big bed I knew so well. Alfonso sat on it while I stood alongside. "Let me see my two soft-eyed little friends," he said, unbuttoning my blouse. I shrugged it off and it fell silently to the carpet behind me, leaving me naked to the waist. Alfonso, still seated on the bed in front of me, cupped a hand under each of my breasts. His thumbs played ever so softly over my nipples. "Mmnnn," I said. Alfonso drew me a little closer to him, his fingers molding my tits, pointing my nipples straight at his face. I closed my eyes, feeling his warm breath washing over my nipples, and then I felt him gently licking. "Oh, Alfonso," I sighed, my eyes flying open.

I don't know quite what Alfonso does with his mouth when he is sucking a pair of tits, but if he could patent and sell it, he'd make millions. I looked down at his dark, curly hair as he drifted from one tit to the next. My nipples felt as if someone were lapping them with liquid fire. Hot tremors of feeling poured through my breasts, seeping down into my body and pooling hotly in my belly. I could feel my vagina spasm in reaction each time Alfonso did something different to my nipples. His hands left my tits and drifted down toward my crotch. As I thrust my tits forward into Alfonso's wonderful mouth, he removed my skirt. My legs were beginning to shake. "Oh, God, Alfonso . . . I'm going to fall down if you don't help me," I whimpered.

He reached around behind me with one hand, burying it in the cleft of my ass, steadying me, his fingers pressing against my cunt from behind. His other hand was coming at my cunt from the front, just pressing, without moving his fingers. My hips began to rock forward and back as I desperately rubbed my twat against Alfonso's hands. "Oh!" I yelped as I had my first orgasm. Jesus, I didn't even have my pants off yet and I was already coming!

I couldn't remain standing another moment. I gave a little moan of sadness as I felt my breasts slip away from his warm wet mouth, and then I was kneeling between Alfonso's knees. "I want to see it," I murmured, unfastening Alfonso's fly. I could see that his cock was already partly hard. I reached inside his fly and pulled it out into the open. As I said, he doesn't have a particularly big cock, but it's a nice shape. I felt it throbbing hotly in my hand. The little slit in the tip was staring at me vertically.

"C'mere, lollipop," I murmured, and bending down, took Alfonso's cock inside my mouth.

"Ah . . . *querida* Christina," Alfonso groaned as I began sucking his prick. "Your mouth is as soft as melting butter . . . as warm as the sun . . ." You have to give these Latin lovers credit. They have the greatest lines and can deliver them with a perfectly straight face. Not that Alfonso wasn't actually enjoying what my mouth was doing to his cock. I could feel his entire body shuddering with pleasure each time I glided my lips the length of his prick. When I felt the shuddering getting a little too heavy, I pulled my mouth away. I wanted him to come in another place.

We tore at each other's clothes and fell naked onto the bed together, arms and legs intertwined. Alfonso began kissing me all over—my face, my neck, my breasts, my belly. "Don't drown," I warned him as his hot trail of kisses neared my cunt. I could feel the hot, warm liquids gushing out of my vagina. My crotch, my thighs, my ass all felt hot and slippery and sexy.

Then his magic lips were pressing against my labia, his tongue thrusting its way into my slit. "Oh God, Alfonso!" I babbled. "You're driving me crazy."

He looked up at me, a lazy smile on his pussy-shiny face. "But my dear," he said, "I have only just begun."

It was true. For the next ten minutes or so, Alfonso's lips and tongue and fingers played an incredible tune on the quivering instrument of my cunt. At times it felt as if a thousand mad butterflies were fluttering around my achingly swollen clitoris. Other times, as Alfonso thrust his stiffened tongue deep into my seething pit, I imagined I was being raped by a living snake. At one point he was sucking on my clit, with two fingers up inside my vagina, and the fingers of his other hand busy with my nipples. I was wailing madly, bucking and writhing on the bed while a seemingly endless string of orgasms rippled through my twat. I was going out of my mind, I was dying—wonderfully.

And he hadn't even fucked me yet. That was rectified a moment later when he took his mouth away from my dripping, spasming pussy. I saw him hovering over me, his face intent, flushed, shiny with my inner juices. And then I felt him slip inside me. It was no great jarring, pounding invasion. I was too wet and there was not that much cock, but what cock there was was endowed with the most intimate knowledge of a woman's inner feelings. "Oh . . . oh, yes!" I panted. "Fuck me, Alfonso . . . make me come."

"With the greatest love, Christina," he said, smiling warmly down at me, his face back-lit with passion. That was another one of Alfonso's secrets as a great lover—he really gets into it emotionally. I could *feel* his feelings pouring into me via his cock.

I held onto him tightly, my hips rocking up to meet his. He was fucking me slowly, gently, his prick doing amazing things inside me, going in directions I didn't know a cock could. For the time being my series of orgasms stopped. I floated on a sea of warm, ever-increasing sensation. We moved together like one interlocked being for what seemed like hours. And then I knew I was in trouble. "Oh-oh," I whimpered as I felt what promised to be the orgasm of orgasms building up deep inside my belly. The inside of my cunt felt incredibly full, swollen, eagerly clasping Alfonso's steadily moving prick. He did something then at just the right moment. I'm not sure just what it was, something with my breasts while his cock seemed to rub against some particularly sensitive place, and then the dam burst and that waiting tidal wave of orgasm swept over me. "Oh!" I cried out. "Ooh . . . ooooo00hhhhhh . . . OOOOOHHHHHH ALFOOOOONNSSOOOOO!" Those were the last meaningful sounds I made for quite a while. I don't know how Alfonso did it, but he kept me coming, just one amazing orgasm, for an immensely long time. My body was far from my control, jerking and twisting, my cunt feeling like the atomic bomb had just gone off inside it, my mind a Technicolor blast, and amidst it all, I was vaguely aware of Alfonso coming inside me, the hot gush of his semen warming my already simmering interior. He seemed to come for as long as I did, and when I finally collapsed in a sweating, panting heap on the bed, he collapsed right along with me.

He still continued doing marvelous things to my body so that I would float back down to earth gradually, but the main show was over. I doubted that I could stand a double feature. My pussy was making desperate, scared little twitchings, like a small animal that's just had a close call. "You Colombian bastard," I moaned. "No wonder the birth rate's so high in your country. It is, isn't it?"

"Oh, yes," he said. "Unfortunately." And then he smiled. "So you like the way Colombians make love, do you?"

That made me feel a twinge of guilt. I had, after all, come here to see Alfonso about another man, another Colombian. The last hour or so had been a wonderful bonus, but I am always nervous about upsetting the male ego. It was Alfonso who made it easy. "Now," he said with mock seriousness. "Tell me the real reason you came here today."

I'm afraid I blushed. "That's all right," Alfonso assured me. "What do I have to complain about, after the gift you just gave me?"

So I tackled it straightaway: "I'm looking for a man, Alfonso, a Colombian."

"Then you are in luck. There are millions of them."

"No, you clown. A specific one. His name is Javier Torralba Bienvia. Do you know of him?"

A fleeting moment of recognition flickered over Alfonso's

features, then disappeared. "The name is vaguely familiar," he said guardedly. "But . . ."

"You're hiding something," I shot back. "Tell me what you know."

Alfonso looked at me thoughtfully. "You genuinely have a thing for this man, don't you?"

"Yes, dammit. Now will you tell me?"

"Very well. But I can't tell you very much. Only that it's a name I've heard. Frankly, Christina, there are somewhat sinister associations with that name."

"He's not in the dope trade, is he?" I demanded.

"I don't think so. But who can tell these days?"

I breathed a sigh of relief, although it wouldn't have changed my feelings if Alfonso had said yes. Javier was still Javier. "Well, then where can I find him?" I asked.

Alfonso shrugged. "That I cannot tell you. As I said, it is merely a name I have heard, and a few stories about someone living in a very remote area, a very rich man. Some of the stories are very strange . . . a little frightening . . ."

"He says he's a cattleman," I cut in, not wanting to hear anything bad. "And he certainly is rich."

"Ah, yes, that's it. A *ganadero*. He probably lives in the eastern part of the country, then. You have to understand, Christina, I'm from the southern part, and communications inside Colombia are not the best. Also, I spend so much of my time here."

I was thinking while Alfonso was talking. It seemed that Javier was as remote a figure to his own countrymen as he was to me. He was probably remote in his very soul as well. I had sensed that when I was with him. I could not just go and find him and say, "Hello . . . I'm here. Do you want me?" I was going to have to enter, in some way, into his mystery. And his mystery was Colombia and its land. "I want to go to Colombia," I said abruptly. "I think I might want to invest in some land."

Alfonso's eyebrows raised sharply. "You're so intense

about this. Well, it can be done, but not in any abrupt gringo way.''

''What do you mean?''

He hesitated, as if searching for the right words. ''What matters in Colombia is who you know, what introductions you have, who owes who what. If you were just to try and jump in blindly, I think you would get nowhere. God knows, Colombia could use some foreign investment from people willing to put time as well as money into the country. It's possible . . .''

''Please, Alfonso. What exactly do I do?''

He smiled. ''Well, the first thing you should do is meet some Colombians. The right kind of Colombians. Rich ones. Do you like parties?''

CHAPTER EIGHT

Fortunately I do like parties, because for the next several days Alfonso took me to quite a few, all given by rich and influential Colombians.

Introduced as someone who was interested in investing in Colombia, I met bankers, ranchers, and industrialists, all of whom showed considerable interest when they learned I had money. Actually, they showed a rather well-bred greed.

I had ample time to observe the average rich and powerful Colombian male. It was an interesting species, usually quite cultured. Most of them had been educated at the best European and North American schools, but underneath their gloss I thought I detected a certain savage hardness.

I think they had a little trouble relating to me. I sensed that Colombian men were not accustomed to dealing with a woman as a business equal, and it made them a little nervous. Their instinctive interest was in the possible availability of my body; to them all non-Latin women were by definition whores. After all, we slept with men we were not married to, didn't we?

The Colombian women I met were birds of a different feather from the men—a bright and chattery group obviously designed for male pleasure and not much else. They were incredibly overdressed, over made-up, tottering about on amazingly high heels; and the behavior of even the intelligent ones was carefully calculated to show they didn't have a single dangerous idea in their pretty little heads. They were like present-day versions of highschool girls from the fifties (whom I've only seen in photos). However, some of the older women exhibited that effortless grace and class peculiar to mature Latin women. They no longer needed to catch themselves a man.

The women had as much trouble adjusting to me as the men. Once or twice I caught some of the younger women looking at me with a kind of dumb envy for my freedom. Then they would revert back to their hip-switching and giggling.

There were a few other non-Colombians besides me at the parties, usually people with some connection to the country. My favorite was an old American doctor who had worked and taught in Colombia for more than twenty years. I remember him at a particular party where he'd had a little too much to drink. He was not a timid man in any case, but that night a young Colombian came up to him and began to attack gringos in general. The young man was a phony little prick, all decked out in his official Latin American Student-Artist uniform, which consisted of trendy (very expensive and artificially aged) bohemian clothing, a Ché Guevara hat and beard, and Lenin glasses. The typical rich Marxist. I had earlier wondered how the kid had gotten into the party. It turned out that he was the son of one of the richest men present. He was obviously an embarrassment to the father, but he was still family, and that counts for a lot with Latins.

Anyhow, this little creep had buttonholed the doctor and, using all the most popular Maoist catch-phrases, was going on at great length about how all of Colombia's, and Latin America's, problems were really the fault of the American Imperialist War Machine. I ached to tell the little shit what I thought of him, but the doctor did it for me. "Look, kid," he said. "Wise up. Sure, there are gringo businessmen who rip off Latins. They'd rip off their own mothers. There are people all over the world who'd do anything to make a buck, who'd rip off anybody—if you let them. That's the important thing, they'll do it if you let them. And maybe Colombians are worst of all where ripping off their own people is concerned."

The kid started to make some kind of retort, but the doctor kept right on talking. "Face it. It's not the gringos who are the exploiters of your country, it's the goddamned corrupt Colombians who run the place. Hell, you prey on one another like no other group I've ever seen. And as far as gringos are concerned, you Colombians will join in with any foreigner that wants to plunder your people—as long as you get a piece of the action. And the worst ones, sonny, are the young punks like you, with your servants and your gaudy clothes and your discos and your contempt for the slowness and cowed passivity of the peons who support you. If you act at all, you don't bother to do anything for the unwashed masses. You don't show the slightest sense of compassion or helpfulness. No, you choose to start killing other Colombians, usually as members of some pseudo-Marxist group, the greatest international exploiters of all, and let me tell you, kid, I know that your aim has nothing to do with the welfare of your fellow citizens. It has to do with your own personal drive towards absolute power."

The young man, never having met an articulate opponent without a mob of sympathizers at his own back, was left with his mouth opening and closing foolishly, which suited him very well, I decided. Seeing my smile, the doctor came over to me.

"Goddamned asshole creeps," he snarled. "They're the next generation of despoilers. God, they're undoing decades of hard work! You know, Colombia used to have probably the best medical school in Latin America, but these damned leftists demanded that all the foreign teachers be expelled, and they got their way. They also abolished any standards of excellence. They refuse to take examinations or be graded. The result? Let me tell you, the average current Colombian medical school graduate is a danger to the public health. Now, what the hell are *you* doing here?''

His sudden change of subject caught me by surprise. I quickly blurted out that I wanted to go to Colombia and start some kind of agricultural business.

''You?'' he asked incredulously. ''Well, watch your back and hang onto your wallet. You won't *believe* the corruption. That's what's wrecking the country. It seems to be in their blood! Colombians love to steal, they think it's clever. I've had rich Colombian friends come to visit me in the States. I don't dare take them into a store. They try to shoplift. And in Colombia if you throw a party for your friends, your *friends*, mind you, they'll steal anything in your house not nailed down.''

''It sounds like a pretty horrible place,'' I said. ''So why do you spend so much time there?''

He looked at me in amazement, as if I'd said something very stupid. ''Why?'' he replied. ''Because I *love* the place.''

For me, that was a good introduction to the paradox of Colombia. One has to have a love-hate relationship with the land, and those closest to the country have the most extreme case of it. Only the grandeur of the land begins to make up for Colombia's shortcomings.

It was at this same party that I met Gabriel. My eyes immediately drifted toward him because he was so damned good-looking. He was tall and elegantly built, quite dark-complected, with large warm eyes, and he was young, about twenty-two, but exhibiting a careless kind of precocious maturity lusciously mixed with late adolescence. My libido, which had been unfed for a day or so, immediately soared.

When I looked in Gabriel's direction, he was already looking in mine. He seemed as interested as I was. With commendable skill, he came up to me and started a conversation.

"I'm sorry about Enrique," he said, pointing toward the pouting Marxist. "He can get pretty boring."

"True. He can," I replied. "But you're never boring, are you?"

I was looking at him pretty intently. It's so much fun to seduce younger men and I had at least several years on Gabriel. His eyes widened a little when he sensed my mood, but he didn't let himself get flustered. I found out later that older women had been seducing him since he was fourteen—he was so damned beautiful.

"I try not to be a disappointment, señora," he said, meeting my calculating look with one of his own.

"Señorita," I corrected. "And what do you do?" I asked. "I mean, who are you?"

He introduced himself and told me that he had just finished a degree in agriculture at an American university. "And what do you intend doing with your degree?" I asked.

"Go back to Colombia and work in agriculture," he replied.

"Oh, really? In what manner?"

The conversation was proceeding on two levels—one was quite ordinary party chit-chat, the other an intensely sexual sizing-up. Gabriel was taking a good long look at what he could see of my body, and I could tell he liked what he saw. I was doing the same with him, with similar results. "I have . . . a rather unusual objective," he said, moving a little closer to me. "I want to start a new industry in Colombia."

"Uh-huh," I said. We were quite close now. I let one of my breasts brush against his arm. "And just what is this objective?" I knew what my objective was. What a beautiful young man he was, and so innocently sensuous.

"Wine," he said, somewhat jerkily, staring down at where my nipple, quickly puckering underneath the thin material of my blouse and quite visible, was digging into his arm.

"Wine?" I replied, thinking he was offering me a drink. "No thanks . . . I had something different in mind. Quite different."

"No," he replied, flustered. "I mean I want to make wine. I want to start vineyards in Colombia, using really good vine stock from Europe and California. I want to make good wine."

"A commendable idea," I replied. "I love wine. But can you grow grapes in a tropical place like Colombia?"

"Oh, yes," he replied quite eagerly. "In the higher mountain areas, where the climate is more temperate. There are already some fine vineyards, but only table grapes. I want to . . ."

"You know," I said, "I find this a really fascinating conversation. It fits in with some plans of my own. I'd like to discuss them with you some more but . . ." I said, looking around the crowded room, "not here. It's so noisy. Is there somewhere else in the house we could go?"

His large dark eyes looked directly into mine. The time for games was over. "There's a bedroom down that hallway," he said. "It's quiet and very, very private. Would that suit you?"

"Perfectly," I replied. "I've had some really wonderful discussions in bedrooms."

We intended to slip away unobtrusively, but by this time I really didn't care. My cunt was seething, and all I knew was that I wanted this handsome young man. I gave a little involuntary shudder as he placed his hand in the small of my back while ushering me into the promised bedroom, and then I heard him locking the door behind us. I turned back toward him just as he was reaching out for me, and we were suddenly pressed tightly together, his mouth against mine, his hands kneading my ass, pulling my loins tightly against his. I opened my thighs, pressing my crotch against his leg. His leg pressed back and my hips began to move. I could feel the heat and wetness from my pussy soaking into my skirt.

Then I was being pressed backward. My knees hit the edge of the bed and I sat down hard. Gabriel pushed me over onto my back. I felt my skirt being raised. "You don't have any underwear on!" he exclaimed.

"It wastes time," I panted. I was really excited now that I knew he was staring up my naked crotch. "I *hate* wasting time. So . . . don't waste any."

He piled a lot of skirt on top of my belly. I could see my pussy, too. "I love blond cunts," Gabriel said in a hushed voice. "There are so few in Colombia."

He was kneeling between my legs, obviously mesmerized by my golden pussy thatch. His face was getting closer and closer to my crotch. "And I love your curly black hair," I hissed. "Right now I'd like to be looking at the top of your head."

It took him a moment to figure that one out, and then he suddenly buried his face against my crotch and I was indeed staring at the top of his curly head. Except I couldn't stare for long. "Aaahhh!" I gasped, and fell back onto the bed as his strong young tongue pried its way into my slit.

He didn't suck me for long. I could tell he was as anxious as I to start fucking. He pulled his mouth away from my cunt, licking my juices from his lips. He stood up, unbuckling his belt. His zipper hissed downward and a length of long, slender, dark-skinned cock leaped out into the open. It was a lovely cock, a young cock, a new-looking cock. "I want it in me," I panted.

Again he knelt between my legs, which were still trailing over the edge of the bed. I felt him fumbling with my pussy lips with his cock, but it was his face I wanted to watch. It was flushed and excited, the eyes hot, the full lips a little parted. I saw a dreamy, faraway look grow in his eyes as his cock slipped into my twat. "Ah . . . *rico* . . . *rico* . . ." he moaned as he began to fuck.

I was to get used to that word, "rico." It's what Latin Americans say when they really like something, like a good fuck. It means "How rich." And this was rich, looking up at this beautiful young man, watching the passion grow on his face, feeling his cock reach deeper and deeper up into my vagina. He fumbled with the buttons of my blouse, tearing the fabric a little. "*Qué bonitas*," he muttered when he saw my naked tits.

"Oh yes, squeeze them," I moaned, guiding his hands to my breasts. His fingers closed around my throbbing nipples. "Mmmnnnnn," I whimpered. "You're going to make me come."

As often happens with these spur-of-the-moment party fucks, the action doesn't last long. The real thrill is the drawn-out verbal foreplay. Not that the feel of cock against cunt isn't the richest part. It is. But now it was finishing time. Gabriel rose up on his feet and tucking my legs under his arms, began his final frantic thrusts into my already spasming pussy. "Aaaaahhh . . . it's sucking me," Gabriel moaned loudly, and I watched his face grimace in ecstasy as he began to come inside me. Through the flickering color pattern of my own orgasm, I watched him pump his load into my body, the cords of his neck straining, his hips pumping, his hands digging into the naked flesh of my thighs.

"Whoof," he grunted, finally sinking down onto his knees again. His cock was quiet inside me, still hard, probably still dribbling a little of his semen into me, but the main show was over. I sat up and caressed his handsome face. "That was nice," I said. "I'm glad we decided to talk about grapes. Grapes are so sexy, don't you think?"

He laughed, which suited him. Then his face sobered. "Grapes are magic, they're holy," he said fervently. "They make wine, which is the most wonderful, magical thing in the world."

"Well," I said. "So you weren't just feeding me a line out there."

"A line?"

"About your vineyards . . . your winery."

"Oh, no. I want to do it. I *know* I can do it. Chile has good wine. So does Argentina. Why not Colombia? The stuff they make there now is from grape juice sent from Spain. It's horrible, not drinkable at all. I know I can change all that. I . . . well, I would *like* to change all that."

"Now you don't sound so sure. Why is that?"

He looked embarrassed. "As always with something you really want to do, it turns out to be a question of money. I don't have the capital."

"What? I thought all you Colombians were fabulously rich."

That made him a little angry, which was incongruous, because his cock was still inside me. I tightened my pussy muscles and expelled his softening prick from my vagina. He winced, but smiled. "No, we aren't all rich," he said. "An uncle with a little money paid for my schooling here. My parents are both dead. My uncle thinks my idea is crazy. I suppose you do too."

I stood up and began buttoning my blouse, very aware of the warm, sticky sperm trickling from my vagina and

starting to run down my leg. I was going to have to visit
the bathroom. "Not at all," I said. "I think it's a fabulous
idea. It has class. It's the kind of thing I could see myself
being a part of. And I do have money. Now zip up your
fly. We'd better go back out to the party before they miss
us, and I think now that we, um, know one another a little
better, we can talk just as well in the living room as in the
bedroom."

CHAPTER NINE

So Gabriel and I made a deal and got into the wine business together. Of course, I forged my usual hard-nosed terms; after all, there was no point in throwing money away, and since I *was* putting up most of the money, I had the lion's share of the ownership. But Gabriel had the right to buy out a percentage of my end as he accumulated profits, up to the point where he could own 49 percent.

I say I put up the money but that's not quite true. I have long been a follower of Aristotle Onassis' dictum, "Use other people's money." Almost all of the funds were borrowed in the name of a holding company which was to control the corporation that controlled the operation, etc. This was because 90 percent of today's business has to be designed around tax laws.

But enough of the details. Gabriel and I were in business—but only if we could find the right property for our vineyards. He said he knew of a place that was perfect on the lower mountain slopes of eastern Colombia. The next step was to gain control of that land.

Of course, all these various agreements weren't worked out in one night at the party. The details took many more meetings between Gabriel and me, and since it had been in a bedroom that we'd had our first initial success in outlining our business relationship, many of our subsequent meetings took place in bedrooms. Gabriel was an enthusiastic lover and could not seem to get enough of me. For my part, I was charmed by his youthful enthusiasm. I remember one of our business conversations. It took place on the big bed in the bedroom of my Manhattan apartment. We were both comfortably naked and I was sitting astride Gabriel, who was lying on his back, languidly playing with my tits, while I slowly slid my cunt up and down the length of his seemingly eternally hard young prick. "I have the tickets," I told him. "We leave for Colombia Wednesday."

"You'll love my country, Christina."

"I love your cock," I replied, grinding my hips down a little harder and making his cock lurch around inside my vagina.

He looked up at me, his big brown eyes going puppy-dog soft. "I love *you*, Christina," he murmured.

I let that one go by me. I really didn't know quite what to say, and then I didn't care because he suddenly seized hold of my hips and with wild abandon began fucking up into me. I could feel his cock swelling inside me. "Oh, yes . . . yessssss," I hissed. "Give it to me good, Gabriel. Come in me . . . let me have all you've got. Fill me with your milk."

I loved the way Gabriel came—in buckets. His long slender cock would suddenly grow very hard and a lot thicker, and when he started to ejaculate I could actually feel it pulsing inside me. Gabriel would writhe wildly, his back arching, his eyes open wide in shocked pleasure and he would start to moan loudly. And every time this happened I would start to come, too, and we would both get very emotional. I mean, after all, we were *fucking* and it's hard as hell to fuck without *some* kind of emotion. This time I cried out as I started to come, "Oh, yes, lover . . . come . . . come . . . *come*!" And after it was over Gabriel continued looking up at me with those puppy-dog eyes. I thought nothing of it at the time, which was a big mistake.

The first place we went in Colombia was Gabriel's hometown of Cali, where he had to pick up some documents. Cali is a city of about 800,000, situated in a long, broad valley sandwiched between two large mountain ranges, the Cordillera Occidental and the Cordillera Oriental, or as we would say in English, the Western mountain range and the Eastern.

It was the rainy season, so as we came in to land the cloud cover obscured the usual sweeping view, although I did see a lot of green below. "Sugar cane," Gabriel said when he saw where I was looking. "That's the valley of the Cauca River below. It's the richest agricultural valley in Colombia. Fifteen feet of topsoil."

To me it just looked flat and featureless, and my opinion didn't change when we were on the ground and heading in a taxi for the city. Flat farmland all around, with mountains to the west and mountains to the east. The western ones were a lot closer, and as we approached the city, I saw that it was situated right at the foot of the steep western chain, which towered over us rather menacingly, I thought, and was bare of vegetation except for some scrubby grass and brush. Even before we got into the city center, I knew I didn't like the feel of the place.

The city center itself was quite new and clean, with wide avenues and shining high-rises and plenty of parks—a little island for the wealthy and upper middle class in the midst of the surrounding sea of poverty. Our taxi pulled up in front of the rather featureless concrete façade of the Hotel Intercontinental, one of the better places to stay, Gabriel told me. He had explained to me that we could not stay at his uncle's. "He would not approve," he said. That annoyed me a little, because I suspected that it was me Gabriel thought his uncle would not approve of, and I don't like being disapproved of. I discovered the real reason for Gabriel's decision much later. Colombian families tend to be fiercely possessive of their family members, and any outsider trying to break into such a group is immediately excluded. Gabriel wanted to protect me from this treatment.

It was afternoon when we checked in. After we'd unpacked, I decided to see the city. "Of course," Gabriel agreed, so I picked up my purse and headed out. "Uh . . . Christina," Gabriel said, catching me before I walked out the door. "You can't go out like that."

I looked down at myself. "What's the matter? Are my tits hanging out?"

Gabriel winced. He was always a little uncomfortable with my rather frank anatomical speech. I found out later that like most Colombians, he was particularly impressed by surface appearances. "No," he said. "But you can't go out wearing those earrings and that wristwatch."

I looked down at my Cartier watch and fingered my diamond-drop earrings. "Why not?" I demanded. "If they're good enough for London and Paris . . ."

"No, they're fine. That's just it, if you go out on the street with them, somebody will take them from you."

"You're kidding," I replied.

"No, no, I'm serious. Put the earrings and the watch in one of the hotel's safe deposit boxes," he insisted.

I could see that he was obviously worried. I sighed. When in Rome . . . "Okay, the earrings go in," I said. "But I'm wearing the watch. I like to see what time it is."

We had quite a little argument, but I still went out into the street wearing the watch. The first thing we noticed was the contingent of armed guards in front of the hotel. "Is somebody important showing up?" I asked. Gabriel assured me it was just the usual number of guards to protect the guests. "We're safe around the hotel," he said. I laughed. I have been in some pretty rough places, and neat, clean downtown Cali seemed like the last that would need protecting.

It was a gorgeous day and we began to walk up the avenue alongside a pretty little river gushing by below sidewalk level. Since Cali is at about 3,000 feet altitude, it seldom gets terribly hot even though we were very near the equator. I was enjoying the feel of the sun and admiring the plants and flowers lining the sidewalk when Gabriel tugged on my arm. "You shouldn't carry your purse that way," he said, "with the strap just over one shoulder. Wrap it around you as much as possible."

"Oh, I've had enough of this paranoia, Gabriel," I snapped, but he looked so hurt that I did as he asked. We were getting near the center of the city now and turned right to head up toward the central plaza. The streets were thick with people, many going home from work. Most of them were dressed with the attempted elegance common to an upward-striving middle class, and the women were particularly amusing in their state of overdress. However, I delighted in the throngs. I like people, and in the States one so seldom sees multitudes in the streets. I was looking at everything—the buildings, the handsome parks with their exotic tropical trees and plants, the sidewalk vendors hawking appetizing-looking deep golden-colored slices of pineapple and other strange fruits. I wasn't paying too much attention to the people closest to me when I suddenly felt a sharp tug, followed by a burning pain in my left wrist. I immediately looked down and saw that my watch was missing, and that the metal band had deeply scratched the skin. "Gabriel!" I shouted. "My watch!"

"I knew this would happen," he groaned, looking at the thin flow of blood on my wrist. "We call it wristwatch bite," he said.

"But I never even saw who did it," I gasped.

"You're lucky," he said. "If you'd resisted . . . Well, just be glad you didn't have your earrings on."

I flinched at the thought of someone tearing my earrings

out of my ears. The streets suddenly looked very different to me. I glanced around at the people, noticing now how they hurried past one another, how they seldom allowed eye contact. They were nervous. They were afraid of each other. I hugged my purse a little tighter. "Let's go back to the hotel," I said.

That night we went to a small bar. It was incredibly boring. "This is one of the most interesting places in town," Gabriel said apologetically. "I'm afraid Cali is not a very swinging place."

"I've seen towns like this in our Midwest," I agreed glumly, "and that's the most boring place on earth."

I insisted we walk back to the hotel. I don't like to let fear dictate my actions no matter where I am. My mood lightened once we were outside. It was a balmy night and the air felt soft against my skin. As we started to walk, however, I noticed that there was a guard in front of the bar we'd just left, a poorly dressed young man wearing a large machete. There were guards in front of other buildings and houses, too, some with clubs, some with machetes, some with guns. Gabriel explained that many homeowners hired men to guard their houses all night. "What a way to live," I murmured, then realized it was the way *I* had chosen, at least for the next few months. It made me very angry to think that I would have to be constantly wary of thieves.

"Too bad there wasn't a cop around when my watch got stolen," I fumed to Gabriel.

He shrugged and smiled. "The thief may have been working with the police anyway," he said.

"Oh, great," I replied. "Welcome home, Christina."

I felt better the next day after a night of Gabriel's satisfying lovemaking. While he went to the bank to retrieve documents related to our new business, I did a little shopping at one of the jewelry stores inside the hotel.

Colombia, by the way, is the world's emerald center, and I found myself buying a beautiful emerald pendant, a gorgeous four-carat deep grass-green stone set round with a circlet of diamonds that brought out the emerald's color even more. It was an incredible bargain at $4,000. But I didn't dare *wear* the thing, of course.

The next day we flew to Bogotá, Colombia's capital city, to beard the bureaucrats. "We have to get the right permits," Gabriel said vaguely. I didn't pay much attention because I was looking out the window at a wilderness of incredibly rugged mountains below. We were passing over the Cordillera Oriental and were heading for Cundinamarca Province where the capital is situated. The air was clearer in this region, and I got a good view of a huge sprawling city as we came in for a landing. There was green everywhere. Ah, the tropics, I thought. But I received a jolt when we left the airport. "It's cold!" I wailed as a chill blast of air hit me.

"We're over a mile high, Christina," Gabriel explained. That impressed me, and I began to appreciate the diversity of Colombia.

"When do we see the jungles?" I joked.

"Never, I hope. I can't stand the heat."

Bogotá was huge, with over two and a quarter million people, most of them unbelievably poor. I was determined not to be put on the defensive by the place, however. After all, I was from New York, so I took up my New York street manner—always aware of who was around me, varying my speed, never allowing myself to get pinned against a wall, and trying to look as aggressive as possible. My manner worked well the first couple of days, as Gabriel and I made the rounds of interminable ministries. I enjoyed all the walking we did because Bogotá is a much more cosmopolitan city than Cali, with scads of sidewalk cafés and delightful little bars. I had noticed, however, a

great number of ragged little children in the streets. One
night I saw several lying huddled on the ground in a
doorway.

"Why are they doing that?" I asked Gabriel.

"To keep warm while they sleep."

"But why don't they go home if they want to sleep?"

"This *is* their home, Christina," Gabriel explained
patiently. "They're *gamines*—street children. You know—
abandoned. They have no place to live except in the
streets."

"My God," I said, horrified. "How do they eat? Doesn't
anyone try to help them?"

Gabriel gave that unconcerned Colombian shrug I was
getting to know so well. "Things are different here," he
said simply. "We don't worry so much about other people."

"The poor little tykes," I said. "Maybe I can give them
some money!"

"Christina . . . don't!" Gabriel said sharply as I started
to walk over to the tangled mound of sleeping children.
They saw me coming and sat up, suddenly alert, like
cautious wild animals. I saw that some of them couldn't be
any more than six or seven years old. I was reaching into
my purse for a handful of pesos when they suddenly boiled
into instant activity, leaping up and surging around me. I
saw a pair of tiny, grubby hands delve into my purse and
come out holding all the money I had with me. I instinctively tried to grab at the money, but two of the *gamines*
were pushing me from in front while another knelt behind
my knees. I found myself sitting down hard on the pavement,
the wind knocked out of me. Gabriel came running up and
started helping me to my feet. "Now you know how they
eat," he said grimly.

"You great hero," I shouted, "Why didn't you stop
them?"

"Are you crazy?" he snapped back, and then glancing
past me, shouted, "Look!"

Running hard, the *gamines* were darting down the crowded sidewalk just as a couple, obviously foreign tourists, stepped out of the doorway of a restaurant. One of the *gamines*, seeing a chance at a double score, grabbed hold of the large handbag the woman was holding. She shrieked and held onto the strap as the large, beefy, red-faced man with her reached down and seized the boy by the collar of his ragged jacket. "Let go, you little bastard," he snarled with an obvious American accent.

It's hard to describe what happened next, because it all happened so fast. The other *gamines* were suddenly all around the American couple. I saw something glitter, and then the man cried out and bent forward, holding his stomach as he let go of the *gamine*. The whole pack immediately fled with the woman's purse. The man slowly turned around, a look of incredible strain on his face. I saw a large red stain spreading across the front of his white shirt where he was pressing hard with his hands.

"They stabbed him," I gasped as he slowly sank to his knees.

His wife was screaming, but no one else paid any attention, even though the streets were crowded. People hurried by, avoiding looking at the American couple, and soon they were isolated in a large quarantinelike space.

"Why doesn't anybody help?" I demanded of Gabriel. "Why don't *we* help?" and I started toward the man, who was still bending forward and groaning softly, but Gabriel held me back. "No . . . it's dangerous to get involved," he said. "The police might decide to arrest *us*."

"Oh, God, I think I've heard *that* excuse before," I said disgustedly just as I spotted a policeman sauntering in the direction of the wounded man. Sauntering, although he could see at a glance what had happened. I took one look at the policeman, at his brutal and ignorant face, and decided that maybe Gabriel was right. "When in Rome

. . ." I murmured to myself and let Gabriel draw me away. Gabriel's only comment about the entire incident was, "They were stupid. They resisted."

"That's a philosophy very hard for an American to swallow," I said angrily. "Come on, let's finish our paperwork tomorrow and get out of this jungle."

CHAPTER TEN

Getting our requisite permits didn't turn out to be quite that easy. Having been rather brutally introduced to Colombia's endemic street crime, I next came to know well its amazingly ponderous and corrupt bureaucracy. We encountered delay after delay. Papers vanished. Others needed impossible verifications. The whole experience began to seem like something straight out of Kafka.

I was getting itchy feet. I'd had enough of Bogotá. I'd had enough of government agencies. I was eager to be off to the actual land where I was about to become a tycoon of viniculture. Of course, beyond this, always in the back of my mind, was my real objective: to re-establish my abruptly sundered relationship with Javier Torralba.

I had not told Gabriel about Javier. Several times I'd started to, but I always held back. My instincts told me it would upset the boy, and I was enjoying having him with me. It was like taking a personal supply of sex with me in a suitcase. But it was always Javier my mind and body yearned for.

It was I who finally broke the bureaucratic impasse. We needed the signature of one official in particular, and he had been holding us up for days. Gabriel and I spent most of the next morning, as usual, sitting in the Great Man's waiting room. When we were finally let in to see him, I rather liked his looks. He was a very good-looking man, around forty years old, with a head of somewhat longish curly black hair and a crisp, curly black beard cut short and neat. He was pompous and officious, but I knew he couldn't help that. He was, in the local manner, merely upholding the dignity of his august office.

I'd noticed quite early on that he was as interested in my looks as I was in his. With that glitter in his eyes, he no doubt cheated on his wife, like any healthy, normal man. I began to get a glimmer of an idea.

The problem of the moment was that we needed this minister's signature to complete our paperwork package, but he claimed he couldn't sign unless another document was authenticated by another agency, but of course that other agency couldn't authenticate unless the minister signed first. It was a typical bureaucratic bind. Gabriel was fuming and near eruption, but I remained cool, playing little eye-contact games with the minister, Señor Pacheco.

"Gabriel," I finally said, "why don't you go over to the other ministry and see if they'll authenticate that document I'll wait here. It *is* all right if I wait here, isn't it Señor Pacheco?" I asked the minister.

"I don't see why not," he replied coolly. "We can talk over some of the other problems of your documentation. Perhaps I will call ahead and urge the other department to initial your document."

Gabriel hesitated. I knew he hated to leave me alone with Pacheco, but at the same time he was anxious to get this mess over with, and he also knew that once we lost our place in line in this office, we would have to begin the whole waiting process over again. "Okay," he agreed finally and sped from the office clutching the document in question.

Pacheco and I were alone. "He's a nice boy," Pacheco said.

"Yes," I replied. "And a damned good lover."

That rocked Pacheco a little. Like most Latin men, he was not used to frank talk from a woman. Anyway, not from a woman met in respectable society. "So . . . he is more than just a business partner to you," Pacheco said carefully.

"He's a business partner . . . and whatever else we choose to make it."

"You think that is wise?"

"I think that's my own business. Now, let's cut out the small talk. You want me and I want you, and it won't be too long before Gabriel comes back. Does the door to your office lock?"

He sat behind his desk staring at me, a look of mingled amusement and shock showing in his eyes. "My God, but you American women are blunt," he finally said.

"Not all of us. We've got plenty of doormats among us, too, but I'm not one of them. I'm used to getting what I want."

He stood up behind his desk. "Is this an attempt to buy my signature?" he asked.

"No . . . it's an attempt to get laid. Now, let's stop talking and start fucking or we'll both miss the bus."

We stood looking at one another for another few seconds. I wondered what was going to happen. I have seen many men, the kind used to complaisant, docile women, become completely cowed by a forthright offer of free sex. Their scared little weenies don't know how to react and just won't get hard. I hoped that was not the case with Pacheco. I genuinely wanted him to make love to me. It had been over two weeks since I'd made love to a man other than Gabriel, and while he was a fine lover, monogamy is not one of my strong points.

Fortunately, I had chosen the right man. Pacheco was not the kind to be so easily cowed. "You're right," he admitted. "I want you."

He came around from behind his desk and passing by where I was sitting, quickly locked the door that led into his office. I was on my feet by the time he turned back toward me. We came together instantly, and from then on it was pure, hot, quick lust. He kissed me very hard on the mouth, his hands dropping to press against my breasts. First my jacket dropped to the floor, then I helped shrug the strap of my lightweight top off my shoulder as his fingers dipped down into my cleavage. "Mmmmnnnnn . . . that feels incredible," I murmured as his fingertips began to tease my nipples. They quickly stiffened in response, and I arched my back, pressing my breasts forward. My mouth was all over his, sliding wetly and messily while I murmured against his lips. One of his hands slid down over my ass and began pulling my skirt upward. I felt cool air against the backs of my thighs, and then against my naked ass. His hand slid in between my buttocks, seeking out my pussy from behind. I helped by spreading my legs. I had started getting wet while Gabriel had still been in the room and I'd first begun toying with the idea of fucking Pacheco, and my cunt was now a swamp. I could hear Pacheco's fingers slithering through the goo, and then his finger was in my slit. My pussy hole was wide open and very hungry, and a moment later it was full of his hard, thrusting finger. I leaned against Pacheco, panting hard while he finger-fucked me. "You're so hot inside," he hissed.

"Let's warm *my* hand, too," I moaned, groping for his zipper. My trembling fingers managed to work it down and I reached inside his fly. His pants were impossibly full of swollen meat. My fingers wrapped around the hard, hot, throbbing shaft of his cock but had trouble working it out through the small opening. "My belt . . ." he mumbled.

"No . . . don't take your finger out of my cunt," I begged.

Using my free hand, I managed to unfasten his belt and the button that held his pants closed at the top. With him half out of his pants, it was now easier to get at his cock. I was leaning against him, my shaking legs barely holding me up as his finger continued moving in and out of my twat. I pressed his rock-hard prick against my belly, massaging it, only easing up on the pressure when he began to groan loudly. I didn't want him coming all over the front of my dress. "Get it inside me before it goes off by itself," I panted.

I had been wondering where we were going to fuck. His office was decorated in that spare, hard Spanish manner, with uncomfortable straight-backed chairs that were totally unacceptable for screwing. The floor was even worse; it was hard cold tile. Pacheco solved the problem quite easily, suddenly scooping me up in his arms and spreading me out on the top of his large wooden desk. A few objects went flying to make room for me and I could feel something annoyingly hard pressing against my side, but I didn't care. All that mattered now was the throbbing, aching hunger inside my cunt. "Oh . . . fuck me . . . please . . . fuck me now!" I whimpered as he tucked my legs under his arms. I quickly reached down, my trembling fingers unerringly finding the hard meatiness of his cock and guiding it toward my gushing hole. There was no more foreplay, just a grunting thrusting motion from Pacheco as I felt my pussy burn and stretch as it filled with his big shaft. Then we were fucking and my hands lowered to tightly grip the edges of the desk. "Oh . . . oh . . . God . . . I . . . love . . . this . . ." I moaned, the words being torn one by one from my throat by his hard jolting thrusts into my vagina.

"Holy Mother of God," he panted back, staring down at me spread-eagled on his desk top while he fucked me. "You are so beautiful. Your belly . . . your cunt . . . your incredible breasts."

My breasts. I had forgotten them for the moment, but his words reminded me of that very sensitive part of my lovemaking equipment. They were naked, jutting up from my pulled-down top, jiggling and jouncing each time his hips thudded against my ass. I let go of the edge of the desk and began tweaking my own nipples, feeling hot bolts of sensation shooting down through my belly to join the ecstasy inside my cunt. Unfortunately, I began to slide across the shiny desk top as I was driven an inch or two farther back with each of Pacheco's powerful strokes. He had to draw me forward toward the edge of the desk several times. I imagined his balls and the base of his cock slamming against the sharp, cool edge of the desk.

That moment's imagination triggered my orgasm. I cried out loudly and began to buck on the hard desk top, my hands leaving my tits and searching desperately for something to hang onto. Papers scattered, a picture fell to the floor. Pacheco's sharp intake of breath and the growing heat inside my cunt told me he was coming, too. Using my legs for leverage, he pulled my ass into the air so that he could thrust his cock deeper inside me, which started another orgasm on top of my first. We struggled together for several more seconds, then as abruptly as it had begun, our spur-of-the-moment fuck was over. Pacheco pulled away, his cock slipping noisily from my hot, slippery cunt. He helped me up off the desk. Our separate toilets took only a few seconds, with Pacheco zipping up his pants and fastening his belt, and I allowing my skirt to fall back into place, hiding my happy pussy, while I readjusted the top of my outfit, covering my tingling, swollen breasts. Finally I put on my jacket.

"You're going to have to get the cleaning woman in," I said to Pacheco, looking down at the smear of combined sperm and pussy juice that had pooled on the highly polished wood of the desk top right near the edge where my ass had been.

"I think it's something I should take care of myself," he replied, mopping up the mess with his handkerchief. I rummaged in my purse for Kleenex, and rammed a wad of it up between my legs to soak up the flow of warm cum seeping steadily from my vagina.

Pacheco and I had very little to say to one another now. We had each got what we wanted and, besides, Gabriel came back only a minute or two later. We heard his voice in the waiting room outside, then the door handle rattled and Pacheco had to go over and unlock it. Gabriel came in immediately, a strange look on his face. He and Pacheco locked eyes for a moment before Gabriel finally looked at me. "They wouldn't authenticate the document," he said to me.

"I've decided that doesn't really matter," Pacheco said flatly. He picked up our papers and going behind his desk, abruptly signed the document we needed. This brought all our attention to the desk, of course, and I became acutely aware of how disturbed the top still looked, and how intently Gabriel was staring first at the disordered desk top, then at Pacheco, then at me. I suppose I had that just-fucked look about me. I know Pacheco did, and I knew I had to get Gabriel out of there right away.

"Thank you very much, Señor Pacheco," I said hurriedly and, scooping up the documents, shepherded Gabriel out the door. I might still have avoided trouble from Gabriel but Pacheco just had to exercise some machismo. "Thank *you*, Señorita van Bell," he said with a smile of great masculine satisfaction.

I felt Gabriel tense, and just managed to get him out the door. "Christina?" he said in a tight voice as we left the reception area.

"Later, at the hotel," I replied, guiding him out into the street and into a taxi. All the way to the hotel he just sat there and looked at me, and I could see how pale he was. He seemed to be sniffing the air, too, as if he could smell the satisfaction of my well-fucked pussy. I suspect the cab driver's presence kept him from saying anything, but once we got back into our hotel suite, the truce was over.

"You . . . let him use you, didn't you?" Gabriel said in a low, hard voice.

"I don't let *anybody* use me," I said coolly enough.

"*Puta* . . . whore!" he suddenly shouted. "That's why he signed the document!"

"Careful, Gabriel . . ."

His voice was suddenly very hushed and hurt. "How *could* you, Christina?"

I was becoming annoyed, partly because I felt a little guilty. Not because I'd fucked Pacheco, which I'd enjoyed, but because of my clumsiness in not foreseeing how Gabriel would react, so I overreacted. Where I should have been soothing, I fought back. "I do what I want, Gabriel," I seethed. "Nobody owns me."

His voice began to rise again. "So," he grated. "You do what you want. You take what you want. Is that something you admire in yourself? Perhaps you admire it in others, too."

"This has gone far enough, Gabriel . . ."

"Perhaps you would admire it in *me*," he shouted. "Perhaps you would respect me more if I took what I wanted."

I was beginning to get a little nervous. "You're acting like a child, Gabriel."

"So that's what you think I am," he snarled. "A child. But Pacheco is a man, I suppose, because you threw yourself at him . . . let him take you like a bitch in heat."

"Pacheco means nothing to me, Gabriel. It was only . . ."

Gabriel was coming toward me. "I'll show you I can take what I want, too, Christina," he hissed. I began to back away, frightened by the wild look in his eyes. He lunged at me. I turned and ran into the bedroom, which was a poor choice; there was no other way out. He caught me by the bed, and when I tried to jerk away I fell onto it. He was right after me, grabbing my skirt as I tried to crawl away. I heard material rip, felt cool air on my suddenly naked ass. Gabriel's powerful arms kept me from going any farther. I'd never realized how strong he was. I was being held captive on all fours. I heard the sound of a zipper behind me. I started to shout at Gabriel to stop, but I was a little frightened of him at the moment. And something else prevented me from stopping what was obviously about to happen—I was getting turned on. Some primitive streak in me was reacting to the thought of being violently taken by the strong young male crouched behind me. After all, it wasn't as if he was a stranger. And the tinge of fear was definitely acting as an aphrodisiac. I yelped half in fear and pain, half in passion as Gabriel held my buttocks in a viselike grip and abruptly rammed his cock into me from behind. "Now, you bitch . . . you whore," he panted, "I'm going to give you what you deserve."

If I truly deserved the wild fuck that followed, then I must be a good girl indeed. Gabriel fucked into me like a man possessed. "I can feel his slime inside you," he snarled. "I'm going to wash it out with my own cum."

Not a bad idea, I thought, but I was in no condition to reply verbally. Gabriel was ramming his cock so hard into me, and so deeply, that I could barely get my breath. My hands were digging into the bedding as I tried to keep myself from being shoved forward flat on my stomach by the wild thrusts of Gabriel's pounding organ. I compromised by laying my upper body on the bed, ass thrust high behind me, tits ground into the bedding.

The next few minutes seemed like one long uninterrupted orgasm. I began to come very hard as I crouched there. Gabriel was jerking my ass back toward his loins each time he thrust his cock forward, fucking like a jackhammer. I started to cry out, a long, keening moan of mindless reaction, which seemed to encourage Gabriel. He started to fuck even harder, and my cries turned into a kind of staccato grunting as I continued to come.

Finally, I had to help. I straightened my arms to raise my upper body, and slammed my hips back hard again and again as my shuddering cunt repeatedly swallowed Gabriel's madly thrusting rod.

In a way, you might say the mood had thawed between us, but there still remained a powerful element of primal savagery. I was the captive bitch being fucked by the powerful male, the completely possessed female, and for the moment I loved it. "Oh . . , yessssss," I shrieked. "God . . . come in me. Wash his sperm out of me with your own. Aaannnggghhhhhh . . . make me *howl*, Gabriel."

We both began to howl as Gabriel started coming. I could feel his cock inside me, huge and throbbing and driving, spewing its hot load deep into my trapped body. Every inch of me was a mindlessly reacting, panting, climaxing piece of flesh, my mind washed away in a flood of physical sensation. It was great, it was wonderful, one of those things you can never plan, that just happen, one of those things that makes sex such an ever-changing, ever-new delight.

Finally, sated and exhausted, I collapsed forward onto my face, panting for breath. Gabriel followed me, lying on top of my back, his cock still inside my vagina. I thrilled to the feel of his weight above me, pinning me to the bed. Finally he rolled off, his cock slipping from my cunt, and lay beside me, looking up at the ceiling and still breathing hard.

I felt a great surge of compassion for this boy-man. "Gabriel . . . I'm sorry I hurt you," I said, softly stroking his face. He looked over at me, his eyes no longer fierce. He looked like a little boy about to be hit. "How could you do it?" he asked quietly.

I replied, just as quietly, "Gabriel . . . I just can't let myself be owned by anybody. I have to take what chances life offers me. That's the way I'm built."

He gave me that hurt, confused look for another few

seconds, and said, "Well, that's not the way I'm built."
Then he looked away again.

I thought to myself, oh God, what have you got yourself into this time, van Bell? But I was feeling so sexy and
so warm toward Gabriel that I leaned over and kissed
him lightly on the mouth. With a sudden desperate motion
he seized me and attacked me with a wild, searching kiss.
I tensed a moment, then thought, oh, what the hell, and
went along with it.

CHAPTER ELEVEN

I felt an intense burst of pride and belonging as I pulled my horse to a stop at the edge of the cliff and looked out over my land. Well, Gabriel's land too, but, with my controlling interest, it was more mine.

There was so much of it, 2,000 hectares, which came to about 5,500 acres. We didn't need that much for our vineyards; they only took up a few hillside slopes. The rest of the land, the great bulk of it, was either planted in coffee and bananas, or, in the flatter portions, served as grazing land for cattle.

"Why so much land?" I had asked Gabriel when I had first seen our huge holdings.

He'd shrugged. "This is what was for sale," he'd replied. I suspected that Gabriel had a basic hunger for land. At first I'd been a little angry, but then I understood. I was catching that land hunger, too. Perhaps it was a result of the vast sky, the steep mountains, the feeling of bigness that emanated from the Colombian landscape.

Once Gabriel and I had finally won our paper war in Bogotá, we'd headed straight toward our new holdings. We'd flown east from Cundinamarca Province, landing in the rough little frontier city of Villavicencio in Meta Intendencia, which was situated at the western edge of the hot, wet lowland plains, the Llanos Orientales, below the towering bulk of the Cordillera.

Villavicencio was the modern equivalent of an Old West

frontier town, with false-front buildings scattered among the more substantial ones, a general air of wildness about the dusty streets, and a number of hard-looking men walking about. We only stayed in Villavicencio for one night. I woke up once thinking I'd heard gunfire in the distance. From what I later heard about Villavicencio, I probably had.

The next day we set out by Land-Rover, followed by a small caravan of four-wheel-drive trucks. We headed south over a horribly rough road toward the small settlement of Acacias. When we arrived, Gabriel pointed at a distant group of forbidding-looking buildings off to our right. "There's a prison up there," he said. "For the really hard cases."

I shuddered. "How awful for them."

He laughed. "Not really. When they escape, they have all this to hide in," and he pointed off toward our left into the green, undulating, empty plain that stretched off to the east as far as the eye could see. "Most of the escaped killers, and the bandits who haven't been caught yet are out there," he said. "This is Colombia's Wild West, but out here it lies to the east."

We continued south, then cut west at the small settlement of Guamal. For a while, there was no real road, but the open plain provided such a firm footing that we made better time than we had on the pitted road.

At Castilla we began to get into mountains again, heading back up into the Cordillera, but at a point far south of Bogotá. We were still driving when night set in. "Damn," Gabriel said worriedly. "I'd hoped we would make shelter before dark. We'll have to stop here for the night."

"How romantic," I said. I had seldom been in such a wild and beautiful place. We were in rugged foothills a little above the plain. The mountains beyond were etched sharply against the sky by the setting sun, and below us the plain was turning a series of variegated purples.

"Not romantic—just dangerous," Gabriel growled. In a moment he called our crew of a dozen men, and he began handing out rifles.

"Is it that serious?" I asked afterwards.

"Maybe, maybe not," he replied. "But we'd better be on our guard. We're our own law here."

It was quite a night. The vehicles had been formed into a circle, just like a wagon train, and, thrilled more than frightened, I woke up several times and watched the sentries prowling about our little camp. However, we passed the night safely, waking to a glorious dawn, with an enormous sun rising quickly above the vast plain and lighting the backdrop of mountains behind us.

It was hard going up into the mountains. We simply had to stop during the middle part of the day because it was too hot to proceed any farther, but after that the air cooled rapidly as we gained a great deal of altitude. It was near the end of the day when we finally reached the center of our land. The convoy stopped at the top of a steep hill, and I found myself looking down into a shallow valley with a river running right through the center. On a small rise below stood a cluster of building surrounded by tall, feathery trees. "Oh, Gabriel, how lovely," I whispered, awestruck by the grandeur of the sight, the obvious age and grace of the buildings, the lushness of the land, and the magnificent mountains all around. "Is this . . .?" I started to ask.

"Our land," Gabriel replied, emotion making his voice hoarse. I think it was then that I began to catch his land hunger.

Weeks of hard work followed. We had to terrace hillsides, plant vines. The *campesinos*—the peons—did the actual labor, of course, but I grew tan and strong just from riding around watching the work progress. The best way to get around was on horseback. For this purpose we had a considerable stable of fine *pasofino* horses, a uniquely Colombian breed, big strong horses crossbred from the original Arab stock. Their specialty was their unusually smooth gait, hence the name *pasofino*, which, loosely translated, means fine walking.

Gabriel insisted that I always take armed guards with me. "Even though we're above the plains," he told me, "there are still quite a few hard men up here."

I instinctively started to rebel against this restriction of my freedom, but then I remembered the scene in Bogotá, the knife sinking into the American tourist's belly. And this land looked a lot harder than even Bogotá. So I gave in.

That day when I rode my horse to the edge of the cliff and looked out over the plain, I had only one armed man with me, Hernán, our foreman, or *capataz*, as he was called locally. We'd had a few other men with us earlier in the day, but we'd sent them back. They'd protested, having been ordered to stay with us by Gabriel, but since the new orders came from the boss woman and were seconded by Hernán, whom the men seemed to fear, they grumbled and rode away. I turned toward the cliff now and sat my horse, looking out at the wild vastness of savannah far below and thought about Javier. He was down there somewhere, that much I had learned. He was lost in that immensity far off to the east in Vaupes Intendencia. I knew I'd never find him by simply going down into the wilderness. For one thing, it was too dangerous. Most of the big ranch owners in that part of Colombia didn't even live on their land. They would be targets for kidnapping and ransom. Or robbery and death. They left the running of their vast land empires to an overseer, or as they were called, *hombres de confianza*, men to put confidence in. I wondered how Javier managed to remain on his land. No, I would have to wait for him to come to me. The important thing was to let Colombia know about the *gringa loca*, the crazy white woman named Christina van Bell, who was growing grapes and running cattle up in the mountains.

Not wanting to think too much about Javier, feeling he

was becoming a not too healthy obsession with me, I suddenly wheeled my horse and galloped away from the cliff. There was a startled cry from Hernán, and then I heard him pounding along behind me.

The wild ride over the high pastures immediately began to improve my mood, or at least to channel my attention in new directions. No matter what the propaganda is to the contrary, riding a horse feels awfully good to a woman. Her cunt is pressed right against the saddle, or even better, against the horse's back if she is riding bareback. After all, think for a moment how few young boys are horse-mad as compared to so many young girls, the latter too innocent yet to completely understand why straddling a running horse is so exhilarating. No wonder that, in more repressive ages, women were forced to ride sidesaddle.

As the *pasofino* surged along under me, not even his smooth gait could keep my cunt from mashing repeatedly against the pommel of my saddle. I wriggled around, letting the pressure press my labia out of the way, so that my clitoris could have firmer contact with the hard leather. I knew the crotch of my tight jeans was growing wet.

And then I saw it—my favorite feature of this beautiful mountain land, a high, slender waterfall cascading down from between two green and lofty peaks. The sight of this silvery, phallic column of water, coupled with a final jolt against my cunt as I pulled my horse to a stop, brought on a paralyzingly strong orgasm, and I slid moaning from my saddle, fell in a heap on the ground, and twisted helplessly there, shudders of pleasure rippling through me.

As my vision cleared, I turned at the sound of pounding hooves and saw Hernán's horse sliding to a stop. Its owner dismounted in one smooth, graceful movement. He stood looking down at me. I lay looking up at him, and we both knew then why it was I had insisted the other two guards leave.

It would not be completely accurate to describe Hernán

as handsome. Not in the same way Gabriel was. What Hernán had was power. His complexion was dark and his face was hard like his body. His eyes betrayed a hint of barely suppressed cruelty, and he moved like a leopard. I had been watching him move since I'd first met him, and despite my better intentions, and my memories of Gabriel's jealousy, I slowly began to realize that I wanted Hernán, not as a true lover, not as a companion, but I wanted him to just take me, the way the stallions in our horse herd took the mares—wildly, savagely.

All this was going through my mind as I lay on the hard sun-baked ground, still trembling from my orgasm and watching Hernán come nearer. He stood right over me, looking down, his eyes hooded, his expression impenetrable. But he knew what I wanted, and when he finally made his move, it was without hesitation or caution. He suddenly knelt, one knee on either side of my body, effectively pinning me to the ground, and with one powerful motion ripped open my blouse. I watched his eyes as he stared down at my heaving, naked breasts, and saw the first hot spark of passion flare in those obsidian depths. Hard, callused hands dug into the tender flesh of my tits. I squealed with a mixture of pain and ecstasy as Hernán mauled my nipples. There was nothing gentle about him.

Then with a grunt of desire he leaned forward and began sucking hard on my nipples. I laced my fingers behind his head, realizing that his thick black hair was not very clean, but not really minding. He smelled of the land around us.

Suddenly he moved to the side and abruptly turned me over, urging me onto all fours. I felt his hands at the buckle of my belt, unfastening it, then he was tugging my tight jeans down over my buttocks. It was hard going, and I helped by squirming from side to side. The jeans descended inch by inch, pinching my flesh. I felt the sun hot on my naked ass, the wind cool against the gushing sump of my pussy hole. When the jeans were finally down around my knees I spread my legs as far as I could, which was not far. I wanted to open myself as much as possible, because Hernán was already shoving his hand up between my thighs. I gasped as one of his callused fingers rammed its way into my vagina. There was no gentleness, no real foreplay. This was animal to animal. Thank God I was so wet.

I heard Hernán breathing hard behind me as he finger-fucked my cunt. My own breathing had the force and tempo of an out-of-control steam engine. Then I felt something new behind me—a hard, rubbery length of flesh sliding up the back of one thigh, heading for my twat. Once again I tried to spread my legs a little farther, but the jeans bunched around my knees wouldn't let me. It was too late anyhow. The bulbous tip of Hernán's cock was already pressing up between my pussy lips, entering my slit. I felt Hernán guiding it with his free hand while the finger of his other hand finally slipped from my vagina. Then the tip of his cock found my pussy hole, and Hernán lunged forward.

"Uuuunnggghhh!" I grunted as my body was invaded by Hernán's rock-hard cock. The force of his entry rocked me forward on my hands and knees, and I almost fell, saving myself only by bracing my arms with all my strength. Hernán helped a little by sinking his amazingly strong fingers into the soft flesh of my hips, holding me in place as he partially withdrew his cock for the next stroke.

I met him halfway, lunging my ass backward greedily as his hips pounded forward. I felt cock flesh lance into me all the way to the end of my vaginal channel. It hurt a little but I loved it. I loved everything about this wild, savage fuck. I continued ramming my hips backward in perfect cadence with Hernán's heavy thrusts. I started coming within the first ten seconds, a long series of sharp jolts shuddering their way through my insides. At the same time I was strangely lucid, vividly aware of everything that was happening, as if my mind were split into two parts. I remember watching a little ant working its way through the coarse grass just a few inches from my face. I remember the feel of the tropical sun, the soothing wind, the feel of the earth beneath me.

And then Hernán began to come and I let everything else fade away, concentrating only on what was happening inside my cunt, aware only of the hot spurts of slippery maleness filling my twat and the increasing power of my own final orgasm, until I was howling like a mad bitch in heat, barely able to hear Hernán's hoarse cries behind me.

He pulled away from me as abruptly as he had entered, his retreating cock trailing a sticky line of sperm down the back of one of my thighs. More warm juices gushed from my suddenly unplugged hole. I swayed back and forth on my hands and knees for a moment, dizzy from the after-effects of the chain of orgasms. Then I got shakily to my feet, staggering because my jeans were still tangled around my knees. I thought for a moment of pulling them up again, and then realized they would only get soaked by the pussy juice and semen running from my vagina. That would not do. Gabriel might see the stains, smell the odor of my arousal. I needed to wash . . .

The waterfall! There was a deep pool of beautiful clear water at its base. I sat down, the grass tickling my naked pussy, and pulled my boots off, then my jeans. My blouse, being already undone, was easy to shed, and a moment later I had left Hernán and was running naked toward the waterfall, thrilling to the feel of the air and the sun and the vastness against my naked flesh.

I entered the water in a long flat dive, the sudden coolness a delicious shock. I came to the surface, spluttering and laughing. How wonderful, how free I felt, and how satisfying it was that this beautiful waterfall and this pool and the very ground where I had just been fucked actually belonged to me. It was mine, mine, mine . . . and Gabriel's, too, of course.

I saw movement by the edge of the pool and looked up to see that Hernán had come over to the water's edge and was looking down at me, his expression once again unfathomable, a primitive blankness. I felt excited having him look at me naked in the water while he himself was still clothed. The falling water had long ago swept the basin I was in free of any sediment and the water was crystal clear. Hernán would have no trouble seeing the rest of my body shimmering nude beneath the surface.

Facing him, I reached underwater and began to rub the slipperiness from my cunt. I was standing in a some-what shallow area, submerged up to my breasts, which were half-floating, bobbing a little each time I stirred up the surface. All this time I was looking Hernán straight in the eye. The hard, black, piercing quality of his gaze was intensely exciting, so exciting that I began to get turned on again. Soon, I was no longer rubbing my cunt to get it clean, I was rubbing it for pleasure. "Mmmnnnnn . . . it feels gooooood, Hernán," I said throatily, spreading my pussy lips with one hand and stroking my slit with the first finger of the other. I don't know just how much the water let Hernán see of what I was doing, but he definitely got the idea. I saw his eyes go hot and alive again, and then a moment later he was pulling off his clothes. In seconds he was standing completely naked at the edge of the pool, his cock lurching once again toward erection.

I sucked in my breath. Hernán looked incredibly potent, incredibly male standing there, his body hairless and bronzed by the sun, his belly flat and hard looking, his chest broad and well muscled, his legs the hard, knotty-looking legs of a horseman. He wasn't muscular in the inflated manner of a body builder, but in the flat-muscled way of a man who uses his body for hard, grinding work.

I expected him to leap into the water and come to me at

once, but to my surprise Hernán began doing the same thing I was doing: masturbating. I watched his powerful fingers close around the thickening shaft of his cock and start sliding up and down its exciting length. I watched the bulbous tip swell and darken, until it was purplish in color. I saw his stomach muscles jump whenever a particularly strong jolt of pleasure shot through his now enormously swollen cock. My fingers were hard at work on my cunt down under the water, and my own body was shuddering with pleasure. We continued looking at one another in fascination as our passion mounted, and then suddenly Hernán was in the water, heading toward me. I moved forward to meet him, then gasped as he abruptly seized me in his powerful arms and hoisted me higher in the water. When he let me down, it was onto the tip of his upthrusting cock. I opened my legs, wrapping them around him, wriggling hard as I tried to swallow the tip of his cock with my pussy hole. He freed one hand to help, and I cried out in pleasure as I felt him slip up inside me.

I was by now so excited that my cunt was producing more than enough lubrication to overcome the natural rinsing action of the water. Hernán's cock moved easily in and out of me. I was riding high in his arms, so it was easy for his mouth to move over my breasts, which were well above water level now. "Oooohhhhh . . . hurt them . . . hurt them!" I panted. He complied, his teeth sinking painfully into my flesh, but not enough to break the skin. I immediately climaxed, moaning and thrashing, my wild motions foaming the water around us. I thrilled to the feel of his hands underneath my buttocks as they held me upright balanced on his prick, which was lurching up into me wildly.

Once again it was a short, savage lovemaking. Hernán abruptly stiffened, and I could feel how huge and swollen his cock had become, how wildly it was shuddering inside me as it spewed its hot load into my vagina. Hernán was crushing me to him tightly, his arms hurting me. I writhed once again in the throes of a fantastic orgasm, my head thrown back, my tits pressing into his face, my legs thrusting straight out behind him.

And then we were slipping apart. It was over so quickly. He let me down and we looked into one another's faces for a moment. There was no softness, no love, just a sense of wonderfully satisfied lust. I turned away and once again washed myself, this time quickly and efficiently. Under the hot sun it took only a few minutes of standing on the bank beside the edge of the pool before I was dry. I dressed quickly. Hernán had already dressed and stood watching me silently. "Let's go back to the ranch," I said briskly, once again the boss lady. He looked at me steadily for a moment, then without a word, mounted and, riding beside me, accompanied me back to the main buildings.

My jeans were clean but my blouse posed a problem. In his haste to tear it from me, Hernán had ripped some of the buttons loose and torn the material. If asked, I planned to say that I had snagged it on a limb during the ride. But this subterfuge was unnecessary. Gabriel was out checking the vines, so I was able to quickly change into a clean shirt, throwing the old one into the trash.

I glanced out the window and saw Hernán walking from the stables toward the bunkhouse. I realized it was time to think about what had happened between us. It had been an intense experience. Pure lust realized. A mating with the spirit of this hard, vast land. But I knew it must not happen again. I had taken a chance today and had jeopardized my relationship with Gabriel, a relationship that was business as well as personal, and I had done it in the most foolish way—by becoming involved with an employee. No, it must not happen again.

But my brave resolution was not to be realized. Now that I have time to think back on it all, I have come to the conclusion that it was the fault of the land. I cannot overemphasize its effect on me. The meadow where Hernán had taken me, the waterfall, the cliff with its incredible view of those forbidding and seductive plains below. The cattle, the vines, the mountains all around—they were mine and I could do what I wanted with them. And Hernán was part of that land. I think that some of the savagery of the country was seeping into me, taking me over. Before a week had passed, I lay panting under Hernán again.

I began to lead a double life, spending most of my time with Gabriel, making plans for our *latifundio*, as large holdings are called in Colombia, arguing part of the time, and of course making love, because I still found Gabriel a satisfying lover. And whenever the opportunity presented itself, I snuck away to be made love to savagely by Hernán.

Actually, the exciting dualness of what I was doing, alternating between the two men, served only to increase my passion with each. Gabriel, not knowing quite why it was happening, was nevertheless pleased by my increased ardor each time we made love. I suppose he believed that I must at last be falling in love with him.

During this time, Gabriel and I began to have serious differences of opinion on the operation of our holdings. I wanted to leave as much wild and free as possible. Gabriel wanted to work the land to its utmost.

"I can't stand the thought of disturbing any more of this incredible beauty than is absolutely necessary," I said to him heatedly one day. I'd seen enough of Colombia to know how much the population abused the land. I rememberd the deforested, eroded mountains around Cali.

"The sentiments of a spoiled, rich *gringa*," Gabriel sneered. "Land is for working. It is for feeding and employing people. Land is to be used as much as possible."

"But what happens when it's all used up?" I shot back.

He shrugged. "Then you find more land. Colombia is a big country."

I thought for a moment of the devastation in so many parts of my own country. But what could I say? What weight would my ideas about land management have in a country which permitted the plight of the *gamines* in its own cities, that let its children starve.

As usual, our verbal excitement slipped into physical excitement, and within minutes Gabriel and I were making love. That always seemed to be the end result of our disagreements, and not a bad one, I suppose.

While Gabriel did not know I was making love to Hernán, the opposite was not true. Hernán, like everyone else on the *latifundio*, knew that Gabriel and I were lovers. After all, we shared the same bed. Little by little I began to realize a certain possessiveness was growing in Hernán. Serveral times, after I had been with Gabriel, Hernán's lovemaking became almost brutal.

"Do you love that boy?" he asked me once bluntly.

"I don't know," I replied truthfully.

Hernán began to intrude on Gabriel's domain, coming to the main house more and more often. That both bothered and thrilled me. One time it nearly led to disaster. Hernán and I were in the hallway. Gabriel was in our joint office, which was a couple of doors away. Suddenly Hernán siezed hold of me and began caressing my breasts and kissing me fiercely. "Hernán . . . stop!" I hissed. "Gabriel . . ."

But excitement was building up inside me. I let Hernán slip one hand down inside my jeans. They were tight, but not tight enough to keep him from ramming a finger down as far as my clit. I began to pant and to kiss him back hard. I pressed my hand against the front of his pants, right over the bulge his cock made. Suddenly there was the sound of a door closing, footsteps approaching on the resonant wooden floors. "Gabriel!" I whispered in a panic. I leaped away from Hernán, quickly tucking my shirttails down inside my jeans again and beginning to arrange my hair. Hernán tried to push his partially swollen cock down one leg of his pants.

The door behind us opened and Gabriel walked into the room. He was immediately suspicious, although I thought I had done a good job with my clothes. "What's been going on in here?" he asked in a tight voice. And then I realized that my face must still be flushed from my passion of a few seconds before. On sudden inspiration I said angrily, "I'm having trouble with this damned mule-headed peon," and I pointed toward Hernán. He tensed. Gabriel tensed too and took an involuntary step in Hernán's direction.

"What kind of trouble?" Gabriel asked in a low, dangerous voice.

"I say we should move those calves out of the upper pasture," I replied hotly. "He says it's too early. I don't think he knows who gives the orders around here."

Gabriel looked searchingly back and forth from me to Hernán. For a moment I was horribly afraid he wasn't going to buy my subterfuge. Then he nodded toward Hernán and said tersely, "Do as she says."

Hernán nodded and turned to walk out into the hallway. Gabriel's eyes followed him all the way. Then when he was gone, he turned toward me. "If he gives you any more trouble, let me know," he said. I felt relief, but not unmixed relief. There was something in Gabriel's expression as he looked at me that I had never seen there before, a kind of coolness. Almost a distrust. Once I was alone again, I vowed that I would end my relationship with Hernán once and for all.

CHAPTER TWELVE

The promise I had made to myself lasted a week. I must have been a little bit crazy to be courting such danger, but I just couldn't get it out of my head that I had two men I could flit back and forth between. The element of danger only seemed to heighten my desire. That final fateful morning I was lying in bed a bit late, about six-thirty (which *is* late on a Colombian ranch), making love to Gabriel. I put it that way purposely, because it was usually I who made love to Gabriel while it was always Hernán who made love to me. He *took* me. In tandem they were two halves of sexual perfection.

The sun was shining in through our bedroom window. I was sitting astride Gabriel, his cock far up inside me as I slowly, lazily, sensuously moved my hips, making my sex-slippery ass cheeks slide deliciously over Gabriel's loins, while his cock felt just right moving up inside my twat. He, as usual, was half propped up on pillows so that his mouth could reach my tits, which he was licking and sucking just the way I liked him to. We had by now developed a quite satisfying routine between us.

I had already come once or twice, and the pleasant little orgasms were serving to increase my level of pleasure. I knew that the big one was on the way. I was just waiting for the right combination of stimulations to set it off. I got that stimulation when I glanced out the window and saw Hernán leave the bunkhouse and enter the barn. The sight of him coupled with a deep thrust from Gabriel's prick suddenly sent me into orbit so powerfully that my sucking, shuddering cunt pulled an orgasm from Gabriel. When it was over, and I had collapsed panting, onto Gabriel's chest, he was overwhelmed. "That was the best we have ever had, Christina," he said. "Hey . . . where are you going?"

I was already getting up from the bed. I felt hot and wet and alive inside, wild with passion. I knew of only one thing that would completely satisfy me today. "It's such a beautiful day," I said. "I'm going out to the barn to check my horse. I want to go for a ride."

Gabriel looked up at me quizzically. "Okay. But don't forget to take some of the men with you. Hernán, too."

That jolted me a little, but Gabriel had already turned away and was getting out of the other side of the bed. "I have some paperwork to do in the office," he said. "See you for lunch."

I pulled on a light dress to suit the warmer weather. Besides, I didn't want to bother with jeans. They're too hard to take off. I left the house wearing just the dress and a pair of boots, nothing else, no underwear, nothing to cover my tingling, expectant skin. I walked straight across the broad grassy expanse that separated the house from the barn and went directly inside. "Hernán?" I called out softly. It was much darker in the barn than it had been outside and the sun's glare had temporarily blinded me. Then I saw movement over by one of the hay ricks. "Hernán?" I said again, and he stepped into the open.

For a moment I couldn't move. My body felt helpless, weak from desire. Hernán looked so powerful, so hard. I had the sperm of one man inside me already. Now I wanted the sperm of another. I had given to Gabriel. Now I wanted to be taken by Hernán.

He was a little less certain. "What the hell are you

doing in here?" he asked. "Mother of God . . . I can smell your cunt from here."

"It wants you, Hernán," I said throatily. "And I'm damn well going to have you, and your cock."

"Are you *loca* this morning? We're too near the house."

But there was no real conviction in his voice. My mood was infecting him with the same lust I felt. I saw the usual bulge in the front of his tight pants growing larger. I walked over to him and opening the front of my dress, forced him to lay one of his hands on my naked breasts. His hand drifted from one to the other, then finally squeezed so hard that I whimpered in pain . . . and loved it. "You fucking hot bitch," he snarled, and then suddenly he had seized me and I was in the air for a moment, coming down to land on my back on a pile of hay. Hernán's hand was suddenly full of erect prick. His other hand was hoisting my dress. My legs opened hungrily, my cunt seethed. "Your pussy's dripping with *his* cum," Hernán said half in disgust.

"To make it all the easier for you to fuck me, my dear," I hissed. "Come on . . . shove it in me!"

With a snarl of combined frustration and lust, Hernán suddenly crowded forward. I felt a fumbling between my legs, then a sliding, stretching feeling and a moment later my twat was full of hot, hard cock, just what I wanted it to be full of. My back arched powerfully as I had an immediate orgasm. "Goddamned hot bitch!" Hernán repeated, grabbing hold of my flailing legs as he fucked into me hard.

The whole thing was over in seconds. We were both incredibly excited. I heard Hernán groan, then his cock was pumping and jerking inside my cunt, adding to the slippery brew already pooled there. I was spasming in final orgasm when suddenly the main door to the barn crashed open, letting sunlight flood inside onto us. *"Que pasa . . . ?"* Hernán started to shout, leaping away from me and tucking his cock back into his pants. I shrieked and leaped up off the pile of hay, smoothing my dress down. But it was too late. Gabriel was standing in the doorway, and the look of rage and hatred on his face told me that he had seen enough. I saw something else too that turned me cold.

Gabriel had a pistol in his hand.

"*Puta* . . . whore . . ." Gabriel said in a low, deadly voice. It would have been less frightening if he had been screaming at me. "I saw this son of a pig go into the barn, too. I knew . . . I knew . . ."

"Gabriel . . . this is not the way to handle things," I said desperately.

"Shut up!" he shouted at me. "This is my country, and I know the way things like this must be handled." His voice grew calmer again. "I will take care of you later," he said. "But first, this traitorous pig . . ."

He raised the pistol and aimed it at Hernán, who throughout all this had been standing rock-still, his body tensed and ready to move, his eyes on the pistol. I couldn't believe this was happening. The look on Gabriel's face left no doubt in my mind that he was going to shoot Hernán. "*No!*" I shrieked, running toward Gabriel and reaching for his gun hand. At the same moment Hernán sprang into action, bending low and moving fast, running not away from Gabriel, but straight at him.

The gun went off with a deafening roar. A second later I had hold of Gabriel's wrist, and he easily threw me aside, but by then Hernán was on top of him. There was a short, fierce struggle, the sound of blows, harsh breathing. The gun went off again, making me jump as if the bullet had hit me. Then the gun was spinning through the air while the two men remained locked together, Hernán bulling his way forward, forcing Gabriel back. They staggered through the open barn door and out into the open.

The sound of the gun had brought many people running,

and now they gathered in a circle around Gabriel and Hernán. "Stop them!" I shrieked, but no one moved. Gabriel was the *dueño*, the owner, but Hernán was the *capataz*, the immediate supervisor whom everyone feared.

The two men were still struggling together when Hernán suddenly broke loose and snatched a machete from one of the men in the surrounding circle. He turned, facing Gabriel. "You tried to kill me, you son of a whore," he snarled. "Now . . . it's your turn to face death."

I was too horrified to make a sound. I fully expected Hernán to rush forward, unopposed and cut Gabriel to pieces with the machete. But as violent a land as it is, the underlying moral code of Colombia would not permit such a one-sided encounter. A low growl of anger went up from the watching crowd. Men with drawn machetes stepped forward and placed themselves between Gabriel and Hernán. But instead of stopping the fight, which was my most fervent wish, one of the men simply put a machete in Gabriel's empty hand, and the two men were left to face each other again.

I was horrified as they began to circle one another, the machetes held out in front of them, each waiting for an opening. In the Colombian countryside, the machete is the ubiquitous companion of almost every man, a wickedly sharp, slightly curved length of steel between two and three feet long, a few inches across, and very thin. It is used for everything from cutting brush, to opening coconuts, to mowing grass, to what I was seeing now—killing other men.

I had heard of several machete fights since I had been in Colombia. The machete has no guard to stop blows, just a smooth plastic handle so the fights are usually very bloody. I had heard of one where the loser had lost one hand, part of the other, one leg, and had died of loss of blood from the numerous deep body cuts. There is very often no winner, just two hacked-up losers.

I could see that each of my men was determined to kill the other. I could understand this in Hernán, who was such a hard man, but was surprised by Gabriel's sudden cold fury and courage as he faced the older man. At that moment I was really in doubt as to who would win. I only knew that in some way I had to stop this horrible thing.

There was no use in appealing to Hernán or Gabriel, or to the crowd either. The latter's blood lust was up. So I ran into the barn for the pistol. But no matter how hard I looked I could not find it. It was probably buried in the hay somewhere, and I knew I didn't have time for a systematic search. Already I had heard one hard ring of steel against steel, and the exultant roar of the onlookers. I had to stop the fight now!

Then my eye lighted on an item neatly hung on a wall peg. A bullwhip. I immediately snatched it down from its peg and ran back out into the yard. Now, you may not think a bullwhip would be of much use to a leggy blond from the city, but a couple of years before I had had a short affair with a man who had grown up on a ranch in Texas and who had worked the rodeo circuit as an expert with the bullwhip. In between our bedtime struggles, he had coached me in the use of this fascinating weapon. I was never as good as he, of course but I was pretty damn good. "Stop, God damn it!" I shouted at the top of my voice as I ran toward the circle surrounding the combatants. Of course no one paid any attention to me—not until I snaked the whip out to its full length and cracked it over their heads. The resulting pop was as loud as a pistol shot, and people hastily turned around to see what was happening. The whip snaked out again, and this time the vicious tip met flesh. The crowd scattered as it bit out again and again. I saw bright gleams of blood through torn shirts, but I didn't care. I just had to get to Gabriel and Hernán before it was too late.

Suddenly there was no one between me and them.

"Throw down those machetes!" I shouted. Neither paid me any attention. I think each was afraid to take his eyes off the other. They stood about three feet apart, weapons poised, weight forward on the balls of their feet. Each had been slightly cut on the arms and shoulders, and there was a killing light in their eyes.

"I said throw them down!" I shouted once again, and then I struck with the whip. It snaked out, a perfect cast, the last two feet wrapping around Gabriel's machete. I pulled hard, and it spun out of his hand, thudding to the dirt somewhere behind me. I expected that would be that, but Hernán suddenly looked over at me, then back at Gabriel, who was of course disarmed and at his mercy. With a gloating cry, Hernán sprang forward, machete raised high. He was going to cut down his helpless opponent!

Gabriel dodged the first deadly blow. "Stop! For God's sake, stop!" I shrieked. But to no avail. Gabriel dodged another sweep of the deadly blade, but then he slipped and fell to one knee, looking helplessly up at the blade suspended above his head.

I have no memory of moving, but suddenly the whip had started its wicked snakelike movement again. There was no time for pretty aiming. The slender poppers at the tip sliced deep into the skin of Hernán's back. He shouted and flinched, which made his aim go off. The machete thudded into the ground next to Gabriel. But Hernán held onto the deadly blade and lifted it again. At the continued danger, something snapped in me. My arm rose and fell. The whip sliced into Hernán's body again and again, into his arms, his back, his sides, his face. He dropped the machete and tried to protect himself with his arms, finally falling to the ground in a fetal ball. I was still wielding the whip, terribly angry that Hernán had tried to kill the unarmed Gabriel, forgetting for the moment that Gabriel had also intended to kill Hernán only a short time before.

But it was I who had just now disarmed Gabriel and the weight of his death would have been on my head.

It was Gabriel who finally stopped me. "You'll kill him," he said, jerking the whip from my hand. I stood stupefied for a moment until my mind cleared, then I nearly threw up as I saw Hernán's bloody, cowering form on the ground in front of me.

The crowd was moving away, suddenly nervous. There had been too much trouble among the powerful. They didn't want any of it to spill over onto them. I looked around for help but didn't see any. "Get a doctor for him," I ordered, pointing to Hernán. Someone nodded. We had an old woman on the ranch who had some kind of healing abilities. I knew they would fetch her. Then I ran toward the house, where I had just seen Gabriel going.

He was nowhere downstairs. Then I heard sounds from upstairs—from our bedroom. Panting, I ran up the stairs two at a time. So much was happening . . . too much. Only a short time before—what had it been? ten minutes?—I had been reveling in making love. Now death and danger was all around me.

I found Gabriel next to the bed packing a bag. "You're going?" I blurted.

He turned toward me with a weary, almost pitying look on his handsome young face. "Do you think I could stay here? You have publicly humiliated me with another man. You, a woman, used a whip on me. You interfered in an affair of honor. Me? I have no honor left here. The only way I could regain it would be to kill you, now that you have kept me from killing the man who shamed me, and I don't want to kill you. I have been away from my own people too long . . . too long in the softer northern world."

"But," I blurted out, "you don't have to leave! These are your people, this is your land. *I* should leave."

How dearly those words cost me. I loved this land as

much as Gabriel. But I had wronged him, and I must pay the price.

"No," he said. "I could never again command their respect. They would not obey me. It would actually be dangerous for me to remain."

He had picked up his bag now. Just before turning toward the door, Gabriel gave me a piercing look that penetrated right to my soul. "You've won," he said quietly. "I know you want this place all to yourself. And now you have it. You may buy out my share. The bank in Bogotá will handle all the details."

And then he was out the door. I was too shocked and ashamed to try to stop him. I sat down heavily on the bed. Now that the crisis was over, neither my body nor my mind could take any more. Pretty soon I began to shake. A few seconds later I was curled up on the big, empty bed, crying.

I cried for hours. The light outside was beginning to grow dim when I heard a knock on the bedroom door. "Gabriel?" I called out hopefully.

But it was only the old Indian woman who did the cooking in the main house. "The young master's gone," she said quietly. "No use in calling for him. But I brought you something to eat."

"I don't want anything to eat," I said morosely. "I don't deserve anything."

"I'll just put it down here," she said patiently. "You can eat it when you're ready."

She made no move to go out after she'd put the soup down. Finally she cleared her throat. "The other one's gone, too," she said.

"Who? Hernán?"

"Yes. He left about an hour ago. Took one of the horses."

"He can have it."

"Good riddance," she continued. "We'll be better off here without him. He was a bad one."

"What do you mean?" I demanded.

Her eyebrows rose. "You didn't know? He's from the plains below. Grew up with a band of *ladrones*—thieves, killers. Never really stopped being like them."

"Oh," I said. Now I thought I understood why so many of the hands seemed afraid of Hernán. "Maybe it's better he's gone," I sighed.

Another silence from the old woman. Her lined, brown face was expressionless when she answered, "Oh, he'll be back. He was shamed too much not to come back. Beaten by a woman—he'll be back all right . . . for his revenge."

CHAPTER THIRTEEN

The land was mine now, all five thousand five hundred acres, but there was a hollowness to my possession of it. I rode over my territory every day, always in the company of several armed men. The land was still beautiful, the views still awesome, the waterfall where I had made love to Hernán still spreading a silver sheen of mist across its backdrop of vivid green foliage, but the land was empty now, at least for me, stripped of the presence of Gabriel and Hernán and all the ways they had affected my life. I began to realize once again that it is people who make life worth living. Mere possessions are of no value when you have no one to share them with.

Sexually, I was being extremely careful. I was growing hornier by the day, and men abounded, but after what had happened with Hernán, I was afraid to pick any one of the men as a lover. With no dominant male hand at the helm, I knew that further sexual experiences would lead to more fights to the death over me.

I would have left but there was still the land, and I loved it. In my self-imposed isolation I depended on its presence, but it wasn't enough. I was growing lonely.

Finally, I had no choice but to go back out into the outside world, at least for a little while. There was the matter of buying up Gabriel's shares in the holding company that controlled the land. I knew he would need the money if he were going to make a new start on his own land elsewhere.

As I began to prepare for the trip to Villavicencio, I began to think about the feasability of putting a small airstrip somewhere on the property. This would enable me to fly straight into Bogotá in an hour or two rather than endure the two-day trip overland to Villavicencio first. The problem would be to find enough level ground nearby that was not blocked by hills at either end.

With this project to occupy my mind, our little convoy of the Land-Rover and a few trucks set out again; the trucks were to bring back supplies. Some of the men were still nervous over the Hernán affair and had mounted a light machine gun on the back of one of the trucks. Being playful, they tried it out on a couple of rabbits as we jounced across the open plain. I was relieved for the rabbits' sake when they missed, but concerned for my own if we were attacked. However, I reassured myself, a man is a much bigger and easier target than a zig-zagging rabbit.

I had myself driven straight to the airport as soon as we reached Villavicencio. I was suddenly eager to see civilization again. After the short flight to Bogotá, I checked into the best hotel in the city, anxious to settle into a tub of hot soapy water and soak off the accumulated grime of the trip. After my bath I carefully applied my makeup and dressed myself in my most elegant clothing. I felt as thrilled as a small girl playing dress-up in her mother's clothes when I finally viewed myself in the full-length mirror. It had been a long time since I'd seen myself in anything but jeans, boots, and a rough twill shirt.

I liked what I saw. The days and weeks in the saddle had toned my body and tanned my skin. My blond hair was almost platinum in places. My dress was cut low enough to emphasize the taut swell of my breasts, and clung well enough to show the sleekness of my hips and thighs. "Let's go knock these city fellers dead, cowgirl," I said to my reflection.

I had no great desire to go out into the city and find "fun" places. My last experience with Bogotá had rather soured me on that. It was not that I was physically afraid; the events of the past few weeks had certainly matured me along those lines. It was simply that I had no desire to go out and see starving children. So I opted for the self-contained little luxury world of my big fancy hotel, being content to go down in the smooth, silent elevator to the ground floor with all its shops and bars and discos and lounges and its dozens of armed guards.

I have no hesitancy about drinking alone in a bar. I have had some very interesting experiences that way. I found one ground-floor bar I liked, with a mock-German motif and some really good sausages and smoked meats, which I took full advantage of. This first evening I was rather enjoying my solitude, deep into my third drink, when I noticed that a man was looking at me intently in the bar mirror. I had been in Colombia long enough to think that he might be connected with the police. Then I realized he was just interested in me as a woman.

That pleased me. He was a nice-looking man somewhere in his late thirties or early forties, with light-brown hair slightly frosted at the temples. He was well dressed in a suit, an item of apparel that had not existed on my ranch, and his pleasant, almost handsome face spoke of honesty and decency as he kept looking at me in the mirror, obviously trying to get up the courage to make an approach.

I decided to do it for him. Picking up my drink, I walked over to him. Since I judged him to be an American, I used English. It was nice to speak it again. "Hi," I said. "Can I buy you a drink?"

He was taken aback for a moment. "Why . . . sure," he finally said. "But is that the usual drill around here?"

"Uh-uh. But I'm thinking of starting a local chapter of Women's Lib."

"From what I've seen, the local women could use it."

My opening gambit got us off to a good start. Will's drink came—that was his name, Will Sturtevant—and before long we were talking like old friends. "What are you doing here in Colombia?" I asked him. "Are you a Yankee salesman?"

He shook his head. "No, I work for AID." When he saw my puzzled frown, he added, "Agency for International Development. We evaluate how U.S. foreign aid is being utilized."

"A CIA front, no doubt," I hinted darkly.

He winced. "Ouch. Don't say that. It's all we hear down here, CIA, CIA. We do have some contact with the State Department, but we're supposed to be independent."

I laughed. "Relax. I've been called CIA myself. That happens to any American who travels a lot and isn't immediately identifiable as something else. Too bad the CIA isn't as inventive as it's made out to be."

"Come to think of it," he retorted, "how do I know you really aren't CIA and are trying to infiltrate AID? What *do* you do, Christina?"

"Well, normally I run a magazine, but—"

His eyes widened. "Of course! You're Christina van Bell. I *thought* I recognized you."

"And stuck-up little me thought it was because you thought I was attractive."

"Both. But you haven't told me what you're doing here."

So I told him. And not just that I had a ranch up in the mountains. I told him about Javier and about Gabriel and Hernán and even about my love for the land. He was a nice man and I knew I would probably never see him again, so I made him my father confessor. He was solid and kind, and he made me feel that maybe, just maybe, the whole thing would turn out all right.

We were sitting side by side on bar stools by then, leaning closely toward one another. His head was right over my shoulder. "You keep looking down the front of my dress," I said a bit boozily. "Like the view?"

"One of the seven wonders of the world," he replied.

"You should see the rest of the terrain," I said. "In fact, that's a pretty good idea. Your room or mine?"

"Women's Lib again?"

"Uh-uh. Just loneliness, plus the fact that I like you, and the fact that no one's made love to me for a long time, and that I really want you to."

He looked at me, his expression soft and warm. "Well, beautiful lady," he finally said. "You're going to get your wish. Come on . . . my room keys are right here in my pocket."

So we went up to his room. As we walked down the hall from the elevator, I could feel my thighs slipping wetly against one another. I wasn't wildly aroused the way I'd so often been with Hernán. I was simply looking forward to a nice, uncomplicated fuck. And that's what I got. We took our clothes off in a very civilized way, no panting moans, no flailing bodies, no torn material or flying buttons.

"God, you're beautiful," Will said quietly but fervently as I stood in front of him for a moment.

"You're not so bad yourself," I replied. His body was nice, like his face, well-muscled but not rawhidey, the body of a healthy man who probably spent a little time in a gym. It was hard to tell about his cock because it wasn't hard yet. Will was obviously a man who took his time, which was just the kind of man I needed at the moment.

He lay me down on the bed and then began kissing me, first on the mouth, rather gently, then his kisses trailed downward, light but sweet. He kissed my neck, my shoulders, my upper chest, and by the time he got to my breasts my nipples were already hard and expectant. "Oh, yes," I sighed as he began nuzzling those puckered, sensitive mounds. "Pay a lot of attention to me . . . that's what I need most. Attention."

He made me come just by sucking my nipples—not the biggest orgasm I'd ever had but a nice one nevertheless. Then his kisses slid lower, down over my belly, his tongue playing inside my navel for a couple of minutes before I felt his face rasping over the upper boundaries of my pubic hair. My legs opened readily. I trembled a little, waiting for his tongue to enter my slit, but he was a lot more subtle and a lot more patient than that. His lips and tongue slid down the inside of one thigh. My hips bucked upward, trying to place my cunt in the path of his tongue, but by then he was too far down, and it felt wonderful anyhow. He remembered to lick behind my knee, which had me moaning from the intensity of it. Then he was at my feet, stroking them with his tongue, sucking gently on my toes.

By now my entire body was a supersensitive ball of pleasure, but I wasn't out of control. I shivered when, after finishing with my other foot, his mouth started working up that leg. After a while his mouth was poised right over my throbbing twat. He blew a long stream of cool air into my slit. "Oh, God . . . you torturing bastard," I whimpered.

I was prepared for more of this delayed culmination when he foxed me again, this time by sticking his tongue directly into my seething pit. "A-aa-aaa-aaaa-aaaaa," I moaned loudly, my hips jerking involuntarily. Thank God. At last.

His tongue-work inside my slit was a masterpiece of inspired understatement. There were no wild sorties, no heavy licking, no gross sucking, just the most delicate, lightly probing movements, which after about ten minutes had my whole body vibrating like a violin string. I had not yet come, except for that one small winner when he licked my nipples. He'd had me on the edge a dozen times, but each time he'd toned down the intensity, leaving me close but not quite there. "What are you trying to do?" I panted. "Drive me crazy?"

"Exactly," he said, raising his head from between my legs and looking up at me. I loved seeing my pussy juices spread all over his face practically up to his eyebrows. "You see," he explained, "I don't have a very big cock, so I want to make sure you're feeling something before I put it inside you."

"I'm feeling something . . . I'm feeling something," I babbled. "For Christ's sake, put *something* inside me or I'm going to use the handle of my hairbrush."

He gave a very knowing smile, which told me he knew he had me in his power, and then crawled up higher on my body and gently put his cock inside me. "Mmmmmnnnnnn," I sighed. "It feels plenty big to me."

"That's why I do all the preliminary work," he explained. "Right now, my little finger would feel like an entire salami."

"Ooooohhhhh . . . bake your salami in my oven," I begged, raising my legs and locking them behind his back. "This feels so good . . . so nice."

He used his cock the same way he'd used his tongue. I suppose it was pretty small, but he knew all the right places to put it. I started coming pretty quickly, and each time I came it made the next spasm all the more powerful.

Just before he had his own climax, he sat up straighter between my legs, and using his saliva-moistened thumb, began paying attention to my clit again. It felt as if my entire pubic area were locked in a vise of almost unbearable pleasure. Just as the first hot jets of his sperm started to spew up inside me, he pressed down in just the right way on my clit, and I had a writhing, screaming orgasm. Fortunately, he was big enough to hold me down until we had both finished.

After that we lay side by side, talking lazily. I think we

were talking about the study he was conducting for AID when I fell asleep, feeling more human than I'd felt in a long time.

The next morning brought an early leave-taking because we both had a lot to do. "Thanks for ironing out the kinks," I said at the door, holding his hand lightly. "I'm going to remember you."

"And I'll be the only person who'll be able to legitimately masturbate while reading the editorial page of *World* magazine," he replied.

We parted then, like those famous ships passing in the night, and I felt marvelously full of energy and tolerance as I set about my day's work. I went to the bank that held the loan papers on the land and arranged to have money transferred from New York to buy Gabriel out. I used my own money this time. Then, I drafted a document that would return sole ownership of the land to Gabriel if anything happened to me. I even included a clause that would permit me to activate this arrangement by mail if I so chose. I felt terribly guilty about Gabriel.

I left Bogotá that afternoon. My sojourn in the city, especially my night with Will Sturtevant, had made the ranch fade a little in my mind. I wondered if I really wanted it any more, or did I want to go back to my old New York–based jet-setting life. The only way for me to decide was to get right back to the land and see how it hit me.

By the time I arrived in Villavicencio late that afternoon, it was too late to start for the mountains. There was no one to take me anyhow, and I spent my first night in Villavicencio alone. It was certainly not the place for a single girl, particularly for a blond *gringa*. As I checked into a hotel, I noticed many strange, unfriendly looks cast in my direction by rough-looking men. However, I preferred those to the friendly looks I got.

I was lucky in my choice of hotels. The wife of the

proprietor, a big heavy woman took charge of me. While I was eating in the dining room, a drunken mestizo lurched over to my table and leaned over me, leering down at my body. My guardian came up behind him and laid him out with an enormous rolling pin. "The same for the next one," she said loudly, glaring around at the suddenly silent dining room. I decided that some of her authority rested on the huge double-barreled shotgun her husband had hanging behind the bar.

It was a restless night. Once again I heard shots out in the street. Once, probably at two or three in the morning, I heard two or more men struggling quietly together in the alley outside my window. I could hear only the sound of their hoarse panting and the scrape of their feet, followed finally by a bubbling cry of agony. I made certain I did not look out the window the next morning.

Luck smiled on me when, right after breakfast, I ran across two of my men in the street right outside the hotel. They were very surprised to see me. "We thought you would not be back for another week," one said.

Unfortunately, the loaded trucks had already left town before dawn on their way back to the ranch. The plan had been for them to return for me in a few more days.

"Can we catch the trucks today?" I asked.

"Perhaps," one of the men answered. "But to be out there alone with just the three of us in the Land-Rover and with the guards in the trucks . . ."

All I knew was that I didn't want to spend another night in Villavicencio, and I'd have to spend several if I waited for the return of the trucks. But if I left now, we might catch up to the slower moving trucks before the day was out.

"We're going," I told the men decisively.

They shrugged and left to prepare for the trip. We were off by ten, bouncing over the rough road on our way toward Acacias and Guamal. At the risk of a broken spring or axle, we were really pushing it but I didn't mind. There was a certain thrill about rushing through the wilderness toward my land again. Memories of the cities began to fade toward the middle of the afternoon as we started up toward the mountains just beyond Guamal. The deep tire tracks of the heavily loaded trucks told us they were not far ahead of us. We were slipping and sliding along the track when a narrowing of the road between two huge boulders forced us to drop down into low gear and go very slowly. We were directly in between the two huge rocks when I caught sight of a flicker of movement out of the corner of my eye. Instinct made me yell at the driver, "Let's get the hell out of here!" But it was too late. A roadblock of rocks had been piled ahead of us, and even as we came to a jolting halt, armed men sprang from behind the boulders and stationed themselves on either side of the Land-Rover, pointing rifles straight at the heads of my men. *"Bandidos,"* I heard the driver murmur under his breath. But I knew it was far worse than that.

One of the riflemen was Hernán.

CHAPTER FOURTEEN

"Out. Out of the car," one of the riflemen said to my men. Keeping their hands in plain sight, the two men carefully stepped out onto the ground. I started to follow but was shoved back into my seat. "No . . . you stay there," the same man growled.

I was relieved to see that Hernán was obviously not the leader of this group. He stood to one side, keeping his rifle trained on my men. They glared back, having recognized him, and I hoped they wouldn't start any trouble. I could tell from the evil, twisted grin on Hernán's whip-scarred face that he would have no hesitation about shooting them. Nor, seemingly, would any of the other men who had jumped us.

There were five of them in all, including Hernán. Their apparent leader was a short, thickset, very dark man with a hard, seamed face. But at least he looked sane, whereas Hernán did not. The former *capataz'* controlled inscrutability had completely disappeared, as if the humiliating events of a few weeks ago had broken something inside him. Frankly, he terrified me.

"You two . . . start walking," the leader said to my men.

"What?" Hernán burst out. "Why don't we shoot them?"

"If they were even a little less poor, I might," the leader replied. "As it is, they are simply poor *campesinos*, not much different from us."

144

"But they saw my face," Hernán protested. "They know who I am. They will give my name to the police."

The leader shrugged. "That's the chance you took when you joined up with us. Look, we've got what we came for," and he gestured toward me. "Now it's time to get out of here."

"You can't leave my men out here," I said, aghast, looking at the immensity of the empty land around us.

"If they walk straight along this track, they will come to the parked trucks sometime tonight," the leader replied. "Besides, it's their only chance," and he pointed suggestively toward Hernán, who was fingering his rifle as he stared angrily after my two men, who were already quite a way down the trail.

"What about me?" I demanded. "Take the Land-Rover and everything in it. Let me go with my men."

The leader chuckled. "There is no way that will happen. You are the prize we came for. Not this other junk," and he contemptuously kicked one of my suitcases out of the Land-Rover to clear a seat. "Get in," he abruptly ordered Hernán and the three other riflemen.

They piled into the Land-Rover, surrounding me in a tight press of raggedly dressed, unwashed bodies. I nearly gagged at the smell. With one of the riflemen driving and the leader giving directions, the Land-Rover spun around in a large circle and, picking up speed, headed off the road in the opposite direction from my land. We were going due east, straight out into the immense plain of the Llanos Orientales.

My mind felt like it was short-circuited because it kept failing to conceive of ways out of this horrible situation. Here I was, surrounded by obvious cutthroats, with Hernán sitting right behind me and leaning forward so that his face was right next to and slightly behind my own.

"We are going to have some fun together, you and I, Christina," he half-whispered hoarsely into my ear.

I turned and stared into his cruelly scarred face. Scars I myself had put there when he'd tried to kill Gabriel. I knew that I was going to pay dearly for every one of those ugly marks. My only hope was the leader. I knew that if he hadn't been present, Hernán would already be taking his revenge on my body. The only heartening sign I had seen so far was the leader's consideration in letting my men go and in keeping Hernán from killing them. But would a rich *gringa* like me merit his consideration? I hoped so.

The jeep sped across the open savannah. We were well into the dry season now, and the flat open floor of the plain stretched on and on like a green, grassy, slightly undulating tabletop.

We were actually making better time than we had earlier on the rutted road. But a month earlier and any progress at all would have been impossible. The enormous downpours during the rainy season turn the plains into an impassable morass.

"Where are you taking me?" I finally asked. "I demand—"

"Shut up, bitch," Hernán snarled. His fingers dug into my right shoulder next to my neck.

"Ow!" I yelped as his fingers found a nerve and pressed hard.

"Do as he says," the leader drawled lazily, not even bothering to glance in my direction. "Shut up."

So I shut up. For the next few hours I concentrated on hanging onto my sanity. Great waves of fear kept boiling up inside me, threatening to push me over the edge and turn me into a babbling, begging, crying mess. I sensed that it was going to be very important that I keep my wits about me.

Just before dark I was able to make out something ahead, a darker smudge against the bright emerald green of the plain. As we drew closer, I could see that it was a small encampment. A few shabby tents straggled around a water hole with horses tethered nearby. As the car pulled up a few yards away from the water hole, the leader leaned forward and gave a blast on the horn. "We have her," he shouted.

A number of men who had been lounging around started toward the Land-Rover but held back when the flap of the largest tent was raised and an old man stepped out into the open. I could tell by the immediate deference of the others that this was the man who mattered most around here. So I studied him closely.

He may have been as young as sixty, but the harshness of an outdoor life had wrinkled his skin and thinned and bleached his hair until he looked at least seventy. However, up close his body no longer appeared frail but rather exuded a lean and whiplike strength.

I was hustled rather roughly out of the Land-Rover and jerked to a halt about a yard away from this man. He gave me a little mock bow, not too badly executed but rather incongruous considering our rough surroundings. "Don Narciso Gomez, at your service," he said to me, his voice full of mocking humor.

"I suppose I don't need to introduce myself, do I?" I replied.

"Not at all. Our esteemed friend here," and he waved toward Hernán, "has already made us aware of who you are. In fact, it was he who suggested we invite you here. He wanted very much to see you. You seem to have done something that has bound him very close to you. Is that not right, Hernán?"

Hernán stepped forward. "All I want is an hour alone with her," he said in a tight, hate-filled voice.

"Ah . . . wouldn't we all," Don Narciso said with an overdone sigh as he looked me up and down. "But it will have to wait."

"But you promised," Hernán protested.

"I promised nothing," Don Narciso said, his voice

sharp. "I only said we would bring her here. But did you think it was only for you? Do you think we do this kind of work for nothing? This is a rich lady."

"Very rich," I said hastily. "Richer than you imagine. If I am returned safely, you will profit greatly by it."

Don Narciso smiled. "Just what I had in mind. All that remains is to arrive at a mutually satisfactory figure. What did you have in mind?"

I thought quickly. There would be no point in trying to be cheap. After all, my skin was at stake. Hernán's glowering presence was a continual reminder of that. "A hundred thousand U.S. dollars," I said.

Don Narciso's eyebrows raised. "A princely sum," he said. "But hardly enough for a princess. Shall we say two hundred thousand?" I nodded. There went the new presses for the magazine. Malcolm would throw a fit.

"It's done, then," Don Narciso said. "We will travel to a place of greater safety, then deliver the news of our transaction to your bankers or managers." He turned to Hernán. "You may play with her for a while if you wish. But she is to remain alive. You will be playing with two hundred thousand dollars. *My* two hundred thousand dollars, so be careful."

Hernán's brutal face lit up with unholy glee as he started toward me. Sick with dread, I wondered just how much agony he could cause me without quite killing me. No doubt it would be a great deal. Hernán had me by one arm and was tugging me toward a nearby tent. "Wait!" I said desperately, taking a step toward Don Narciso, who had started back toward his tent. He turned and looked back at me. "If I am returned completely unharmed, completely unmolested," I said, "then the amount will be four hundred thousand dollars."

A huge smile creased Don Narciso's already well-creased features. "Ah," he said. "That puts a different light on matters. Let her go, Hernán."

"No!" Hernán snarled. "I have a score to pay."

"Not with another of my two hundred thousand dollars," Don Narciso said, and now there was no humor in his voice at all. "And in my camp, you runt of a sow's litter, you do not say no to me. Not ever. Do you understand?"

Hatred and frustration continued to twist Hernán's features, but by now Don Narciso was fingering the large pearl-handled revolver he wore at his belt. A number of the men moved forward, their attitude toward Hernán clearly one of menace. "All right," he snarled. "I will not touch her. She is safe from me . . . for now."

He spat these last words in my direction before spinning on his heel and stalking away. Don Narciso came up to me, looking troubled. "It is always so disruptive to have a woman in the camp," he said. "I'm afraid some of my men are . . . a little less than gentlemen. Many have not had a woman for a long time, and none of them have ever had a woman like you. I think you would do well to keep this in mind if you wish to continue enjoying my protection."

I looked around at the men. They were indeed a horrible-looking band of cutthroats. There was no mercy at all in their hard, cruel faces. All except for one young man, younger than many of the others, whom I had not noticed before. He looked completely out of place. He was quite handsome, with thick, curly dark hair and an open countenance. He was much better dressed than the others, his clothes cleaner, but he wore a huge knife in his belt and carried an automatic pistol. He was no tourist in this camp.

Don Narciso saw where I was looking. "Forgive me," he said. "I have been amiss. Let me introduce my son, Rodrigo. You two should get along. In fact, I think it would be best if I put you in his care. Rodrigo?"

The young man came over to us, and Don Narciso gave him strict orders to see that no one harmed me. Rodrigo nodded. He looked at me and smiled, and I felt heartened by that smile. Although Rodrigo was obviously a part of this murderous-looking bunch, I sensed that there was the possibility he and I might share some tenuous strand of humanity.

While he was still outside his tent, Don Narciso gave rapid orders to the band. "Take the Land-Rover into Surimena and sell it to our usual contact," he told two men. "Then meet us at the usual place."

Having tethered their horses to the Land-Rover, the two men drove slowly toward the north and Surimena, which I knew to be the nearest town. The rest of the group quickly broke camp and lashed the resulting baggage onto the pack horses. Then everyone mounted and we set off toward the southeast. "We must be long gone from here before the alarm is given," Don Narciso said as we left.

We rode all night. Like the others, I was on a horse, but the reins were lashed to Rodrigo's saddle horn. "Just so you don't get lost in the night," he explained, showing a little of his father's mocking humor.

For several hours, the adrenalin of fear kept me awake and alert, but toward morning I began to grow terribly tired. A couple of times I started to fall asleep and nearly fell from my horse. While the whole group stopped and waited for me to be put back in place again, I heard a lot of inventive cursing. "Why don't we just rape her and shoot her?" one man muttered. "I've never had a four hundred thousand dollar fuck before."

That woke me up a little. The man had voiced my greatest fear: How long would the promise of money keep this band of wild animals from doing what their guts told them to do—use me and throw me away when they were finished? Thank God for Don Narciso's protection, but would that be enough? I suspected that his first interest was in maintaining the unity of his band. He had already warned me that if I became a disruptive factor . . .

Rodrigo was holding something to my mouth. A bottle. The contents smelled awful. "Here . . . drink," he was saying. The bottle tipped and something liquid flowed into my mouth. I couldn't help gagging as I swallowed. It was *aguardiente*, the raw local booze made out of distilled sugar cane squeezings. It must have been 180 proof, for it took me several seconds to stop choking and coughing, but I definitely felt more awake now. I saw Rodrigo's teeth reflect moonlight in a brief smile. God, he was handsome. What the hell was he doing here?

We rode the rest of the night and most of the next day. No one but me seemed to be particularly tired. This was a genuinely hardened bunch. For part of the day we joined the tracks of a large herd of cattle. "Our own tracks will be lost," Rodrigo explained to me. He had been talking quite a lot, perhaps just to keep me going, but I was grateful for his attention. It took my mind off the ugly realities of my situation.

Don Narciso must have decided we were safe enough from pursuit for the time being. We made camp later that afternoon. In awhile Rodrigo led me to a smallish tent. "You'll want to sleep," he said, the understatement of the year. He laid down a couple of old ponchos, and I dropped off on the spot. His last words to me before I fell asleep were, "I don't think it's necessary to tie you up. You won't go anywhere. You know Hernán's just waiting for you to make a mistake."

What wonderful material for nightmares that warning was. However, I slept like a log for hours, and it was fully dark when I finally woke up. I sat up stiff and sore, on the pile of ponchos. My mind was confused for a few seconds, and then I realized that something had awakened me. What was it? Then I remembered. I thought I had sensed someone coming into the tent!

"Who's there?" I whispered, my heart pounding. I fully expected Hernán's cold, deadly voice to answer out of the darkness, so I sank back in relief when the response came. "It's me . . . Rodrigo."

It took a moment for me to get my voice back to normal. "What time is it?" I finally asked.

I could sense him shrugging. "Who knows? We don't worry much about that out here. It's a few hours after dark. Did you sleep well?"

"Yes. I feel a lot better."

"Why do you seem so nervous, then?"

I hesitated. Then I told him, "I've got to pee."

He laughed. "Come on. I'd rather you did it outside my tent."

"Your tent?"

"Of course. Did you think we have so many you would be given one of your own? You really are the princess, aren't you?"

There was no answer to that. He had his hand on my arm as we went out into the night. "Over this way is a good place," he said. "Some nice soft sand."

"You're coming with me?" I asked. "I'd really rather pee alone."

"Of course you would. You'd probably also like to take off on your own and save yourself a lot of money. But I wouldn't recommend it. This is a very harsh land. There are dangerous animals out there, some of them walking on two legs. I think you've already met some of those."

"Yes, I have." I thought of Hernán and suddenly felt better about having Rodrigo near as I squatted and peed. He was quite chivalrous, turning away to stare into the night until I was finished. Then we walked back into camp. I smelled food and was suddenly ravenous. "May I?" I asked, pointing to a large pot boiling over a fire.

"Of course." He ladled out a bowlful for me. "But I think we'd better take it back to the tent. The men are not used to you yet. They might get nervous . . ."

He was right. Already, greedy eyes were trying to see

through my clothes. I quickly followed Rodrigo to the tent. Once inside, he lighted a lantern so I could see while I was eating. "Mmmnnnn," I murmured, spooning down the rich stew. "Good. What is it?"

"One of the men killed an iguana this afternoon."

I nearly choked on a mouthful of stew as I visualized the iguana, an enormous lizard several feet long. Oh, what the hell, I thought. If I can eat snails and like them . . .

Rodrigo produced the bottle of *aguardiente* after I had finished the stew. This time it felt a little better going down, and I began to feel almost good. A little sleep, good food, the company of a handsome and personable man . . .

I looked a little more closely at Rodrigo. "Can I ask a personal question?"

He shrugged. "We'll see when you've asked it."

"Well," I said, "it's a variation on the old line, 'What's a nice girl like you doing in a place like this?' "

He'd just taken a mouthful of *aguardiente*, but he laughed so hard he spewed half of it out onto the tent floor. "Well," he replied, when he'd stopped choking, "I'm my father's son, aren't I?"

"Perhaps. But you know what I mean. You're so different from the others. You've . . . obviously had some education."

"Yes, I have," he said, his mood suddenly darkening. "Perhaps too much."

I waited without saying anything. I knew he would talk if he wanted to. He finally said, "I was almost a lawyer at one time. I nearly completed my course at the university. Only a few more weeks to go."

He stopped talking, a brooding look on his face as if he were looking hopelessly into a past that was no longer possible. "And . . . ?" I prompted.

He looked at me bleakly. "I had been celebrating. I'd just passed a difficult exam, one of my last. I'm afraid I was a little drunk, but not much, really. I was with a girl, a girl I liked very much. We were walking along the street, singing, when a squad of soldiers came by in a jeep. They stopped us and asked us for our papers. She had hers, but I'd forgotten and left mine at home. That was very unfortunate because now the soldiers had an excuse.''

"An excuse for what?" I asked when he didn't continue.

"An excuse for anything they wanted to do!" he replied harshly. "The military has so much power in my country. You cannot conceive of it; you have nothing comparable in yours. The army is a separate, independent, and all-powerful branch of our government. Military personnel walk the streets like policemen, but with far more power than police. They take ignorant peasant boys, some of them in their teens, put them in uniform, give them guns and very little training, and let them think they are gods. But they are still poor and ignorant and at the bottom of the heap. Now, that night they had what they thought was a brat of the privileged classes, walking the streets fat and happy in the company of the kind of girl beyond their wildest dreams. And I had broken the law by not having my identification with me.

"They roughed me up a little, but I didn't fight back. I didn't want to give them any more excuses. Then they started on the girl. They asked her what she was doing with this drunken lawbreaker. They told her they could take her in, too. She was crying by this time. Then they started touching her, feeling her breasts. One of them, a little bastard who'd obviously grown up half-starved, an Indian, tried to stick his hand up underneath her dress. That was more than I could take. I hit him. He fell down and stayed down.

"Now they had their excuse. I saw one of them swinging his rifle toward me. I tried to deflect the barrel, and it went off. It went off," he repeated in a dead voice.

"But he missed you, obviously."

"Yes. He missed me. He hit the girl. She fell with the side of her head blown off. Her beautiful face . . . horrible."

"My God!" I exclaimed. "Then what happened?"

He was staring off into space, but not really looking at anything. "No one moved for a few seconds. Then things began to happen. The soldiers had gone too far, and they knew I knew it. The only way they would be able to cover themselves would be to shoot me, too, and then put the guns in our dead hands, the way your American police do sometimes when they shoot the wrong person, and then they could say they'd stopped two terrorists and we'd tried to fight. But they never got the chance. When I saw that Ana—the girl—was dead, something snapped inside me. I tore the rifle away from the one who'd fired. I never even thought about shooting him. I beat him over the head with the stock so his brains came out.

"When the others finally reacted, they panicked and were poorly trained. They were not used to having their victims fight back. Colombians have been trained to be either victims or aggressors, but not me. Not with the father I had. I took a machine pistol away from one of them and started firing. They fired back, but they were incompetent. They missed me and missed me, but I didn't miss. I killed five of them and two got away. They ran down the street and around the corner and I tried to get them, too, but the machine pistol ran out of ammunition and by the time I'd found a full magazine, they were gone."

"And then you were in real trouble," I said.

"Oh, yes. Rightly or wrongly I'd committed the unforgiveable sin of fighting back against the military. I was a dead man. If they ever got their hands on me, that is. So I left the city and came out here to be with my father. That was two years ago."

"Mmm," I said. What else was there to say? Then I thought of something. "But how could you go to school and almost become a lawyer if your father, was, well, you know . . . ?"

"A bandit?" he said, chuckling bitterly. "He wasn't always that, you know. A long time ago he had a big ranch right out here on these plains. He built it up himself from scratch. Even educated himself. Pretty good for a mestizo who'd been born in a mud hut. But he became a rich man and married a fine woman from a good family—my mother."

"I suppose he had some kind of trouble like yours, didn't he?"

"Yes. During *la violencia*. A group of neighbors with different political sympathies attacked the ranch. They burnt it, destroyed everything we had. They killed my mother. But they made a big mistake when they let my father get away. He was wounded very badly, but he managed to make it out onto the plains and they couldn't find him. He recovered his health and for a while he considered trying to get the men punished who had done this to us, but they were of the party in power then, and he realized he'd have to do it himself. That's when he formed his first band. It took him years, but he finally killed every one of the bastards who'd raided us."

"How did you get away?" I asked. "Surely . . ."

"Yes. They would have killed me, too. But at the time I was visiting the home of my mother's brother in the city. He brought me up after that, and I lived a very ordinary life until that night when the soldiers—I suppose that even then I had hatred for them in my blood." He sighed and shook his head. "Old memories," he said. "It's better to think only of the present. I'm so tired . . ."

"Perhaps we should go to sleep, then," I said. He let me pull him down next to me on the soft pile of ponchos. I held his head against my breasts, feeling very motherly as he just lay there quietly curled against me for a while. I don't know what changed it, but suddenly the mood was different. Rodrigo moved away a foot or two and looked at me.

"You are very beautiful, Christina," he said. "When I was lying against you I could feel your body very clearly. You are strong but you are soft, too. Particularly right here."

He reached out and touched my breasts. I made no move to stop him, so he slowly unbuttoned the front of my shirt, baring my breasts. "So beautiful," he murmured, content with just looking for a moment, then he began running his hands wonderingly over my breasts. It wasn't terribly sexual at first, but when my nipples began to harden, his touch took on a new urgency. "With your mouth . . . please," I said, pulling his head down onto my breast. "Oh, God! Your mouth is hot!" I burst out.

My words had a galvanizing effect on Rodrigo. He began sucking my tits hard, moaning and sighing with passion. I held his dark curly head close against me, feeling my breasts swell, feeling my pussy awakening. I don't know if my answering passion was simply an atavistic reaction to the fear and violence that had marked the last two days, or if perhaps I was unconsciously acting out the role of the helpless, threatened female seeking the aid of a powerful man. Whatever it was, I was turned on.

Our clothes came off as each of us helped the other. Rodrigo had a lean, hard-muscled body, with not an ounce of wasted flesh. His cock was already jutting up starkly as we came together again. I could feel it pressing into my belly.

"It's been so long since I had a woman," he murmured as he pressed me down onto my back.

Rodrigo's lovemaking was very simple and direct. He laid me down and he fucked me. There was none of Will Sturtevant's subtle, maddening artistry, nor was there Hernán's wild animal passion. There was, however, something so straightforwardly exciting in Rodrigo himself that none of that mattered. For one thing, he had a fabulous cock, long and hard and thick, and he used it with a gusto that soon had me well on my way to an orgasm. "God . . . what the girls have been missing," I whimpered, remembering his comment about his not having made love for so long. I was lying flat on my back, my legs splayed out, my knees drawn up slightly, my hips pumping in response to his hard, steady thrusts. I could feel his pubic bone thudding against my pussy mound, stimulating my clitoris. As his cock moved in and out, he looked down at me, something like worship in his eyes. "Lovely . . . lovely . . ." he half whispered.

Then he put his full weight on me, pinning me down, his hands hooked underneath my shoulders so that he could pull my body toward his thrusting prick. I felt smothered by maleness, covered, possessed. I felt his cock begin its final swelling up inside me. It was surprising how long he had lasted since he had not made love recently. I waited, my hands fluttering up and down the length of his muscular back until I heard him give a hard little cry then his maleness was spouting into me and I let my own orgasm go, my gift to him. I spasmed wildly, my fingernails digging into the skin of his back. That only seemed to increase his passion. He reared up again, his powerful hands slipping under my buttocks, raising my hips up off the ground. He rammed into me again and again, his face reflecting the agony of his pleasure, his cock impossibly huge inside me, still spewing its slippery load deep into my belly.

With a groan of contentment, Rodrigo rolled, exhausted, to the side. I flinched as his cock jerked unceremoniously from my still-spasming vagina. This boy was going to have to learn better manners, I thought, but didn't have the heart to say anything at the moment. Rodrigo looked so relaxed, so complete. He suddenly smiled at me and hit his forehead in mock panic. "My God!" he said. "Does this mean my father doesn't get the extra two hundred thousand for sending you back in good condition?"

"Uh-uh," I replied. "After the way you just improved my condition, he'll probably get another two hundred thousand."

His face clouded. "Too bad it has to be this way, Christina."

"It's okay. We'll worry about it later." But I suddenly realized Rodrigo wasn't worrying much about anything. He was sound asleep.

I had too much to think about to be able to go right to sleep. Despite the events of the past hour or two, I was still a captive. My life was still forfeit if things went wrong. However, my one big plus was that I now had additional protection between me and Hernán. I hated to think of Rodrigo that way because there had been genuine passion in our lovemaking, and I had been deeply touched by his account of the tragedy of the girl and the soldiers. But realities were realities. As Rodrigo himself had said, it's too bad it had to happen this way.

However, that didn't stop me from reacting all over again when I felt Rodrigo's reawakened prick pressing against me during the night. We were lying together spoon fashion, each on our sides, with me curled up in front of him, and though Rodrigo himself was asleep, his prick was jutting between my thighs from the rear, half buried in the deep cleft between my buttocks. It took only a little wriggling on my part to line up my cunt with that probing hardness and then I reached down from in front and fed the tip of his bloated shaft into the entranceway to my vagina. I was still very wet with Rodrigo's copious semen, and the whole length of his prick slid into me easily.

With both of us half-asleep, we fucked gently for several minutes. Then I began to grow very excited. Still lying spoon fashion I raised one leg, opening myself wider so that his prick could reach further up into my suddenly cock-hungry depths. He did his part by seizing my hips right where the pelvic bone provides a natural handle, and he held me in place while he made several wild cock-thrusts up into my twat. We both came in seconds, the wet heat of his semen gushing back out my vaginal opening and dripping down both our thighs.

After that we slept until dawn, lying close together but as relaxed as an old married couple. However, when we heard the sounds of the camp coming alive outside our tent, Rodrigo leaped up like a startled rabbit. "Be a good idea to get our clothes on," he said somewhat gruffly, perhaps to hide his shy embarrassment over what had passed between us during the night. For my part, I was just as anxious to get dressed before anyone came into the tent. This was not the time to be rocking boats.

Just as we stepped outside, Don Narciso came striding toward us. Rodrigo looked at his father, blushed, then quickly walked away. "Got to saddle the horses," he grunted.

Don Narciso gave me a long, searching glance. "So," he said in a low voice, "that's the way it is. I thought he might take you, and I thought it would do the boy good. But he seems . . ."

He looked at me again, his lined old face stern, his eyes intelligent but merciless. "You had better not do anything to hurt that boy's head," he said flatly. "Or your estate is going to save four hundred thousand dollars."

With that, he walked away. Boy, talk about shotgun marriages, I thought to myself.

The sun—an enormous red ball that seemed to fill half the sky—was just coming up over the horizon when we started out. "It's really very beautiful," Rodrigo said as he rode alongside me. "There's no other land like it."

"I'll have to agree with that," I replied, looking around at the seemingly endless and empty plain. It was still quite green although the heavy rains had stopped some time ago.

The grass was rich and very high. The only other vegetation was a scattering of bright green shrubs.

"It's not really very fertile," Rodrigo said. "The soil is good only for what you see growing here, but that is good in itself. It keeps òut the damned dirt-grubbing farmers and their little shacks and hordes of starving kids. It's perfect cattle country. Lots of grass . . . lots of space . . . lots of sky."

I snuck a look at Rodrigo's glowing face and had a sneaking suspicion that he was not exactly filled with regret over the lost possibilities of a law career in the city.

We had ridden about two hours when a horseman came galloping toward the main body. "One of the scouts," Rodrigo said to me and immediately spurred his horse away to join his father. The two men rode out to meet the scout, the three of them talking animatedly for a short time. Then Don Narciso and Rodrigo turned their horses and snapped orders as they rode back through the rest of the band. Rodrigo had a moment to spare for me. "An army patrol," he said tersely. "They're heading this way."

"What are you going to do?" I asked breathlessly. Was rescue so near at hand?

"Teach them that this land is not open to them," he replied grimly.

For the next few minutes I watched as master tactician Don Narciso set up an ambush. The land around us was very gently rolling, but in no way could it be called hilly. The only outstanding feature was a shallow little draw, probably cut by a seasonal watercourse. "They will have to come this way," Don Narciso said, pointing to the water-formed gulley. He placed his men in a wide horse-shoe which would close off three sides of the draw, leaving only the entrance open.

I was becoming more and more horrified by the minute. "Are you really going to ambush them?" I demanded of Don Narciso as he cantered by, calling out orders.

"As certainly as the sun came up this morning," he
said. He looked at me very hard then and called an old
man over, the oldest in the band. He pointed me out to the
old man. "If she tries to warn the soldiers, cut her throat,"
he ordered and then rode on.

The old man gave me a toothless grin and, drawing an
enormous knife, pulled me down onto the ground and sat
beside me, one skinny old claw digging into my shoulder.
All I could do was stare in horror at the obviously razor-
sharp edge of that ugly blade.

Very soon everyone was in place, the horses far enough
back so that they would not whinny and give away the
ambush. I was at a fairly high point above the gulley, so I
was subsequently able to see everything that happened. It
amazed me that the entire band had been able to melt into
the terrain so completely. The entire area appeared completely deserted.

I became aware of a low humming sound in the distance.
After a few minutes the hum resolved into the sound of
engines. I waited tensely, very aware of the old man
beside me. He was watching me intently, the knife held
only inches from my throat. I knew that even if I wanted
to, I'd never have a chance to call out. I forced my mind
away from thoughts of that cold, sharp edge slicing into
my neck.

A small truck or large jeep, it was hard for me to
classify it, came into view. Three others followed right
behind. I estimated that there must have been about twenty
men in the four vehicles. The lead vehicle hesitated at the
entrance to the gulley. Someone in charge seemed to have
as good a tactical sense as Don Narciso. But there was no
other way around—the gulley provided the best footing for
the vehicles. Despite the troop commander's initial caution,
he must have been in a hurry, for he neglected to send out
flanking foot patrols. His haste cost him his life.

Don Narciso was lying on the ground not far away

from me. He stayed perfectly motionless until the vehicles were all well into the gulley. He then turned to a rifleman lying next to him. "Hit the radio with your first shot," he said. "If they have a chance to call in air cover . . . pphhhtttt! We've had it."

The rifleman smiled, giving a thumbs-up sign. Then he squinted down his rifle sights for what seemed an eternity. The sudden crack of his rifle was so loud that I involuntarily jumped. "Got it!" Don Narciso yelled, and I saw pieces of equipment flying from the second vehicle below; it must have been from the radio. Then the relative peace of this pleasant afternoon was broken by a thunderous crash of rifle fire. I saw men falling from the trucks as puffs of dust from rifle shots boiled in the dirt alongside them.

It was amazing how brief it all was. One soldier managed to stand up in his vehicle and began firing a mounted machine gun, but a firestorm of rifle bullets immediately struck him, and the mass of metal literally swept him out of the truck.

A few of the soldiers tried to bolt back out the way they had come, but horsemen suddenly appeared, shooting and yelling, in the entranceway of the gulley. The soldiers fell.

A few more shots and there was no more movement in the gulley. Nothing. Heads began to appear on the opposite rim of the gulley, and in a few moments bandits were pouring down the sides to surround the vehicles. I saw that one of the men was Rodrigo. He went over to the second vehicle and began to examine the machine gun. "It's undamaged," he shouted triumphantly up at his father.

I saw him turn and walk to the next vehicle as men swarmed around the machine gun and began to dismount it. Rodrigo was peering inside the bullet-shattered hulk when I suddenly saw movement behind him. One of the soldiers was still alive!

My breath sucked in as the soldier painfully propped himself up on one elbow. He was an officer, with a different uniform from those of the other soldiers. I felt very sorry for him. He seemed to be badly hurt.

And then I saw that he had something in his hand. It was a pistol and he was aiming it at Rodrigo's back!

My reaction was automatic. "Rodrigo! Look out!" I screamed at the top of my voice. The old man next to me leaped a foot, and for a moment I thought he was going to use his knife on me.

Though Rodrigo's reaction was instantaneous, for me, everything seemed to be happening in slow motion. The echoes of my cry were still bouncing off the sides of the gulley as he spun around. Suddenly he had his gun in his hand, too. I heard a shot, saw the officer's gun jerk upward. A bullet spanged off the truck right next to Rodrigo. I saw the officer's gun rise again, lining up on Rodrigo. Then Rodrigo's gun roared. The officer was knocked backward by the impact of the bullet. He was still alive, though. He tried to bring his gun to bear once again but could not make it. He rolled tiredly onto his back.

Rodrigo walked up and stood right over him. I couldn't believe it when he pointed his pistol straight down at the dying man. "No!" I screamed. Rodrigo looked up at me, then down at the officer again. He fired three times. I saw the officer's body jump under the impact of each bullet. Then he was still.

I watched with horror as Rodrigo walked up the hill toward me, the pistol still in his hand. I stood up. He stopped only a couple of feet away, and we stood looking at one another. "You wonder why, don't you?" he asked me quietly.

I dumbly nodded yes.

"There can be no survivors in a war like this," he said. "And there's a personal matter involved. Six months ago I lay on a hilltop and watched that same officer calmly shoot down the unarmed mayor of a little village, his wife, and three children. I'm glad that I had the chance to kill him."

He started to turn away but stopped and turned to face me again. "Thanks for saving my life," he said quietly.

The rest was horrible. Several of the bandits were going from soldier to soldier, shooting those still alive. Then everything was stripped both from the vehicles and from the corpses. I went over and sat underneath a particularly big bush so that I would not be able to see what was happening. I had been full of hope and good feelings this morning. Now I realized once again what desperate straits I was in. These people were as hard and as merciless as this land.

The pack horses were heavily loaded as we headed away from the site of the ambush. I rode silently alongside Rodrigo, not daring to look at him. He had the grace to leave me alone. That night, after having made camp, I hesitated to go to our tent. Rodrigo got up from the fire, and after looking at me expectantly and seeing I was not moving, he walked by himself to the tent. For a long time I could not follow. I kept seeing the officer's body jumping under the impact of the bullets.

I might have lain down by the fire and slept, but I suddenly became aware of a face staring at me from the other side of the fire. It was Hernán, his face looking disembodied against the blackness, the leaping flames distorting his scarred, hate-filled features.

I got up and walked quickly to the tent, my back prickling, my ears straining for the sound of footsteps behind me. I wouldn't put it past Hernán to stab me in the back and then melt away from the camp.

Rodrigo was lying down when I entered the tent, but the lamp was still burning. He raised up on one elbow to look at me, and I looked away. However, the tent was not very big, and I had no choice but to lie down next to him. He was the first to speak. "You make me feel that perhaps I did wrong today. I have not felt that way in a long time. It's not a feeling I like."

"It's a feeling that civilized people have," I said curtly.

He laughed bitterly. "Civilized people? Like the civilized men who dropped the atom bomb? Like the civilized men who casually order a bombing raid? Or the ones who sit and grow fat while others starve?"

"You were almost a lawyer," I retorted. "You should know about the rule of law."

He didn't laugh this time. He simply looked disgusted. "I was close enough to being a lawyer," he said, "to know that it is the lawyers who commit most of the real crimes."

"You're just bitter."

He nodded. "Perhaps. But I don't spend much time worrying about it. Life is quite simple—hard, brutal, abrupt out here. One acts. I really don't like killing. But it was about time somebody killed that captain. It was he himself who established the rules he died by. He will kill no more innocent people."

I wanted to say more, I wanted to protest in some meaningful way the terrible things I had seen. But I knew I was out of my depth. Although I couldn't accept such a value system for myself, I detected a certain ring of truth in Rodrigo's words. Somehow his actions, his whole personality, fit the reality of this harsh land. I suspected he was one of its finest flowerings. "All right," I said. "I won't judge."

He looked at me somberly. "Thank you. That is a very fine gift."

I let myself draw closer to him. Soon we were touching, tentatively and perhaps a little timidly at first, as if amazed at this feeling of life after a day of death. I made no protest as he slowly undressed me. He paid special attention to each part of me he uncovered. First he concentrated on my breasts, and by the time he was unbuckling my belt, my nipples, wet with his saliva, were hard, swollen, fully tumescent.

He unzipped my pants but didn't take them off. Instead, he slid his hand down inside, flattening his palm against my pussy hair. I wriggled my hips around, making room for his questing finger inside my slit. I gave a sharp little intake of breath as his fingertip brushed past my clitoris. Then it was moving lower, sliding easily in the slippery moistness of my hot, ready little gash. He managed to work the very tip of his finger up into my vagina. I bucked my hips upward, my cunt begging for more, but the jeans were just too tight. "Oh, God . . . get these things off me!" I moaned, wrestling with the waistband.

He helped me slide the tight material down over the swell of my hips. The jeans bunched up around my ankles in a hopeless tangle, but I finally managed to kick them loose. How wonderful it felt to have my cunt completely in the open.

He leaned down, moving his head close to my crotch. I thought that perhaps he was going to press his mouth against my pussy, but he merely wanted to watch as his fingers roamed through the convoluted folds of my snatch. "In Spanish," he said in English, "we call it *concha*. That means shell. It certainly does look like the soft, moist, sweet flesh inside a beautiful shell."

I wasn't inclined to answer. My body was twitching and jerking as his fingers probed deeper and deeper into the mysteries of my cunt. He isolated my clitoris, pushing my pussy lips back out of the way with the fingers of one hand, then managed to work that ultrasensitive little button free of the prepuce partially covering it. "Oh! Oh! I'm going to come!" I whimpered as the forefinger of his other hand circled lightly around and around my undefended clit. "You can come just from this?" he asked.

"Uh-huh . . . oooohhhhhh, I . . . OH!"

He had just shoved his thumb up into my vagina while keeping up his wonderful torture of my clitoris. My hips must have raised a foot off the ground as a powerful orgasm ripped through my lower body. "My God," he murmured. "The inside of you is actually sucking on my thumb."

"That's just its way of saying hello," I panted. My stomach muscles were twitching and jerking wildly as rippling chains of orgasmic aftershocks flowed in waves through my cunt. It was getting to the point where I could no longer bear just lying there doing nothing. I sat up suddenly. "I want your clothes off," I panted. "I want to see *you*."

He helped me as I stripped him naked. The same hard-muscled body, the same lovely cock, already half-hard. "Now it's my turn," I half whispered, bending my head down toward his cock. "Lie on your back."

His breath sucked in as I began gently, slowly running my fingers up and down the hardening shaft of his prick. I paid a lot of attention to the tip, circling my fingers under the helmet-shaped head, seeking out the most sensitive areas. I was kneeling next to him, so he was able to reach up and caress my breasts at the same time. "What are you going to do?" he asked as I moved my mouth right next to the tip of his cock.

He was so innocent in so many ways, this killer of men. "You wait and see," I murmured. He gave an involuntary little cry when I extended my tongue and began running it around and around the swollen knob of his cock tip. His hands spasmed, digging a little too hard into the soft flesh of my tits, but I didn't mind. Everything felt wonderfully sexy.

When I began sucking his cock, sliding my mouth gently up and down the full length of the swollen shaft, he seemed amazed at the pleasure he felt. "I can't believe it," he kept repeating. "I can't believe it."

I began to suck harder. I was growing as excited as Rodrigo, and was helped by the fact that he had abandoned my tits and was now pushing a finger up into my vagina.

"You're so hot and wet inside," he moaned. "Your cunt's as hot as your mouth. Two mouths . . . two mouths . . ."

As he approached orgasm, Rodrigo began to grow more and more incoherent. I hesitated. Did I want him to come this way? God, I wanted him to fuck me, but I realized he had never done this before, had never come in a woman's mouth, so I increased the pressure of my lips and tongue against his cock, at the same time lightly squeezing his balls.

As the saying goes in New York, he went ape-shit. "Aaarrrrggghhhhh!" he bellowed hoarsely, his hips pumping upward madly. His fingers slid out of my cunt, and he seized hold of my head with both hands, forcing my mouth down tighter against his loins. I nearly gagged as the swollen tip of his cock pounded against the back of my throat. I saved myself by opening my throat and taking his cock partway down it. That saved me the trouble of swallowing, because he was coming now in short, hard spurts, his cock twitching and jerking inside my mouth. Strange inarticulate cries burst from his throat and his head thrashed wildly from side to side, the cords in his neck standing out starkly.

His cock was still rock-hard and shiny with a mixture of semen and saliva when I pulled my mouth away from it. "Don't let it get soft," I begged as I wiped a trickle of his sperm from my lips.

"But . . ." he stammered.

"Just concentrate on what I'm doing," I said as I quickly straddled his sweating body. My cunt was poised right above his cock. When I took it in my fingers, the shaft felt a little less hard than a moment earlier. I quickly fed the tip up into my pussy hole and slammed my hips downward, surrounding his prick with cunt flesh. "Feel what my pussy is doing to your cock," I hissed as I pumped my hips up and down, sliding the slick hot walls of my vagina against his shaft.

His cock continued to grow softer inside me, but it was enough for me. It felt wonderful. Perhaps it was the look of ecstasy on my face, perhaps it was the moment when he murmured how beautiful my tits were and started caressing the nipples again; whatever it was, he began to grow hard inside me again. "Oh, God . . . God . . . I love your cock!" I cried out, moving my hips in a wide, wild circle, making his prick jerk excitingly inside me.

We fucked for a long time in that position. After about ten minutes, I remember having a sudden clear vision of Rodrigo shooting the officer. It happened just as I was starting to come. Frankly, I don't know which happened first, the vision or the orgasm. I'm a little ashamed of that, but I guess it goes to show just how close together in our minds, or perhaps in our bodies, sex and death are.

We must have fucked for at least an hour, wildly, unceasingly. We changed to other positions, Rodrigo's cock never leaving my vagina. He was very strong; he could move me around any way he wished. That in itself, the sense of his power, was as exciting to me as the feel of his cock inside me.

We had one final, screaming, moaning, flailing orgasm together and then we collapsed in a tangle of sweat-soaked flesh. When the blood hammering in my ears had diminished a little, I heard the sounds of laughter outside. My colloquial Spanish is a little weak, but I could detect ribald comments featuring my and Rodrigo's names. "I think our secret is out," I said.

"We were a little noisy," Rodrigo admitted.

"I feel wonderful."

"You look wonderful. Come to think of it, you do feel wonderful, too," my lover said, stroking my trembling body.

"Stop it or we'll have to start all over again."

Our postcoital banter went on for a while, but our exertions, and the long and emotion-charged day, had taken its toll. There was no more lovemaking. Rodrigo and I fell asleep curled tightly together, secure in our closeness. As I was soon to find out, however, there is no security. Only change.

We were like two children when we awoke the next morning. We had been through both hell and heaven together. We were delighted with one another. However, morning in the camp was no time for sex play. We knew the camp would be moving on soon, so we dressed and went outside. The sun was not quite up yet. People smiled at us. I suppose we looked like lovers, and everybody loves a lover, right? Well, almost everybody. I began to feel accepted in the group as I looked around me and saw that faces were friendlier, that some had lost their earlier hardness.

All except one, of course. One of the first people I saw after Rodrigo and I came out of the tent was Hernán. He was sitting on a pile of equipment a few feet away. He must have been sitting there watching the tent entrance, just waiting for us to come out. "Ah," he said with an ugly sneer. "The *gringa puta* and her puppy dog."

I felt Rodrigo stiffen beside me. "Don't pay any attention," I said hurriedly. But Hernán was far from through. Looking straight at Rodrigo, he said, "She has beautiful tits, doesn't she? And when you pinch the nipples just right, you can make her come. Right? At least she did for me, this *gringa* whore. And when she comes she sometimes says, 'Oh God!' and she bucks and her cunt runs juice like a ripe pineapple."

Although I tugged on his arm, Rodrigo would not move. His body felt like a piece of spring steel about to snap. I looked around me desperately. Don Narciso, sensing that something was happening, was striding swiftly in our direction. Oh, hurry, I thought.

". . . She loves to sit on top of a man," Hernán was continuing. "She loves to have him suck her tits while she whimpers and moans and moves her hips, and she says things like . . .''

"You son of a whore!" Rodrigo snarled. "I should have killed you a long time ago," and he launched himself at Hernán.

As strong and as fast as Rodrigo was, Hernán was faster. Moving with amazing speed, he leaped up from his seat and sprang at Rodrigo, meeting him halfway. There was suddenly a knife in his hand. It must have been there all the time, alongside his leg. I screamed. There was the thud of bodies, an odd cry from Rodrigo, and then he was staggering backwards, the handle of the knife protruding from his chest.

"Oh, God, no," I sobbed, running toward Rodrigo. He was slowly sinking to his knees. He looked up into my face once as I knelt beside him, his eyes big and soft and hurt. Then the light went out of his eyes and he pitched forward onto his face. "Rodrigo!" a harsh voice cried out a few feet away. I looked up. It was Don Narciso. He was standing a few feet away, seemingly unable to move. "Is he . . . ?" he asked in a hoarse whisper.

A man knelt next to Rodrigo, placed his ear against his back. *"Está muerto,"* he said. "He is dead."

"Ah," Don Narciso said. A short, soft syllable loaded with incredible menace. "Ah . . . you . . ." he said, turning to face Hernán.

Hernán had been standing in the place where he and Rodrigo had crashed together. His chest was heaving, and there was a twisted smile of triumph on his face. Now he suddenly realized what his situation was. His face paled and he began to back away, his body moving automatically toward the freedom of the open plain.

But a circle of men had formed behind him, and they pushed him back in the direction of Rodrigo's body—and toward Don Narciso. "Ah . . . you piece of shit," Don Narciso said, a little more loudly now.

Don Narciso was wearing a machete. He now drew it and continued walking steadily toward Hernán. Once again Hernán backed away and once again he was pushed forward by those behind him. He stumbled a little and Don Narciso raised the machete high, the expression on his face terrible. "No!" Hernán cried out.

I quickly turned away, not a moment too soon. I heard the awful, wet *thwack* of the machete biting into Hernán's flesh, heard Hernán's hoarse scream. "Filth!" Don Narciso cried out. Another thwack, another scream, and then blow after blow and no more screams, only one bubbling moan from Hernán before he became silent forever.

I sat shuddering on the ground next to Rodrigo's body and only slowly became aware that there was someone standing over me. I had to will myself to turn. Don Narciso was looking down at me, the machete still in his hand, blood dripping from the blade. I caught a glimpse of a huddled red thing lying on the ground a few feet away, then I looked up at Don Narciso again. His face was terrible.

"I told you once that the presence of a woman in our camp was not a good thing," he said in a flat, emotionless voice. "If I had listened to myself, if I had given you to Hernán right away, to do with as he wanted . . . But, no, I didn't. And now my son is dead, and I ask myself, why do *you* continue to live?"

I kept staring at the bloody machete. I knew Don Narciso was going to kill me. I wanted to scream, but I no longer seemed to have the energy. It had all been too much, all the days and days of death and killing.

Don Narciso went on. "But my son felt something for you. I know he would be grieved by your death. And yesterday you saved his life. I owe you a life, don't I? But I still ask myself . . . why is my son dead and why do you live?"

I crouched on the ground, hardly daring to breathe,

while I watched a terrible struggle pass over Don Narciso's lined, hard old face. All his life he had been a man of action. When someone killed one of his, he retaliated with death. Now his body, his tortured mind, demanded more action. The machete in his hand looked alive; I was afraid of it, as if it had a mind of its own. I still don't know what might have happened, whether or not Don Narciso, given the time, might have decided to kill me.

He never got the chance. Someone shouted from the edge of the camp. Several shots immediately followed, and then while everyone was milling around, a band of armed, mounted men suddenly charged out of nowhere and swept down on us, shooting and yelling.

Pandemonium followed. Don Narciso, waving the bloody machete, began shouting orders, and men ran to snatch up weapons. But it was too late. The invaders were already among us. I saw men falling, guns roaring, machetes flashing in the red light of the rising sun, which was right behind the attackers. Some of Don Narciso's men managed to loose off a few shots, but I didn't see them hit anything, and then they were running for cover.

Don Narciso held his ground as a rider on a huge white horse bore down on him. Don Narciso swung at the rider, who easily dodged, and a moment later the weight of the charging horse slammed Don Narciso to the ground.

I became aware then that the rider on the white horse was continuing his charge, and straight at me! I screamed and, leaping to my feet, started to run. I heard the thunder of hooves behind me, then the horse was suddenly level with me and a moment later a powerful arm encircled my waist and jerked me into the air. I couldn't breathe. I struggled, but to no avail. The rider slammed me down onto the horse in front of the saddle, then he called out to the other attackers, ''Out! Let's get out of here! I have what I came for!''

The other horsemen swept around us in a protective

circle, and we thundered away from the camp, the rider on the white horse still holding me prisoner in front of him. But I was no longer struggling. There was no need to. I had recognized the rider's voice. I turned around to look, to make sure. Yes. It was Javier.

CHAPTER FIFTEEN

As we rode away from Don Narciso's camp, the men accompanying us shouted and laughed while they recounted their exploits during the attack. However, I said nothing and Javier said nothing. I really didn't know *what* to say. Like everything else that had happened to me over the past few days, it had all been so sudden. Now, out of the blue here I was once again in the company of the man who had for so long been the real object of my life. And this after a rescue barely in the nick of time. I shuddered as I remembered Don Narciso's bloody machete.

Finally Javier called a halt. Both he and I slipped down from the back of the big white horse. We stood facing one another for a moment, his hands held lightly on my shoulders. "You are all right?" he asked quietly. "You are not hurt?"

"No," I said, shaking my head. He turned to his men then. "Mario. Have we lost anyone?" he demanded. There was a rapid head count.

"No one missing," a handsome young man replied. "Arturo's arm was grazed by a bullet. Nothing serious."

"And Don Narciso's men?" Javier asked, somewhat tensely, I thought.

The young man shrugged. "Two or three were hit, I think. But probably not badly. It was all over so fast, and for the most part they were just trying to get out of the way."

Javier's breath exploded in a relieved sigh. "Good," he said. I wondered why he seemed as concerned about the welfare of Don Narciso's men as he was about his own.

"We had better continue on our way," he said. "Bring the lady's horse."

It was news to me that I had a horse, but one of the men was soon leading a beautiful little chestnut mare up to me that was very handsomely saddled and bridled. "I brought him for you," Javier said.

"Thank you," I replied politely. I felt uncomfortable; this was all so anticlimactic. I had been saved from the direst straits by the man of my dreams in a rescue straight out of the *Arabian Nights*, and he was treating me as coolly and as politely as a lawyer fishing for a retainer. Nevertheless, I swung into the saddle when Javier called for us to mount up. However, I did make sure we were riding knee to knee as we started off across the plain toward the east.

I was a little surprised by our leisurely pace. "Aren't you afraid Don Narciso and his men might catch up to us?" I abruptly asked Javier, trying to be just as cool as he was.

"There's no danger of that," he replied. "I had two men run off their horses just as the attack started. They're scattered over the plain for miles. It'll take the whole day, perhaps longer, to round them up again."

I chewed on that for a moment. "You had this thing very carefully planned, then," I finally said.

"As carefully as possible, considering the short time we had. Where men's lives are at stake, it is criminal to plan carelessly. We set it up, Mario and I, so that we would ride in with the rising sun at our backs. We thought about a night attack, but it was too risky. For one thing, it would have made it much more difficult to find you. And we were helped this morning by some kind of disturbance in your camp. That aided the element of surprise."

Some kind of disturbance in our camp. I felt a great pang of sorrow as I remembered the look in Rodrigo's eyes just before he died. That look had been for me. But I knew I must not think about it. It was like an unreal episode out of a dream, out of a nightmare. "How did you know I was there?" I asked abruptly, partly to change my train of thought.

"There is not much that happens in these plains I do not know about," he said simply.

I let that sink in. "Does your omniscience extend to the mountain slopes?" I asked. "Did you know about me and my ranch up there?"

"Yes. For quite some time."

"Why didn't you come up there to find me?" I asked a little harshly. "It would have been a lot less dramatic."

"I did not think it would be a good idea."

His words were like an impenetrable wall. There seemed to be no opening, no emotional crack that would permit me to get a purchase on his feelings. Instinct told me not to try. I did say, "You seemed relieved by the news that Don Narciso didn't lose any men. Why?"

"Because he and I have to live together."

"I don't understand. Don Narciso is a bandit." And then I had a terrible thought. "My God! Are you a bandit, too?"

He laughed. "No, I am what I told you, a rancher." Then he waved his arm at the horizon. "Do you see all this? It's huge, isn't it? There is no one in sight, but there are men here. More men than you think. I am one of them, Don Narciso is another. My land begins not far from here and it goes on for a great distance. Don Narciso has no land that is really his own, but he exists out here just the same. There are many men like Don Narciso in these plains, most of them much worse than him. This is a lawless place, so I must either find ways to coexist with the Don Narcisos or wage endless war. I choose the path of coexistence. Now, Don Narciso had something that was important to me. When he understands that, the reasons for my action will have meaning for him. But if I had hurt him too badly, simple pride and machismo, would have required that he seek revenge. I did not want that."

I cleared my throat. "There is something you should know, then. His son, Rodrigo, was killed this morning. That was the disturbance in the camp."

"Ah! That is very bad news."

"And Don Narciso partially blames me."

"Worse and worse. Perhaps we should pick up our pace a little."

We rode for the rest of the day before making camp. Javier said nothing to me that was not required, and for my part I was content to be silent and let the events of the past day sink in. For a time I grieved for Rodrigo. I kept remembering the hardness, the aliveness of his beautiful young body, the ardor of his joyously innocent lovemaking. I grieved for the wasting of his life. However, with each forward step of my horse, he faded a little in my mind. The whole thing began to seem so unreal, so improbable from the start.

Just before dark, we forded a rather good-sized river and made camp on the other side. "This is the Rio Guaviare," Javier told me. "And this side of it marks the beginning of Vaupés Intendencia. My land is a two-day ride ahead."

I nodded and watched him walk away to direct the setting up of the camp. I particularly noticed the security arrangements. Armed guards were posted in strategic positions, as if we were expecting an attack. "I thought it would be impossible for Don Narciso to catch up with us," I said to Javier.

"Nothing is impossible with a man like Don Narciso," he replied grimly. "But he is not the only danger out here. In these plains the man who fails to provide for his own safety is very quickly a dead man."

Well, more cheerful news. I was beginning to feel like I was living in the Early Middle Ages and we were waiting for the Mongols to come charging over the hill. I must admit, though, that seeing Javier's thorough posting of a night guard did make me feel a lot more secure.

That first night we had no tents. We slept out in the open, with myself somewhat screened off from the men by a pile of saddles. I slept quite alone as Javier was with the others. He even took a stint as night guard. Oh well, I thought, with no tents there's just no way we could make it together. So I fell asleep by myself staring up at what looked like a billion stars.

I was pretty grumpy as we continued on our way the next day. "Does this damned plain go on forever?" I groused to Javier. Actually, my problem was that I was with the man of my dreams, the man who had so gloriously made love to me months before, and he was not touching me. I was getting as horny as hell.

"In two more days we will be on my land," Javier said.

"Two more days?"

"It's a big land." That was quite an understatement.

There was some excitement when we reached Javier's base camp that afternoon. He and his men had left it behind when they'd made the final approach to locate Don Narciso's camp. We were met by three men from the base camp, one of them driving a small truck loaded with supplies. That night when we made temporary camp, we at least had tents. Mine was quite comfortable and even had a cot inside. However, it was damned narrow and hard-looking, and certainly not big enough for two. Which was just as well because I again spent the night alone, much to my disgust.

The next day my disgust turned to dismay as Javier seemed to grow more and more cool toward me. On the few occasions we talked, he might as well have been my tour guide instead of the dream lover, who had rescued me from bandits at the risk of his life.

We crossed another river, the Inirida, and several hours later made our third camp. That night I determined to take the bull by the horns. I noticed Javier walking out toward the camp perimeter. I followed, catching up to him just outside the circle of firelight.

"You've been avoiding me," I said curtly. "Why? Don't you like me?"

He looked down. I could just barely make out his features in the darkness. "Too much," he said.

I felt a flash of hope. "No guessing games," I said. "Just what the hell does that mean?"

He looked up now. "Why do you think I left you there alone in the house on Mallorca? Why do you think I remained down here in the plains when I knew you were just up there in the mountains? It's because you and I come from two different worlds, two different ways of life, lives that could never really merge. And all that would come of trying to join them would be our own destruction. That is why I have . . . avoided you, despite my almost overwhelming desire. But enough of that," he said, and abruptly walked away into the night. I stared after him for a while.

"Hey. I think he likes me after all," I thought to myself.

I spent the night alone again, but I no longer felt dismayed. I knew that time was on my side. I had read the future in Javier's passionate manner as he talked. I realized, however, that as usual, fate could use a little helping hand. So the next day as we drew closer and closer to Javier's ranch, I concentrated on making myself the epitome of desirability. I don't really know what it was that I was doing. I was simply following the instinct of a woman who knows that the man she wants is about to fall. And Javier did indeed seem a little confused during the day, as if something were bothering him but he didn't quite know what.

About midday he told me that we were now on his land. "Good," I replied. "I'm tired of roughing it. When do we get to your ranch house?"

"Oh . . . I'd say about tomorrow night."

"What? My God, is your ranch that big?"

"Bigger. It's four *more* days from the house to the boundary on the other side."

I looked around me in awe for the rest of the day. Land, land, and more land. As far as the eye could see, and it all belonged to Javier. My God, no wonder he'd smiled when he'd lost that money at the roulette table!

We began to see cattle. "Yours?" I asked. He nodded. "How many head do you have?"

"I don't know. We are never able to locate them all out here on the open range. But there are enough."

An hour later we saw several horsemen approaching in the distance. I tensed, but Javier was unperturbed. "Some of my *vaqueros*," he explained. "You'd call them cowboys."

I looked at the *vaqueros* with great interest. They were a really rough looking bunch. They were riding barefoot and wore old, patched clothing, but could they ride! They came dashing up to us, the brims of their big sombreros flapping in the breeze. They greeted Javier effusively, and I was impressed by their obvious respect, even love, for their employer.

That afternoon we reached another river, the Vaupés. "We follow it along for another twenty-four hours," Javier told me, "then turn up a little tributary for a few miles, and we are at my home."

We camped at a particularly beautiful spot that night, on a little hillock above a bend in the river. Javier had my tent placed right under one of the rare trees that occasionally dot the plain. Even though the little hill wasn't really very high, it still gave me a wonderful view of miles and miles of rolling green *llanos*. Javier was standing next to me as I watched the sun go down, sending enormous shadows racing across the plain. "My God, this place is beautiful," I breathed.

Javier looked at me intently. "You really do love it, don't you?" he asked.

"Oh, yes. All of it. Except the cities, of course. I wish you could have seen my ranch up in the mountains."

He continued to look at me. Finally he said, "I think I believe you, Christina."

He turned then and left me. I sighed. What an exasperating man. But what a fascinating, challenging one, too. I'd long ago had my fill of the easy ones. To me, Javier was like Mount Everest, there simply to be conquered.

He came to me in the night, slipping silently into my tent. I had a knife in my hand by the time he was within feet of the bed. I was fast learning to be a Colombian.

"Javier?" I said sharply.

"Of course," he replied. "But you sounded sure it was me."

"Well, you *did* have a bigger bed put in here . . ."

He laughed. "Remind me never to underestimate you."

And then he was on the bed with me. "My God!" I said in mock surprise. "You don't have any clothes on!"

"Neither do you, I hope."

"Not a stitch." It was pitch black in the tent. "Here," I said. "Feel."

A hand reached out toward me in the dark. I could sense it coming. "Oh, my God," he said. "I forgot how lovely your breasts feel."

"It's you who make them feel lovely. Try the other one. Mmmmnnnnnn . . . now the nipple. Oh, God, how could anything feel so good!"

"I want to feel all of you. Ah, your skin is so smooth. But what's this? You're all wet down here."

"Yes, why don't you try and find out where it's coming from? Uh-uh . . . a little farther down . . . below the shrubbery. That's right . . . down in the vaaaaleeeyy," I sang softly. "Oh! God! You've found the switch!"

His fingertip traced lightly over my clit, and I began to pant. I had waited so long for this! "Oh, please . . . shove something up inside me before I die," I pleaded. His finger skipped lower down my gushing slit, the tip finally catching at the opening to my vagina. He didn't go right in. First he pressed downward, opening me up. My hips pressed back, then something gave and his finger was inside me.

Then the game-playing stopped. Javier suddenly fell on me, his finger still in my cunt, his mouth working against mine. Then he lowered his head to nuzzle my tits, then lifted it up to my mouth again. "Oh, Christina . . . Christina . . ." he moaned into my mouth.

Up until now both our moods had been light and playful. Now the mood changed to classic Grand Passion. We were all over one another, mouths sucking greedily, hands roaming madly. My fingertips traced over the smooth hardness of his broad chest, riffled through the crinkly fur of his pubic hair, heading south until at last I had hold of his cock. It was like a heated steel bar. "I want it in me," I babbled. "I want it in me now."

I got what I wanted. We had just been through three days of extended mental foreplay. What was happening now was only its logical culmination. I opened my legs wide as Javier climbed into position above me. I felt pressure against the opening to my vagina. I let out a sharp little cry of happiness as the pressure changed to penetration. He was in me! At last! And this time he would not be able to slip away from me in the dark, either physically or mentally.

My hands lay on his steadily flexing buttocks, guiding gently as he fucked his prick in and out of me. I could feel every inch of it going into me. I shuddered with a sense of loss as it began to withdraw, then gasped with anticipation as he hesitated a moment before pressing it deep into me again. "Oh . . . oh . . ." I gasped. "Just like that . . . keep it up. No, faster . . . no, slower and I'll come. Just a few more . . . I . . . there . . . oh, *yeeeesssssss!*"

After that first orgasm, the tempo began to pick up. We had each waited so long for the other that we began to go a little crazy. His hips slammed against my crotch more and more wildly. I began to lose my ability to think. A meaningless chain of words—sounds, really—poured from deep in my throat. I was vaguely aware of him panting hoarsely above me, but most of all I was aware of his marvelous cock ramming deeper and deeper into my cunt. It was growing, becoming harder. The swollen tip felt as big as a small apple as it battered against the end of my vagina. "Aahhhhh," he suddenly groaned. "Here I come . . . oooohhhhhh . . . Jesu . . . JESU!"

Scalding bursts of Javier's semen filled my pussy. "Give me all you've got!" I wailed as a string of sympathetic orgasms rolled through my belly. My fingers were digging deep into his buttocks, pressing him further and further into me. His hands were pounding on the bed. More inarticulate cries burst from his lips. This was a different Javier than the man who had made love to me so elegantly on that beautiful yacht. This was a wilder, more primitive man, perhaps the real Javier. I loved it, I thrilled under the sense of brute power he was pouring into me. It was as if all the time I had so far spent in Colombia, all the hardships, triumphs, and horrors, had happened simply to bring about this wild coupling with Javier Torralba Bienvia, the master of these vast lands on which I was now being marvelously, wonderfully fucked.

Much to my chagrin, Javier did not stay with me in the tent when it was over. "It would offend the men's sense of propriety," he explained. "I started out with them, it is only right that they and I are together this last night before we return to our home.''

I sighed. ''I guess I'll just have to take your word for it.''

''You may take my word for that,'' he said from the tent entrance. ''And you may take my word for one more thing: from now on, Christina, you belong to me. You are mine.'' And then he was gone.

CHAPTER SIXTEEN

I first saw the house from a half-mile away. It was in the late afternoon of the day after Javier and I had once again become lovers. There was something from the previous night that gave a special glow to what I was seeing now.

We had left the Rio Vaupés and had been following a smaller tributary for a couple of hours. I was feeling tired from our long, sexy night when Javier suddenly called for me to rein in my horse. Then he pointed ahead of us, and there it was, on a small rise ahead, catching the golden glow of the afternoon sun. I just sat my horse for a while and stared. "Oh, Javier," I finally murmured. "It's beautiful."

Rancho Del Sol. Ranch of the sun. There were quite a few buildings in the central complex; barns and corrals and bunkhouses and storehouses, but set apart from them a couple of hundred yards up the low hill was the main house. It was two stories high, Spanish colonial in style, with thick, whitewashed walls and a red tile roof. I could catch glimpses of arches and columns framing covered walkways on both the ground floor and second story. I discovered later that the covered walkways sheltered the windows of the house itself from the direct rays of the huge blazing sun that was both the blessing and the curse of the plains.

A heavy, whitewashed wall about eight feet high surrounded the entire house. As I later discovered, it enclosed a lovely tropical garden that meandered all around the house. ''My great-grandfather started it,'' Javier said as he sat his horse beside me. ''It was just an adobe hut then. We've been adding to it for a hundred years, and now I know why, Christina. We've been waiting for you to come and live in it.''

I was too overcome by emotion to answer. This really *was* a home, a place that had known the lives of generations of the same family. The house seemed to have captured the spirit of the surrounding land and of the people who made their living from it. It was almost too much for me. I have been a wanderer all my life and always stand a little in awe of permanence.

We had been seen from the house. Bells began to ring and a number of people, most of them on horseback, came running down the slope toward us. ''Come on!'' Javier shouted joyously and spurring his horse, he galloped up the slope toward the buildings. I rode just a few bounds behind him.

When we had reached the welcoming throng, Javier made sure I was riding alongside him. ''I want them to know that from now on, you are with me, Christina. This house, this land, these people, are all yours.''

Well, the people didn't seem to know that yet. They crowded around Javier, quite deferentially, true, but with warm devotion, too. They eventually noticed me, of course, and the glances thrown my way were a combination of curiosity, friendliness, and awe, particularly when Javier reached across to me and with joined hands, we galloped right up to the front gate of the hacienda.

We dismounted, and Javier led me inside. That's when I first saw the garden. Being enclosed by the wall, it had some of the atmosphere of a cloister garden in a monastery— an island of secluded peace. I fell in love with it immediately.

Servants were waiting for us at the door leading into the

hacienda itself. They were mostly older people, withered and blasted by lifetimes under a merciless sun. Introductions were made, but I had a hard time remembering the names. It was days before I had everybody straight in my mind.

Stepping into the cool, ordered interior of the hacienda made me realize just how dirty, dusty, and trailworn I was. I had been expecting something rustic, more or less like my ranch headquarters up in the mountains, so I was not quite prepared for the magnificence that met my eyes. I have been in a lot of grand houses on several continents, but Javier's house was equal to the best. The lustrous glow of handmade floor tiles was covered here and there by the richest carpets, some Flemish, some Persian, some Chinese, their warm, rich colors softening the harder texture of the adobe walls.

I also saw a century's worth of personal acquisitions, which reflected the increasing wealth and intellectual sophistication of a family; paintings, statues, tapestries abounded along with small, gorgeous works of art behind glass in tall cabinets. I walked up to one painting. "My God," I said to Javier, "where did you get this? I saw it hanging in a museum in Florence only last year."

"The one in Florence is a copy," Javier said matter-of-factly. "We've had this one for fifty or sixty years. We just don't let the outside world know."

I nodded, a little stunned. I knew that the painting had a catalogue value of over a million dollars. And there were more, equally as valuable, stretching down the hallway.

We walked through large, bright rooms, furnished with old, wonderfully comfortable looking pieces. Despite all the elegance and the marvelous collection of art from all over the world, the house still maintained its South American air. It reminded me of a perfect gemstone abiding in a rough yet beautiful setting.

Javier took me upstairs. He showed me into a large,

airy, sunlit room with a large dressing room and bathroom off to one side. "This is your room, Christina," he said.

"My room?" I asked. "Or ours?"

"Yours. But don't worry. I will spend a lot of my time here," and he pointed meaningfully toward the huge canopied bed that dominated one corner. I thought of protesting any separation at all from the man I loved, but I had the immediate certainty that this sort of arrangement was just right for us.

A closet door was partially open, and I caught sight of rich fabrics behind it. I thought for a moment that this must have recently been someone else's room and that they hadn't yet had a chance to move out. I was about to protest imposing on this person when Javier noticed where I was looking, and forestalled my comment. "Look inside," he said, walking over and opening the closet door all the way.

I did, running my hands over one beautiful dress, pants suit, and gown after another. "How lovely they all are," I said. "But whose . . . ?"

"Yours, Christina."

"But—"

"I had them made as soon as I learned that you were up in the mountains of Meta Intendencia. They should all fit. I did a little industrial espionage on your dressmakers and found out your exact measurements and had a dress dummy made. Now having seen you again, having touched your body once more, I'm certain the dress dummy is perfect. Everything should fit you."

I was impressed. There was at least $100,000 worth of clothes in that huge closet, and there was another closet to the side of it. I was beginning to realize that I would not exactly be roughing it here at Rancho Del Sol.

"But now you will want to clean up," Javier said. He motioned with his hand, and a small, dark Indian woman seemed to materialize out of nowhere. Her name turned out to be María, like half the other female servants, and some of the men. She disappeared into the huge bathroom and a moment later I heard water running. Javier withdrew with a low bow, and the moment he did another little woman materialized and began helping me out of my dusty, torn trail clothes. That was the last I saw of these garments. From then on, everything I wore always seemed to be new, to the point where I began to miss the familiarity of old and comfortable clothing.

However, I was not yet thinking of that as I luxuriated in the big sunken bathtub while one of the little women scrubbed my back. For many years I had been accustomed to wealth and the privilege it buys, so it was not the mere physical possessions surrounding me that I found impressive. It was where they were, set in the midst of this harsh and primitive land. It was as if a fairy castle had been set down in the midst of a wilderness, and, of course, the magic that had accomplished this was money. Huge amounts of it. I suspected that Javier's wealth must be enormous.

What a change dinner that night was from dinner on the trail. Javier and I ate alone, seated at a large, beautiful wooden table in an interior room of the hacienda. Dozens of pure beeswax candles flickered about us, shining from the polished surface of the table, reflecting from the silver and gold table serviçe. The finest wines had been decanted into crystal goblets. There was an abundance of rich food, most of it centering on beef.

When I say we dined alone, that doesn't count the numerous servants who were constantly hovering about us, on the alert to make certain that neither Javier nor I lacked anything. I was wearing a beautiful evening gown, cut low, with a flowing Empire skirt. Javier was dressed in a dark, elegant suit of very formal cut, quite Latin in some mysterious way I could not quite put my finger on. We ate and drank while seated impossibly far apart but nevertheless managed to murmur endearments to one another, mostly in

English, which was our one island of privacy from the servants.

Later, when both of us were a little tipsy from the wine and an incredibly old and smokily delicious Armagnac, we walked upstairs together. We stopped outside the door to my room. "You go in," Javier told me. "Prepare yourself. I would like you to get ready for me. I will join you in a little while."

It was all so wonderfully, wickedly formal because after all we were planning to fuck. In the end, it was going to be naked body to naked body, an act performed in pretty much the same way the poorest and simplest people perform it. What a sense of sin, then, of specialness, to have my maid take from me the beautiful gown and then dress me in no less beautiful a peignoir. Never in my life had I felt as naked as I did under that sheer, cool material.

I dismissed the maid and lay down on the big bed. I really didn't know what to do with myself. For the first few minutes I kept expecting Javier to come in, but he didn't. Then I started thinking about him, about his beautiful body, his lovely cock, the way he made love to me, and I began to grow excited.

I squirmed around on the bed, trying to ignore the smoldering fire beginning to grow up between my legs. My breasts felt big and heavy and hot, and the nipples were so sensitive that I gave a little gasp every time the filmy material of the peignoir slid across them.

Finally, training and habit won out over patience. I parted the front of the peignoir and began stroking my nude body. God, it felt wonderful; my skin was so sensitive. I ran my hands hotly over my throbbing breasts, watching the nipples grow harder and harder. Then I spread my legs and began rubbing my cunt, just the outer lips at first, but the hot, slippery liquids bubbling out from between their warm, padded softness encouraged me to let my finger slip into the central slit. "Oooohhhhh . . . Javier . . . where *are* you?'' I whimpered as I slowly sluiced my finger up and down that simmering, hungering little valley.

I caught a glimpse of movement on the other side of the room and thought for a moment that it might be Javier, but then I saw that it was only my own reflection in a mirror. That was captivating enough. I stared at myself, at the way the peignoir fell from my shoulders, parting to bare my breasts and the front of my body. One of my legs was hooked to the side, baring my snatch. Looking into the mirror, I could see the pinkness of my inner pussy meat, the bright glisten of my natural lubricant, and of course, my finger gliding up and down, pressing its way through wet, swollen flesh. I looked at my face, at the helpless, hot expression on it, at the green of my irises gleaming from behind suddenly heavy lids. My blond hair trailed down over my shoulders, parting like a golden waterfall around the upthrusting prominences of my breasts. Most of all I was fascinated by the hungry, wanton way my tongue was restlessly moving over the flushed swollenness of my half-parted lips.

That was the state I was in when Javier finally entered the room. I was lying there, panting with pleasure, half out of my mind as my fingers continued their work inside my slit. "I'm sorry . . . I couldn't wait any longer," I whimpered.

Javier was standing at the foot of the bed, dressed in a long, beautifully embroidered Japanese kimono. The gold and red and blue of the design contrasted perfectly with his dark, elegant handsomeness. I expected to see shock on his face; after all, he was so proper and I so hopelessly wanton, but instead I saw a look of hot answering lust light up his features. "I love what you are doing to yourself," he said softly to me. "Please . . . do it some more."

"You mean you want me to keep playing with my cunt?" I asked. My voice was very low. I was too turned on to trust a normal tone. He nodded. "It's the most beautiful thing I've ever seen in my life," he murmured.

My hand was still lying against my crotch. I opened my legs a little wider, then started playing with myself again. "It feels particularly wonderful when I slowly run my finger up and down my slit . . . like this," I said, demonstrating. "All the way, from the bottom near my pussy hole, right up to my clit. See? Just slowly and lightly."

Javier sat on the bed next to me, looking down at what I was doing to myself. "It's so wet looking," he said. "And so swollen. I can see the way your finger is pushing through all that, and . . . I can see your vagina. It seems to be . . . pulsing."

"Uh-huh. It's hungry, Javier. Really hungry. For cock."

He smiled. "Your language is bolder, more earthy than what I am used to. But I like it. It . . . how do you say it? Turns me on."

"Like this?" I asked, slowly shoving my forefinger up into my pussy hole right in front of him.

He suddenly pushed my hand out of the way. I sighed unhappily as my finger sucked free of my clutching vaginal opening. However, it was soon to be replaced. "Let me try it for a while," Javier said, "while you guide me."

"Mmmmnnnnn," I sighed happily as his bigger, blunter finger began gliding up and down my grateful slit. "That's right . . . just slowly up and down. No . . . not too hard. Yes . . . just right. . . . Oh!" I gasped as he reached down with his other hand and pushed a finger up inside my pussy hole, just underneath where his other finger was working so gently inside my slit.

It was all an easy slide after that. I was by now so wildly turned on that I'm sure the mere sight of me would have made a hermit monk get it up. I could already see action under the front of Javier's kimono, a lovely tenting effect that testified to the growing presence of just the instrument needed to satisfy the raging sexual hunger shuddering through my cunt. I vaguely remember writhing on the bed while Javier's fingers continued torturing my genitals, then somehow we were both naked and that wonderful instrument was pushing deep inside me and I was coming before it hit bottom.

Making love, in that big bed, in that massive house, with its generations of memories of other lovers, the ancestors of the one laboring over me now, was almost mystically satisfying. I remember only a wonderful collage of raging orgasms and panting endearments, and then I was falling asleep, hot and sticky and throbbingly satisfied between my legs, Javier lying warm and real beside me, his whispered words entering my ears, "Remember, Christina. You are mine now."

CHAPTER SEVENTEEN

The next few weeks went by like a beautiful dream. There were long hours with Javier, eating together, riding over his land, talking, and of course making love in my big bed. That was my favorite—except for one thing. Javier never spent the entire night with me. We would make love, sometimes for hours, and then fall asleep together, but sometime during the night Javier would leave my bed and, I supposed, return to his own. I asked him why, once. "Because it is my way," he replied.

Something about his tone made me refrain from pressing the matter, although I liked to joke about it. One night I said, "You wouldn't want me to believe I've unknowingly put myself into the hands of Count Dracula, would you? And think that my lover has to return to his musty tomb before midnight?"

He turned the joke back on me. "You've got it wrong. I have to be in my coffin before dawn. Remember? We stayed up making love until three the other morning." He began to tickle me then, and after laughing and rolling around on the bed together, we ended up making love. And again I woke up alone.

One day, when Javier had gone out riding on the range, I tippy-toed to the back of the house where I knew his private room was, determined to look inside. I had by now made myself so nervous with all this Dracula talk that my heart was racing as I quietly pushed the door open. After the luxury of my own room, I expected something similar in Javier's. Imagine my surprise, then, when I saw only a very small chamber with a desk on one side and a narrow cot on the other. The room of a monk. Or a vampire.

"*Yah!*" I shrieked as someone suddenly touched me on the shoulder from behind. I spun around, one hand at my throat, to face one of the little servant women. "Does the señora want something?" she asked, her face expressionless.

"Uh . . . ah . . . no," I managed to gasp as I fought to get my pulse rate back under control. "Just looking for Javier."

I trailed out of the room rather lamely, and the woman closed the door behind me. There was something very protective in her manner. Ah, well, I thought, at least I didn't find a pleasure palace full of harem girls. Not that he'd be able to do much with them anyhow, after the condition we usually left one another in after a night of our wild lovemaking. So . . . I had a strange lover who preferred his simple little room to mine. Big deal. But I still wished he'd at least once spend an entire night with me.

I began to learn my way around the hacienda. For a start, I made myself remember the names of all the servants, which was a real task, because there were more than twenty. I slowly became acquainted with some of the *vaqueros*, too, a wild but chivalrous bunch. One evening I saw two men sitting under a window of one of the outbuildings, where I knew some of the married couples and single girls lived. It was quite a charming sight. Each of the young men had a guitar, and they took turns singing rather lovely and plaintive songs, all the while looking longingly up at the window, or rather grimly at each other. I later asked Javier what they were doing. "Singing *coplas* to a girl," he said.

"*Coplas?* How romantic."

He hesitated. "Not really. They are in love with the

same woman. Already they have come close to a knife fight over her. I ordered them to settle it peacefully, and singing *coplas* is one way of doing that. It's a kind of duel, but with songs instead of weapons. One will win, one will lose. The girl will choose the one she thinks sings the best.''

Too bad Hernán and Gabriel couldn't have done that, I thought. Or Hernán and Rodrigo. No, I wouldn't let myself think about that. I was too happy.

Most of the people I met were very friendly to me. As Javier's woman, I had a rather awesome status in their eyes, particularly as a foreign woman, a *rubia*, a blond. I was the *dueña* of the hacienda and received the respect due that position. Sometimes too much respect. At times, I longed for an equal to talk to. It might have been Mario, Javier's second-in-command, whom I had met on the long ride to the ranch. He was a good-natured, friendly, handsome young man, who unfortunately reminded me very strongly of Rodrigo. I saw a certain degree of worship for me in his eyes, which made me decidedly nervous. That could be such a problem with Latin men.

There were two young women at the ranch whom I noticed often, and who seemed to have no particular duties. One of them was a lively, lovely young girl named Conchita, which means Little Shell, or if one chooses the slang meaning, Little Cunt. She was such a sexy, flirtatious little thing that I couldn't help thinking from time to time of that second possible meaning to her name.

She responded to my overtures with smiling friendliness and we chatted a few times, but I never could get close to her. When I tried, she would grow nervous, and begin to sidle away.

There was another woman, an extremely beautiful one, named Carmen, who was not at all friendly to me. She had raven black hair, a beautiful, dark, sensuous face, and an incredibly lovely figure. I saw sensualist written all over her, and being one myself, I was naturally drawn to her, but she replied with such coldness and hostility that I backed away and left her alone, wondering what I might have done to offend the girl.

At the time I was floating high above the world on a cloud of sex and love with Javier, so I had little time or thought left over to worry about either Conchita or Carmen. I remember one day in particular Javier and I had been acting like a couple of love-sick newlywed kids, romping in the morning on my bed, then prowling about the house and grounds looking for mischief to get into. We were in the stables when I noticed something hanging on the wall, an odd contraption of leather. "What's that?" I asked.

"My grandmother's sidesaddle," he answered.

"Sidesaddle? My God, it's in good shape."

"Yes. We keep it oiled."

"Oh, Javier, I've never ridden on a sidesaddle. May I?"

"Well . . ."

"Oh, please."

He agreed, laughing, and to play the role a little better, I went upstairs and put on a long, old-fashioned dress. Javier laughed when he saw me. "My grandmother would turn over in her grave," he said.

My mare was now wearing the sidesaddle, and I mounted, not without difficulty. The mare didn't like it and shied at first, and a couple of times I slid out of the saddle, landing hard on my feet. Eventually, after a lot of soothing and a handful of sugar cubes, the mare quieted down and I was able to mount. With Javier riding alongside on his big white stallion, whom I insisted on calling Silver, we trotted out of the yard and headed out into the plain. "Oh, Javier," I shrieked. "I feel like I'm going to fall!"

He laughed and told me it was my own fault, but I rather quickly got the hang of it and in no time was riding along quite easily. I did wonder, though, how English gentlewomen of preceding centuries had ever found this kind of seat secure enough to actually jump horses while riding on it.

We rode out for about half an hour, trailed by the usual two armed men. Javier was very cautious with me, particularly since he had heard, via other landowners, that Don Narciso bore both of us a considerable grudge.

"How do you like the saddle?" Javier asked suddenly.

"Not too bad," I replied. "But it doesn't feel quite the same as a regular saddle. You know . . . between the legs."

He laughed. "Now you know why the oldtimers made their women ride sidesaddle."

"So they wouldn't get turned on and attack the first man they saw. I know, I know. Male chauvinist pigs. But I . . ."

There was a little silence. "But what?" Javier finally prompted.

"Well . . . I've always wondered about one thing. Concerning saddles.'

"And what is that?"

"If two people can fuck while riding a horse."

Javier was shocked, but he laughed if a little hollowly. "Christina . . . you are absolutely incredible!"

"But I mean it. And I don't need a saddle rubbing against my cunt to get me turned on, Señor Torralba. Just looking at you and remembering the feel of that lovely cock of yours going inside me is enough, and I'm looking at you right now, handsome."

"Ah . . . but the men," Javier replied, turning in his saddle to glance back at our guards.

"Send them away. I want to fuck you right here and now. And on horseback."

"Christina. I—"

"I'm getting really wet just thinking about it," I said in a sultry voice.

Javier looked over at me and that familiar look in his

eyes told me I was getting through to him. He wanted me. He suddenly wheeled Silver around and trotted back toward the two guards. There was a short conversation, and when Javier rode back toward me the guards stayed put. "They won't follow. Not for a half-hour," Javier told me, a feral gleam in his eyes. "Now . . . let's see if your lewd and lascivious plan has any hope of working."

We rode just out of sight of the two guards, and then I dismounted. I stood next to the tall stallion, looking up at my lover. "What's that funny bulge I see in the front of your pants?" I asked in a husky voice.

"Climb up here and see for yourself."

"You're on, masked stranger."

He let that go as I clambered up onto Silver. It wasn't easy, particularly wearing that long dress. And to do what I wanted, I had to sit right in front of Javier, facing the rear of the horse. Silver didn't like that at all, but Javier's masterful hand quickly brought his nervous steed under control.

There really wasn't much room up there. The saddle horn was right behind my ass and Javier right in front of me. "Now," I purred, reaching down for Javier's zipper. "Let's see what all this strange swelling is about."

It was hard as hell to get the zipper down, with me sitting practically on top of it, but I managed. "Oh, my goodness," I said. "You've been hiding a snake in there. Is it poisonous?"

"Uh-uh," he said. "Very friendly. Perhaps you would like to play with it for a little while."

"Mmmnnnnn . . . yes, it is friendly. See? The little mouth in the end is smiling at me. But it's so hot and dry outside today! Maybe I can help. I have a nice wet, shady place where it can rest."

Javier had to help me work that damned long skirt up around my waist, but eventually my naked ass was resting against the smooth, warm leather of the saddle. I had to raise myself up high to position my cunt above Javier's upward angling cock. "Careful . . . careful," he grunted as I bent his rock-hard shaft downward a little. I felt the tip in just the right place, then slowly settled onto it. "Ooooooo oohhhhh," we both moaned as his prick slid smoothly up into my twat.

The trouble was neither of us could move. I was sandwiched in between the horn and Javier's loins, with his cock anchoring me firmly in place. It felt wonderful to have his cock inside me, but we were both used to a lot more movement. It was Silver who solved our problem. He had been getting bored, standing there while we hopped around on his back. He took a couple of restless, stiff-legged steps. "Uunnggghhh," both Javier and I grunted as the abrupt motion of the horse jammed me down hard on Javier's prick. "Oh, that's it . . . that's it!" I gloated. "Make the son-of-a-bitch trot."

First Javier coaxed his horse into a walk, which felt good enough as my weight shifted back and forth in the saddle, making Javier's cock slide around inside me. Then Silver broke into a trot. Since he was no *pasofino*, he trotted the way an old jeep goes over rough ground. Naturally I bounced way up and down with each jolting step, which was just what I wanted. "Oh . . . oh my God!" I panted, as I rose and fell on Javier's cock. In addition, the saddle horn was pressing up into the crack of my ass, exerting pressure against my rectum. My nether regions felt invaded by long, hard objects.

I was getting incredibly turned on and so was Javier, judging by the hardness and size of his cock inside me. "Make him run, Lone Ranger!" I shouted.

Javier dug his heels into the stallion's flanks, and we took off like a rocket. I was bouncing so wildly that a couple of times I was afraid the saddle horn was going to go up my ass, but I held tightly to Javier and managed to keep his cock in all the way. Javier's horse was amazingly fast, and I saw the landscape whizzing by me backwards just as my orgasm struck. *"Aaaiiyyyyy!"* I shrieked happily. "Hiyooooo, Silver!"

I felt semen spouting up into me from below as the experience worked for Javier as well. We clung to one another madly, barely able to hold on, our genitals locked together. Finally, Silver saved us from a bad fall by becoming bored with this senseless (to him) running, and slowed to a stop. He stood quietly cropping grass while Javier and I slowly untangled ourselves. "I'll never go riding alone again," I panted to Javier. "Not unless you have a special saddle horn designed for me—modeled after your cock."

"Christina," Javier said with a good-humored shake of his handsome head. "Somehow I don't think you're kidding."

"I'm not sure I am. Anyhow, let's get back to the ranch and see if we still like it lying down."

We laughed and joked until we rejoined the two guards. As they rode with us at a short distance, Javier turned serious. "There's one thing that puzzled me, Christina," he said.

"What?"

"All this 'masked stranger' and 'Hiyo, Silver' stuff. Just what is it supposed to mean?"

Now it was my turn to laugh. "You wouldn't understand," I replied. "Just dreams from childhood, memories of the boob tube."

That left him even more puzzled, but we all need our little secrets, don't we?

CHAPTER EIGHTEEN

That wild ride turned out to be the high point of our relationship, a plateau of sensual and emotional sharing. After that, things began to deteriorate.

I suppose they had to. It had all been too intense, too special. No one can live that way forever. But unfortunately that had been the basis of our relationship from the start. As I said before, it was right out of the *Arabian Nights*. A fairy tale.

It did not fall to pieces all at once. Nor did we ever stop loving one another. But now Javier's mind began to turn in other directions, mostly toward the ranch. With me, he had been on a kind of extended vacation from his normal life, and that life was Rancho Del Sol.

It began when one night he was out late with some of the men, repairing some storm damage in a distant pasture. I waited up all night but he never came to my room. Imagine my hurt feelings when I discovered he had come home during the night but had elected to go straight to his own room. "I was tired, Christina," he told me later. "Very, very tired."

I was very childish about it, I see that now, and my pouting had the effect of souring Javier's usually even temper. We did not sleep together the next two nights, but unable to stand the separation any longer than I, Javier came into my room in the middle of the third night and we nearly devoured one another.

That was only the first of many difficulties between us. Part of the problem was that I had nothing to do outside of being with Javier. Everything else was done for me by hordes of half-invisible servants. I am a woman who is used to being very active in the world. I was now reduced to the role of a much-beloved decoration.

I complained about my situation to Javier, but he had trouble understanding. "You have everything a woman could possibly want," he said, genuinely puzzled.

"Not *this* woman," I said. And then I had a bright idea. "Tell you what. I have some business things to take care of. Maybe I should go to Bogotá for a few days."

I knew I had said something wrong by the stricken look on Javier's face. "You won't come back," he said woodenly.

"What? Well, of course I'll come back. What makes you think that?"

Javier, however, had quickly smoothed his features, and I now I met a blank wall. "Anyhow, it is impossible for you to leave now. The roundup is soon, and you know how far it is to the nearest settlement. I can't spare the men to take you there. Perhaps in a few weeks."

That's where we had to leave it because, as I was beginning to realize more and more, I was completely reliant on Javier for everything. What I did not realize, not yet, was that there existed in Javier a basic insecurity with which he was unable to deal. Yes, he was strong, he was brave, he could face the charge of armed men out to kill him, and he was unafraid to brave the most violent storms nature could throw at him. But there was one thing that had him backed into a corner. He was afraid of the outside world.

He had not been joking when he said I would not come back from Bogotá. Bogotá was part of The Enemy, the corrupt, incomprehensible world outside the open, clear spaces of his beloved plains. Somehow, some unknown and malevolent force would take me from him if he permitted me out of his sight, out of his control.

Almost immediately after our discussion, Javier went out on the roundup with most of the men. He was gone for days, and I spent my time moping around the hacienda, trying to find things to do. There were people aplenty, but no one to really talk to, no one with the same kind of mind, the same kind of background as myself. I was a little like the mariner cast adrift on the sea: Water, water, everywhere, and not a drop to drink.

There *was* one person I began to seek out more and more—the girl, Conchita. She may not have had my experiences, but she had a quick and lively mind. I enjoyed talking to her, and despite her earlier nervousness she and I began to become something like friends. However, she would never talk about Javier, despite my desire to learn more about him from those who had known him a long time.

In the midst of the roundup, Javier came back to the hacienda for one night. He was as anxious as I to get to my bedroom, and we made very satisfactory love. But I sensed something missing. He was gone before I figured out that he had left part of himself out on the plains and that I had received only a portion of his attention.

Somewhat disconsolate, I once again sought out Conchita's company. She sensed I was not happy and did her best to cheer me up. One day we were walking across the big grassy area in front of the main house, just approaching the buildings where most of the staff lived, when I suddenly caught sight of Carmen standing in a doorway, staring at us. Once again I was struck by her incredible dark beauty, and by the intensity of her presence. I was also struck by the violently bad vibes she was hurling in my direction. She saw me looking, and with one last scornful curl of her lovely lips, stepped back out of sight into the doorway.

"What's the matter with her?" I asked Conchita.

"She . . . is not very happy right now," Conchita said haltingly.

"Not happy, hell. I know when someone hates me. But why should she?"

There was no answer from Conchita. "What does Carmen do around here, anyway?" I asked, determined to pursue the question.

"Nothing . . . now," Conchita said softly.

And then it hit me. Of course! How stupid of me not to have realized! "She and Javier were lovers before I arrived, weren't they?" I demanded.

Conchita was becoming upset. "Please . . . don't ask me," she begged.

"Then I'll go and ask Carmen," I said, starting toward the doorway where I had last seen her.

"No!" Conchita said, taking hold of my arm and pulling me back. "It would be dangerous. She is a very violent person."

"Then *you* tell me!" I demanded, growing angry.

"Only if you promise not to talk to her."

I agreed. Conchita looked around nervously, as if afraid someone might be listening. "It's not like you think," she finally said. "She didn't have the position you have, but she was first with Javier all the time. The rest of us . . ."

"What? You too?" I blurted out, amazed.

"Please . . . I've said too much already. You have to understand. There are not many women out here, and Javier is a man. What a man!" she suddenly burst out, and then, knowing what a faux pas that had been to utter in my presence, she had the grace to blush tremendously. I loved her for that.

"Yes . . . yes, I know," I said, taking her hand. "And now I'm on the scene and the fun and games are over. But how come Carmen hates me so much and you obviously don't?"

"Well, Carmen was his favorite, as I said. They shared a great many things. I think she even helped him with decisions concerning the ranch. And for her there was no man, no interest other than Javier. When you came . . ."

"Damn," I murmured. "Why did Javier . . . ? He shouldn't have treated her that way!"

Conchita sighed. "Sometimes I don't think you really understand our Latin ways."

A genuine understatement. But I decided to try. Since it had seemed necessary for Javier to keep the whole thing a secret, I decided to go along and not bring it up either. I also decided to maintain my friendship with Conchita. Not being the jealous type, I was not unduly disturbed that she had previously climbed into bed with my beloved. She was such a sexy little minx that I could understand why he had been tempted, and with his life and death power as *dueño* of Rancho Del Sol, well, I could see it all. But I was still confused by Conchita's lack of jealousy over my stealing this paragon from her. "Well . . ." she said shyly when I pressed her on the subject. "I have a *novio* . . ."

A *novio* is a cross between a boyfriend and a fiancé. It took a little more prying to find out the name of this lucky man, and I was delighted to find out it was Mario, Javier's young, handsome, right-hand man. Conchita, however, was quick to explain that this posed problems. Since she had been the master's woman at one time, Mario was hesitant to step in where his *patrón* had got his feet wet. So far, he had not yet slept with Conchita although he loved her very much. Now that's loyalty, I thought.

Conchita swore me to silence. At least I now had a secret to keep. That was *something* to do. I was annoyed, however, that Javier had held out on me. He should have told me. Carmen might have cut my throat some dark night if I, poor unsuspecting soul, had been careless enough to put myself in her path. I had another bone to pick with Javier, too. His sexual attentions had been falling off so much of late that I was getting downright horny, and that always makes me irritable. So what if he had his cows to play nursemaid to? I wanted to get *laid*.

I tried to broach the subject in a semihumorous way one night when we were at the dinner table. "You're not paying very much attention to me lately," I said.

"I'm sorry, Christina," he replied. "I've had a lot on my mind lately."

"I suppose I *will* have to go to Bogotá . . . just to find a man with a little time," I joked.

I instantly knew I had made a big mistake. Javier sat completely still, as if he had been turned to stone. "If I ever catch you with another man," he said in a cold, deadly voice, "I will kill the both of you."

I sat, petrified, as he abruptly stood up from the table and left the room. He came to me later that night full of warmth and implied apologies, but I had now learned enough about Javier's pride and the customs of his country to know that he had meant what he'd said at the dinner table. And to know that I didn't want any more Hernán-Gabriel duels or dead Rodrigos.

The next morning Javier was particularly considerate. He came to my room, cossetted me, made love to me until I thought I was going to pass out, then he left for a few minutes and came back holding a collection of small boxes. "I have a gift for you," he said. "Something I've been saving for the right moment."

"Oh, Javier," I said when he opened the first box. In it was an emerald pendant on a diamond-encrusted gold chain. The emerald itself was encircled by a lovely melee setting of small, very fine diamonds. It was one of the biggest and most perfect emeralds I had ever held in my hand. "Eighteen carats," Javier said. "A perfect stone from the Muso mines a few hundred kilometers north of here. It's yours, Christina. Try it on."

Oh, you're trying to buy me, you wonderful man, I

thought as I put the chain around my neck. In the mirror the emerald hung just above my breasts, not quite inside the cleavage. Its rich color and the glitter of the diamonds were a marvelous contrast to my naked flesh.

Javier was not finished. He opened the other boxes. Each had two or three fine unset emeralds inside, not as large as the one in the pendant, but with mesmerizingly rich grass-green color. "Just some baubles for you to look at," Javier said. "Pick two or three you might want set. There is lots of time."

For a few days the emeralds were a constant diversion. I would put the stones on top of my dressing table and look into them. Each was completely different inside. Most emeralds, even very good ones, are full of tiny stress cracks and inclusions. They are what's called an emerald's "garden." The big pendant stone had very little garden. That was one of the factors that made it particularly valuable. I supposed it was worth well over a hundred thousand dollars. I have never had it appraised. I still wear it once in a while.

However, Javier's ardor began to wane again. He spent less and less time with me. There was no doubt he still loved me; I could see it in his eyes when from time to time I would suddenly catch him looking at me. It was simply that I was no longer new. Now I was simply a part of what he had always had—Rancho Del Sol. In a way I supposed it was flattering. I was completely accepted. But to me, life must hold more than that. Perhaps that's a fault of mine, but it's a part of me, and I doubt that anything but extreme old age will ever change my questing nature.

The last of my illusions vanished one night about two weeks after Javier had given me the emeralds. He had been restless all evening and did not come to my room later. I was horribly disappointed because I was literally in heat. I was still awake about midnight when I thought I heard the sound of someone passing by in the corridor outside my room. For a moment I thought it might be Javier coming to see me at last, but my door did not open.

Curious, I got out of bed very quietly and opening my door a crack, peered out into the hall. I barely caught a glimpse of Javier as he started down the stairs.

Now, why is he sneaking around at midnight? I wondered. Perhaps he has something to do and doesn't want to awaken me. Early to bed and early to rise on a Colombian ranch, I supposed. I moved over to my window and stood looking out at the night. Under the full moon I saw Javier cross the open space in front of the hacienda and head for the outbuildings. But why? Everything was dark over there . . . except for one lighted window. I saw Javier head straight toward that window and vanish for a moment in the shadow of the building. Then I saw a door open and light spilled out into the night. Javier slipped in through the door and the light was suddenly blotted out as the door closed.

"You son-of-a-bitch," I half whispered. I knew that door. It was the door Carmen had been standing in the other day.

CHAPTER NINETEEN

Let me tell you a little bit about my theory of jealousy. I never get jealous simply because somebody close to me makes love to someone else. As long as they continue their attentions to me, I haven't really lost anything, have I? Jealousy is really the fear of losing something. Well, now I *was* jealous. Javier was spending time with Carmen *instead* of me. She was taking something that should have been mine.

Or was she? Perhaps she and Javier were only talking business. Conchita had said that Carmen often worked with Javier on ranch business. I told myself it would be stupid to be jealous over what might, after all, be nothing. The best thing would be to go to bed and forget all about what I had just seen.

But very few of us function on such a cool, rational basis. Besides, I was simmering inside, from just plain horniness because my man hadn't made love to me for so long. I *had* to know what was going on down in that building.

I quickly pulled on some clothes and went tripping lightly down the stairs. I tried to stay in the shadows as I made my way across the big yard, and as far as I could tell no one had detected me by the time I made it to the shadows beneath Carmen's window.

Crouched low under the partially open window, I could

easily hear Javier and Carmen talking together inside. That was nice, I thought. They *are* just talking.

Then I began to understand what they were talking about. "I thought you would never come," Carmen was saying.

"It was not easy for me to make the decision to do so," Javier replied.

"That woman means so much to you, then?"

"Yes, she does. She's my woman."

"What do *I* mean to you, then?" Carmen asked bitterly.

"A great deal."

"Hah! You say that. But how do you show me? What do you give Carmen?"

"I have something to give you tonight."

"I do not believe you."

"Then I will show you."

I heard the sound of two people coming together. Actually it sounded more like a struggle. "No!" Carmen hissed. "I will not take the leftovers you bring from the bed of that woman."

"I have not made love to her for days, Carmen. I have been thinking of you."

"Then leave her! Leave her!"

A low groan from Javier. "I cannot. I need her, I want her, I have to have her, there . . . in the house. But I need you too . . ."

"No . . . no . . . no . . ." I heard Carmen almost sob. "Don't . . ."

I heard the sound of cloth tearing. "Oh! Your hands!" Carmen gasped. "Your mouth . . . !"

There was nothing but panting after that, then the creak of a heavy weight descending on a bed. "Oh, Javier . . . Javier!" I heard Carmen cry out, and after that only the rhythmic slapping of naked bodies, the heavy breathing and murmured endearments of two people making love. For a moment I almost burst into the room to confront my two-timing lover and my rival, but some basic instinct of self-preservation held me back and instead I walked away from that window on unsteady legs, desperately trying to think.

In the first place, I was not in a position of strength. This was Javier's turf. If I broke in on the middle of his passionate coupling with Carmen and faced him now, I knew I would humiliate him so badly that *he* would never forgive *me*. I would drive a wedge between us that could never be removed. What he was doing, after all, was an inescapable part of his culture. The Latin male was *expected* to have hidden lovers on the side; it was a measure of his manhood. The Latin culture, however, did not extend that same privilege to women. It was the good old Double Standard, or, as it is called in South America, the Law of the Funnel, with the man's part being the big and open end, and the woman's narrow and circumscribed. I had no doubt that if I took the same liberties Javier was taking, he might indeed kill me out of rage and wounded pride. And at the same time he was killing me he would not be loving me any the less.

If I had been back on my own turf, New York, say, or Paris or London, I would probably have shrugged and said, okay, my lover's getting a little on the side, and so will I. There would have been a certain freedom in that, and perhaps it would have even strengthened our caring for one another. It is, after all, very easy to get bored with the same bed partner if that is the only bed partner you have.

But here I had no options. This was a small, inbred community in which news traveled fast, and even if I did find a man willing to brave Javier's rage, I'd never get away with it for long. But dammit! I couldn't permit him to leave me itching with horniness half the time while he was getting it off with Carmen!

I just *had* to have another sexual outlet or something would snap between Javier and me, and I didn't want that because I still loved the arrogant sneak. I could not, however, get over the memory of that knife sticking out of Rodrigo's chest. I didn't want any more of that and if I were even *seen* too much in the company of any one man, all hell would break loose. The only people I could feel relaxed and comfortable with here were women, like . . .

Of course! A woman! Javier had said he would wipe me out if I made love to a man. But he'd said nothing about a woman, and I was a switch-hitter. I like cunt almost as much as cock, and as long as I was thinking of cunt, *concha* in Spanish, I started thinking about sweet, lovely, sexy little Conchita. There was my answer!

Of course, I would have to convince Conchita of that, which might be something of a problem. But at least I had a direction to head in. I'd show that sexy male-chauvinist Javier that I was as good at playing games as he was.

I was feeling pretty good when Javier dropped in on me the next morning and I let him make love to me. After all, why cut off my own nose to spite another's face, as my old grandmother used to say? I still loved the feel of his cock in me, the weight and strength of his body, and, well, him too! Predictably he was acting pretty smug when he left. With both me and Carmen, he had the best of two worlds.

I lazed around the house until Javier had left to make his day's rounds of his empire. Within minutes after he had ridden away, I left the house and tracked down Conchita. God, she was a cute little thing! "Come on," I said. "Let's go up to my room."

That unnerved her. She had never been into the main house. "Never?" I asked. "But where did you and Javier . . . ?"

She was blushing so furiously by now that I gave up on that line of questioning. She was so innocent in so many ways, but that would make it all the more exciting to . . . My *God*, I thought, I was becoming a dirty old woman!

I managed to coax the girl up to my room. She looked around her in awe. "So magnificent!" she breathed softly.

I saw that she was staring particularly hard at my closet. I looked at her rather critically. "We're about the same size," I said. "Would you like to try on some of my clothes?"

"Oh, Christina, I couldn't," she stammered.

"Nonsense. I insist." Of course I did. That's how I'd get her clothes off her. I picked out a nice little dress and held it up in front of her. "Try this one," I said.

Glowing happily, Conchita took off the old, rather shapeless dress she was wearing, exposing a pair of panties that reached from her navel to halfway down her thighs. God, they were ugly! And she was wearing a bra that looked as if it had been made of parts of old inner tubes. It didn't fit her at all and mashed her breasts way out of shape. I let her put the dress on over these monstrosities, and it was such a nice, simple little dress that it looked good on her despite the horrors beneath. "Oh," she exclaimed gleefully, "it's beautiful."

"Then it's yours," I replied. "I never wear it. It's a little too full for me around the hips, but it fits you perfectly."

She protested and protested that she couldn't possibly accept such a queenly gift, but I knew her heart wasn't really in her protests. She wanted that dress. I loved her for being such a modest little sweetheart, but I finally got my way by mentioning how much Mario would like seeing her in the dress, and she accepted.

"Now I want to see you in something really nice," I said. I'm sure you have the figure for it."

This time I selected a really slinky evening gown, cut very low and quite form-fitting around the hips and ass. Conchita took off her new dress, laying it reverently on the bed, and then still wearing her Salvation Army undergarments, she wriggled into the evening dress. "Uh-uh. That won't do," I said, shaking my head. "Not with that bra and those panties."

It was really quite a sight. The bra stuck up out of the cleavage of the gown quite hideously, and lower down one could easily see the gross line of her bulky panties beneath all that slinky material. "Frankly, Conchita," I said, "the only way to wear this gown is without anything at all underneath it. Come on . . . let's try it that way."

By now Conchita was so fascinated by this wonderful game of trying on expensive clothes that she forgot to be bashful. She stripped off the gown and started unhooking her bra. What a difference that made! Without all that cloth and elastic her tits assumed their natural shape. The girl had the most beautiful breasts! Sure, I thought in sudden anger. Nothing but the best for my greedy Javier.

"The panties, too," I said. "They ruin the line of the gown."

Conchita hesitated for a second, then bent down and gracefully stepped out of her panties. What a sweet little snatch! A neat vee of curly black pussy fur nestled right in the center of a lovely curving sweep of hips and thighs and soft belly. My mouth was really watering by now. However, I had to help Conchita on with the dress. I hated covering up all that sexy lushness, but I made sure as I settled the dress down over her shoulders that my hands rubbed lightly over her tits. She was quite sensitive. Even with that little bit of stimulation, her nipples puckered slightly. "There," I said, fondly patting her ass low down so that her cunt would get a little shock. "Doesn't that look nice?"

The girl was staring at her reflection in the mirror obviously unable to believe what she was seeing. "Is that me?" she asked in awe.

"Yes, it is, Conchita. And you are a very beautiful woman."

That was not an overstatement. The girl positively glowed. Her thick, dark, slightly wavy hair, with its auburn highlights, trailed down over her lovely bare shoulders. There was just enough Indian in her to give her large dark eyes an exotic tilt. Her breasts, full and firm and thrusting out boldly from her slender rib cage, filled the top of the dress to perfection. I thought of offering her this dress, too, but realized there would be no way for her to wear it at Rancho Del Sol. Besides, I wanted it back. It was one of my favorites. And I wanted it off her right now.

Conchita was quite a different person as I slowly lifted the gown over her head. She had just glimpsed possibilities in herself that she had never before imagined. As I hung the dress up again, she seemed to forget that she was standing there naked. "You didn't realize you were so beautiful, did you, Conchita?" I asked softly, stepping up next to her. She shook her head in a daze, not denying it. She was still staring into the mirror. It occurred to me that this might be the first full-length mirror she had ever seen.

"You have lovely breasts," I said. "Why do you wear that horrible bra? It pushes you all out of shape—like this." And using my hands, I demonstrated what happened to those lovely tits when she profaned them with her old bra. She looked down at my hands cupping around her breasts, a little look of wonder on her face. "You'd be better off wearing nothing," I said, slowly letting her breasts assume their true shape again, but making sure my thumbs slid lingeringly over her nipples. She gave a little shudder, and her nipples hardened again.

"And those panties. They ride too high—and too low. Good panties should reach no higher than here," and I drew an imaginary line with my finger around her body, just above her pussy hair in the front, and dipping down a little into the crack of her ass behind. Once again she shuddered and her eyes were big as she looked at me.

It was now or never. "You know . . . we're built so much alike," I said. "Particularly our breasts. See?" I quickly pulled off my blouse, baring my tits. I stuck them right next to hers so that our nipples grazed lightly. I passed my hands over my breasts, then over hers. "They even feel the same. Here . . . you feel."

I took the girl's hands and laid them on my breasts. She started to pull away. "I . . . I've never touched another woman."

"Oh, come on," I urged. "After all, if you can wear my clothes . . . what could be more intimate than that?"

Once again I guided her hands to my breasts. She touched them rather timidly at first, then began to get interested. "They're so warm!" she said.

"Just like yours," I replied, reaching out to caress hers. God, they were lovely tits. She gasped a little as my thumbs closed on her nipples, then looked me straight in the eye. I could see from the expression on her face that she was beginning to sense what I wanted to do. I saw an instant's hesitation and fear but it was quickly replaced by a kind of daring curiosity. She looked down at my tits again. "Your nipples are hard," she said matter-of-factly.

"Sure. Because it feels so good when you touch them. Your nipples are hard, too."

"Christina . . . I . . ."

"You're so beautiful, Conchita." I was beginning to kneel in front of her as I said this. As I dropped lower, her breasts grazed my face. I kissed her right nipple, then her left. I felt her body jump a little, but she didn't push me away, so I boldly took one of her nipples in my mouth and began to suck. I heard her breath suck in sharply. She didn't seem to know what to do with her hands. Several times they fluttered undecidedly behind my head. I don't know if she was trying to get up the nerve to push my head away or pull it more tightly against her.

She started shaking all over. I felt her legs beginning to go, so I guided her down onto the edge of the bed. As she sat there I moved in between her legs, still kneeling. Now I had to bend down to reach her tits with my mouth, but it was worth the trip. Her nipples were very hard and she was breathing heavily. "Wait," she moaned softly. "We really shouldn't . . ."

"Of course we should," I murmured around my mouthful of nipple.

"But! But . . ."

Her words continued to register protest, but not her body. She placed her hands behind her on the bed and thrust those gorgeous tits out ahead of her, right into my face. "Oh . . . it does feel so good . . . so wonderful . . ." she whimpered. "Like when . . ."

She abruptly shut up. I had no doubt she had been about to say, "Like when Javier used to do it." Yes, he could really suck a tit, as I well knew. I was afraid that her sudden memory of Javier might break the spell, but if anything, it increased her passion. Perhaps she was also thinking of Mario, whom she loved and desired but who, out of his misplaced loyalty to Javier, had not touched her. As horny as I was, I suspect innocent little Conchita was far hornier.

Sensing this, I gently pushed her over onto her back. She lay there, legs trailing over the edge of the bed, breasts rising and falling rapidly as her beathing got more and more out of control. I was already in between her legs, staring down at her sweet cunt. What a little jewel; it was certainly glittering like one, with all that shiny liquid gushing from deep inside. Conchita was by now so excited that she had pussy juice running halfway down her thighs. I inhaled the rich musky odor of it.

"Even your pussy is beautiful, Conchita," I breathed as I skidded my fingers through the goo.

"Christina!" she burst out once.

"Yes?" I answered.

She hesitated a moment. "Nothing."

I slowly ran my thumbs over the thick pads of her pussy lips. Juice literally squirted out at me. I parted her labia. What a rich feast lay inside, all that shining wet pinkness, the lovely, twisting folds of her inner labia, the slowly pulsing opening to her vagina, the already swollen knob of her clitoris peeking shyly out from behind its protective covering.

"Oh . . . it's been so long!" Conchita moaned as I slowly shoved one of my fingers up into her pussy hole. Her hips bucked upward and her twat opened hungrily, eager to swallow as much of my hand as it could.

"I'm going to show you something now," I told the girl. "I'm going to do something to you you'll never forget."

"Oh, yes . . . please!" she panted, writhing wildly on the bed. I smiled, then moved my mouth close to her gushing cunt, and extending my tongue, making it broad and flat, shoved it deep into her slit just above where my finger protruded from her vagina, and stroked it slowly and lovingly upward. "A-aa-aaa-aaaa-aaaaaaahhhhh," Conchita moaned loudly, her legs rising off the floor and sticking straight out on either side of my body. They began to shudder violently.

The rich taste of the girl's pussy filled my mouth. God, it had been a long time since I'd done this! I squirmed into a more comfortable position, squatting on my heels at the foot of the bed, with Conchita's twat poised on the edge right in front of me. It was a good angle. I always try to avoid the possibility of whiplash from a particularly strong buck when I'm eating a woman. I hoisted her legs up high and settled them over my shoulders.

Then I began to dine in earnest. My tongue darted in and out of the girl's slit, sometimes replacing my finger inside her vagina, sometimes stabbing directly against her clit, sometimes simply doing a quick little dance up and down the length of that hot, swollen, dripping little valley.

I'd chosen well. Conchita went out of her mind, producing some of the prettiest moans and squeals I've ever heard. I managed to reach up high enough to get my hands on her tits, only to find her own hands had beat me there. She was wildly pinching her nipples, which by now were swollen soft and big. So I concentrated on her cunt, finally sucking her clit deep into my mouth where I could worry it with my teeth and tongue.

That was too much for Conchita. She went absolutely wild, her cunt exploding into a series of cataclysmic orgasms that instantly flooded my mouth and nose with gushing pussy juice. More dangerously, her legs, formerly lying on top of my shoulders and trailing down my back, suddenly clamped tightly together with my head in between them like an old-fashioned nutcracker. The pressure was terrible, and with my mouth and nose buried in her spasming cunt, I thought I was either going to suffocate or drown.

But Conchita finally reached the end of her endurance and collapsed onto the bed, begging for mercy. I quickly pulled my mouth away from her snatch, gulping big lungfulls of air.

I climbed up onto the bed next to Conchita. Her eyes were wild as she looked up at me. "Wonderful . . . it was wonderful," she babbled. She took a good look at my face. "Is that shiny stuff all over you from . . . from *me*?" she gasped.

I nodded yes. "I want to taste it," she hissed, and was suddenly kissing and licking my face, my mouth. My God, I thought, once you turn this girl on, you can't turn her off. She was writhing against me, her tits pushing against mine, one of her legs rising to half encircle my body. I could feel the wet, furry heat of her cunt pressing against my thigh. She pulled away for a moment. "Christina," she panted. "I want you to show me how you do that wonderful thing you did to me."

"Well . . . of course . . ."

"Because I want to do it to *you*!"

Jackpot.

CHAPTER TWENTY

For the next couple of weeks I was as happy as a clam. Conchita and I made it together at least twice a day. Under my expert instruction, the girl had become one of the best pussy-eaters I had ever known. She loved it, she couldn't get enough. "I hope Mario will let me do this to you when we finally get married," she bubbled to me one afternoon. "I don't think I could live without it."

"So you two *do* want to get married," I said thoughtfully.

"I love him, Christina."

"You'll probably have to go away from here if that's what you want."

"I know. I have been talking to Mario. I think he will eventually realize that. He's so loyal to Javier, though. And where else could he get such a good job? Times are very hard now, Christina."

That conversation, and others like it, got me started thinking. To realize their dream of being together, Mario and the girl would undoubtedly have to leave the ranch. And what about me? What about my personal dreams, my life, my work? I was a newspaper woman, not the chatelaine of a ranch!

It was Javier who was holding us all here. Mario was devoted to the man, and of course *I* loved him! Now that I had my daily physical outlets with Conchita, I was a lot less tense around him. He seemed to sense this and responded by making love to me more often. For a while it was very nice. We all had a good thing going—me with Conchita and of course Javier was still sneaking out several nights a week, getting his with Carmen. Rather a nice, civilized arrangement.

Until the day Javier caught me and Conchita with mouthfuls of each other's cunts. I thought he'd earlier gone way out into the prairie, but he'd only been guiding a work crew around the outer corrals. He walked into my bedroom to find the two of us entangled in a really lovely 69, which he didn't appreciate at all. I first realized he was there when I heard a low, strangled *"Mierda"* from the doorway. That means shit. I twisted around, my heart knocking strongly as I saw my self-appointed lord and master standing there just inside the doorway, staring at us unbelievingly.

Conchita saw him at about the same time and with a squeaking cry of fright shot out from underneath me with incredible agility and stood trembling next to the bed, half-crouched as if for flight. "You little whore," Javier snarled, starting toward her. But I put myself in between them.

"You hypocrite," I screamed. "If you harm her, I'll kill you if it's the last thing I ever do."

That surprised Javier so much that Conchita had time to snatch up her clothes and dart out into the hall. With her safely gone, I started to breathe a little easier. I felt really protective toward the girl. Javier continued to glare at me for several more seconds, then he stormed out of the room, slamming the door behind him.

I quickly dressed and went after Conchita. I found her sobbing in her room. "He will kill me," she wailed.

"He won't dare," I reassured her. "But he *may* send you away."

"B-But . . . M-Mario," she blubbered.

"If he doesn't go with you, then he's not the right man," I said.

"H-How would we live?"

I dug into my pocket and pulled out the largest of the

uncut emeralds Javier had given me. "A wedding present," I said.

Conchita stared at the stone. It was easily worth forty thousand dollars, a very nice wedding present indeed. "But . . . I couldn't," she hesitated.

"Stop that, Conchita. You're owed it after all the trouble you've been through here. Talk to Mario. See what he says."

She gulped and agreed. Then it was my turn go face the music. I returned to the house and found Javier sitting in the study. To my surprise, he was drunk. I had not seen him drink more than a little wine or brandy since I had come to Rancho Del Sol, but now he was really sloshed. "You perverted whore," he said to me bitterly when I came into the room.

"Don't be so self-righteous," I snapped back. "You told me I couldn't have any other men, and at the same time you started ignoring me. Well . . . I went by the letter of your damned law. I took a woman. Now, tell me, in your male-oriented book of right and wrong, does that make me unfaithful or not?"

That shook him a little. "I . . . you've betrayed me with another person, no matter how you try to twist the facts."

"Oh, you prig," I snorted. "And what did you think you were doing to me? With Carmen?"

That really rocked him. He had not thought I knew. At first he looked embarrassed, then angry. I had embarrassed his macho pride by baring his infidelity and hypocrisy. I saw him retreat into a shell, which he lubricated with another huge slug of whiskey. He shuddered, then murmured, "I won't give her up—Carmen."

"I'm not asking you to. But I won't give up Conchita either."

"You will if I send her far enough away."

"If she goes, I go."

"That will never happen unless I say you can go."

"You son-of-a-bitch, if you push me far enough, I'll get out of here if I have to crawl all the way to Bogotá on my hands and knees."

"Then that may be the way you leave."

Neither of us said anything else for a while, just sat there and felt our love dying around us. Javier continued to belt down the booze. He was really drunk when he looked up at me again. There was a crafty look in his eyes I didn't like. "You really like doing that, then?" he mumbled.

"Doing what?"

"Making love to another woman."

"Depends on the woman. On the circumstances. I actually prefer men, but they're not that available around here."

"We'll see," he said. Then he got up, lurching a little, and going to the door, called one of the servants. He gave him some low-voiced instructions I couldn't hear, then came and sat back down again. A few minutes later I heard a tapping on the door. "Come in," Javier shouted.

The door opened. "You sent for me, Javier," a woman's voice said. Carmen started to enter the room, but stopped dead when she saw me.

"Yes," Javier said. "I don't think you've officially met my companion, Christina van Bell. I'd like you two to get to know one another. Get to know one another very well."

Carmen was poised by the door, like a cat trying to decide between fight or flight. I suddenly felt sorry for her, because I had a pretty good idea of what Javier had in mind.

"Come in all the way, Carmen," Javier said somewhat sharply. She obeyed, moving to the very center of the room where she stood rigidly still. "You love me, don't you, Carmen?" Javier said abruptly.

Carmen started to reply but cast a quick look at me and clamped her lips shut. "Please . . . tell the truth," I said gently.

"You know I do, Javier," she said quietly.

"And you'd do anything for me?" he prompted.

"You know that."

"Yes," he said. "You swore once that you would. Does that still hold true?"

"Forever," she said with great certainty. She had become more sure of herself, as if having faced me on my own ground, she now felt she could handle anything thrown her way. I felt a certain grudging admiration for this proud, beautiful woman. I hoped Javier would not do anything to break the obvious trust she had in him.

"Good," Javier said. "Then I want you to take off your clothes."

A look of immense surprise passed over the girl's face. Perhaps she had been expecting Javier to order her to knife me. I believe she would have done that with great gusto. She stood uncertainly, looking quickly from Javier to me. "Don't do this to her, Javier," I said.

He looked coldly at me, then back at Carmen. "If you love me, do as I say," he snapped.

Carmen shrugged, and then began to disrobe. As unhappy a scene as it was, I could not help admiring the girl's body as it emerged bit by bit, lush and strong with deep, firm breasts, incurving stomach, outcurving hips, a thick dark bush of glossy pubic hair, and such pride of stance that it magnified her already considerable beauty tenfold.

She finally stood naked in front of us. "Do you think she is as desirable as Conchita?" Javier asked coolly.

"You should know. You've had them both."

"So," he hissed. "The little bitch told you that. She'll pay."

"Oh, no, Javier," I burst out. "She didn't volunteer the information, I tricked it out of her. It doesn't really matter to me, anyhow, but for God's sake, don't take our problems out on that innocent girl."

"You want me to spare her. But I have to warn you, Conchita's welfare is completely in your hands at the moment. If you do as I say . . ."

"Which is . . . ?"

"That you do to Carmen just as you were doing with Conchita. In front of me."

I faced my lover. "If you think you're punishing me, Javier, you're not. Carmen is a beautiful and desirable woman. I myself have nothing against doing what you say. What bothers me is what it might do to Carmen. If you force me to do this, Javier, then I have to warn you, it's all over between you and me."

"A very pretty little speech," Javier sneered. "But Carmen will be happy to do as I want her to do." He turned to Carmen. "Lie down on the carpet," he told her.

Before she did as Javier ordered, Carmen actually smiled at me. It was a triumphant smile. She was about to demonstrate the advantage she had over me—her complete loyalty to Javier. By now she knew what was supposed to happen, and when she lay down on the carpet, she opened her legs wide, baring her cunt, a bright pink gash against the darker background of her pubic hair.

Javier looked pointedly from me to Carmen. "Well?" he prompted. I noticed a gleam in his eyes that had not been there before. He was starting to get turned on. I don't know if it was because of what he expected Carmen and I to do to each other, or if it was his knowledge of the absolute power he had over us both.

I dropped to my knees in between Carmen's outstretched legs, running my hands slowly up the inside of her thighs. I could feel solid muscles underneath smooth, soft skin. Carmen let out a little sigh, partly of resignation, but I thought I also detected a note of something else. Fear? Excitement?

"No," Javier said, interrupting. "I want you to take your clothes off, too, Christina. I want to see you both naked together." I had nothing against that. Hell, I'd take away his triumph by not fighting back. Besides, Carmen was so lovely . . . I quickly stripped, then kneeling once again, got to work. There was no point in using a lot of foreplay. I suspected Carmen would only jeer at me. So, bending down I rammed my stiffened tongue deep into the girl's slit.

I got more of a reaction than I'd expected. A powerful shudder shook Carmen's lovely frame. I felt her legs tremble a little. God, even half-willing she was reacting strongly.

I used every bit of art I knew to bring Carmen toward orgasm. My recent exercises with Conchita had gotten me into practice and I soon had Carmen writhing and twisting on the carpet, but she refused to utter a sound. Not until Javier suddenly loomed over us. His mocking manner was completely gone now. He was looking down at us with something like awe on his face. "My God . . . you two are so incredibly beautiful together," he murmured. "Your coloring . . . such a marvelous contrast."

I suppose my blond hair was by now spreading out over Carmen's dark-skinned thighs and darker bush as my face burrowed deeper into her crotch. Javier knelt beside us. Only then did Carmen finally speak. "Touch my breasts, Javier," she pleaded, her eyes fastened hungrily on this man she so obviously loved.

I managed to look up enough to see Javier's powerful fingers sinking into the creamy flesh of the girl's swollen breasts. Her nipples peaked rapidly, and now she began to moan steadily, whether from my licking of her cunt or from what Javier was doing to her tits I didn't know, but I suspected a little of both.

Then Javier was suddenly standing, tearing off his clothes. His cock sprang free, rigid, hard, jutting out from his body. The sight of that familiar organ, which had brought me so much pleasure suddenly inflamed me. Jesus, I wanted it!

I got it. Javier quickly knelt behind me. I had my ass in the air, head down, the better to eat Carmen, and now I felt Javier's hands on my buttocks, steadying me as he fed his cock up into my cunt. "Mmmmnnnppphhhhh!" I mumbled into Carmen's snatch. Oh, God, how everything had suddenly changed. Now there were three of us, and we were no longer separated.

Carmen's hands rose, playing softly over my head. "Oooohhhh . . . suck me," she hissed. "Stick your tongue into me. I look up and see Javier behind you, know his cock is in you, and I can imagine that your tongue is his cock going all the way through you and into me."

Sex had performed its age-old magic, taking our emotions of hate and fear and distrust, and at least for a little while, converting them in the crucible of passion into something approaching love. I reveled in the rich taste of Carmen's lovely cunt, thrilled to the feel of Javier's cock lancing into me from behind. Just as I came, I pulled my mouth away from Carmen's gushing slit and cried out, "I love you, Javier!"

Then he was rolling me out of the way, and I watched his cock plow into Carmen's body. It was beautiful to watch them make love. They melded together like two halves of the same person. I saw her body arch hungrily up toward his, saw his cock plunge deeper and deeper, finally heard the familiar sounds of his orgasm as he started to come inside her. A bright red flush spread upward over Carmen's breast, suffusing her dusky skin with a lovely glow.

And then it was over and we were three very confused people. Javier sat on the floor, hands on knees, staring moodily at the far wall. "I think I've always wanted to do this," he said. "With the two of you at the same time. You see, the problem is I love you both. I can't stand the thought of losing either of you."

I sighed. "You seem to mix up love and possession, Javier. It's taken me a long time, but I know for sure what your real love is . . . Rancho Del Sol. Admit it."

He started to open his mouth, but no sound came out. "And Carmen is part of Rancho Del Sol," I continued. "You and she and the land are all one thing. As for me . . . well, you tried to tell me a long time ago, on that ship in the Mediterranean. You and I are from two different worlds, and I miss that world, Javier. I want to go back to it."

"No, no . . . I can't let you!"

"And I'm taking Conchita and Mario with me," I continued.

"What? But why?"

"They're in *love*, you Colombian klutz! Haven't you got any eyes?"

He seemed thunderstruck. "I never thought . . . But why must they go away?"

"Think! You're a Latin male. Do you think Mario could ever be comfortable being married to Conchita here, taking orders every day from her former lover?"

Javier groaned. "It's too much . . . I'm losing everything . . ."

I put his hand on Carmen's breast. "Really?" I asked acidly.

I suppose we could have gone round and round, but we were suddenly pulled from this homey little scene by an enormous uproar outside. There were shouts and yells and someone was furiously ringing a bell. "The alarm!" Javier shouted, springing to his feet and pulling on his clothes. Carmen began to dress, too, and not wanting to be the only nudist around, I did the same.

María met us in the hallway. "Some of the scouts from

down by the river report that a large group of bandits is heading this way. They think it's Don Narciso.''

"It had to happen sooner or later," Javier said. Then he began rapping out orders, deploying his men. There were people rushing everywhere. He turned to Carmen. "Go to the cellar with the other women," he told her.

"I refuse, Javier," she snapped back. "My place is at your side."

Javier hesitated, then nodded, a glow of pride in his eyes. He turned toward me. "Don't look at me that way," I stammered. "I hate bullets."

I do hate bullets, but I would have remained beside Javier if I'd thought it would have helped. But it was so much better this way—having only Carmen at his side would point out to him very clearly which of us, myself or Carmen, belonged on the ranch. I think he saw what I was doing.

"I understand," he said. "But, then, you must leave here. It is you Don Narciso is after, I sense it. Pack a small bag, just a few things. You have only a few minutes."

I ran upstairs, my mind in a turmoil. I had not wanted to leave this way, in a panic, without one last loving look at this marvelous land, this beautiful house. But Javier was right, I only had minutes, and he might change his mind once the danger was over—if any of us survived.

I took only my emerald pendant and some of the smaller stones and a flower that Javier had plucked for me with his own hand a few weeks before. I had kept it pressed in a book. With these few possessions, I was soon running back downstairs, dressed once again in trail garb.

Mario was entering the house just as I got to the bottom of the stairs. Javier laid a hand on his arm. "I want you to do something for me," he said. Mario nodded. I could see the hero worship in his eyes. "Take my woman, Christina, and her friend, Conchita, and get them safely away from here.''

"But . . . Javier," Mario protested. "My place is here
. . . with you. We have always fought together."

I could see warring emotions flickering across Mario's
face as he said this. Here was his chance to leave with the
woman he loved, but his loyalty to Javier was greater.

"For me . . . do it for me, then," Javier said fiercely.
"I do not want these women here when Don Narciso
arrives. Who else but you could I trust with a task as
important as this?"

Mario nodded, but there was still sorrow in his eyes. He
turned and ran to fetch Conchita. Javier and I were alone
for a moment. We flew into one another's arms. "This is
not easy," Javier murmured into my ear.

"You bet your arrogant ass it isn't," I sobbed back. I
was coming apart and couldn't help myself.

"It would be easier to get killed in the fight."

"Don't you dare!" I warned tearfully.

"It was beautiful, Christina."

"Beautiful."

And then there were others in the room. Mario was back
with Conchita. She was wearing the dress I had given her.
Something was clenched in her fist. I imagined it was the
emerald I had given her. "Come on . . . come on!" Mario
shouted. "We have only seconds."

I let go of Javier and started out of the room. I caught
sight of Carmen standing a few feet away. Our eyes met
for a moment. "Thank you," she said to me. "You are a
lot of woman."

"Take care of him," I murmured, and then we left.

"Go with God, Christina," I heard Javier call out.

The three of us, myself and Mario and Conchita, ran
down toward the little tributary river. There was a flat-
bottomed boat waiting for us. We clambered in and immediately shoved off. The boat spun out toward the center of
the stream, which was about a hundred yards wide, then
the current caught us.

That's when the attack began—a storm of shouting and pounding hooves and gunfire. We crouched low in the boat, watching tidal waves of bandits surge across the open plain, surrounding the hacienda and its outbuilding. I was certain that the white-haired figure leading the charge was Don Narciso. The bandits were met by a wall of lead as the defenders fired back. I saw men and horses go down and heard screams of agony.

And then, as the boat came opposite the main house, I saw Javier standing on one of the upper balconies, a pistol in his hand as he shouted orders to his men. Standing next to him, her long black hair blowing in the wind, was Carmen, coolly firing a rifle into the press of attackers below. At that moment I knew I had made the right decision—Javier and Carmen belonged side by side. Joined together, they perfectly epitomized the spirit of this incredible land.

We were spotted. Several horsemen veered in our direction. Bullets began to churn up the water between us and the shore. Mario fired back with his pistol, but the range was too great. The horsemen tried to follow us. They almost got close enough to hit us, but Javier had planned well. About a quarter of a mile below the house the ground sank away into a sticky marsh. I saw the bandits' horses bog down and suddenly we were away free, moving farther and farther downstream. I suppose I should have felt relief—we were out of danger—but all I could think of was that wonderful image of Javier and Carmen, standing together defending their home.

God, how I loved that man.

CHAPTER TWENTY-ONE

The rest was anticlimactic. We continued downstream until our tributary joined the Vaupés. After that it was a slow cruise to the provincial capital of Mitú on the edge of the Amazon jungle. Using the magic of my credit rating, I chartered the three of us a plane to Bogotá where I had some final business to transact. First, I activated the documents that returned ownership of my mountain property to Gabriel, contingent on his letting Mario and Conchita buy in on the deal with the proceeds from the sale of the emerald I had given Conchita.

In Bogotá, we learned from a friend of Mario's that the bandits had been beaten off from Rancho Del Sol. Don Narciso had died in the fight. Javier and Carmen had survived, although Javier had been lightly wounded.

I gave a sigh of relief, then made arrangements to fly back to New York. There were many tears at the airport as I said good-bye to Conchita and Mario, but once on the plane I sat, stunned, all during the takeoff. However, once in the air, banking toward the northeast, I could not help looking out the window at the rugged, wild land below, particularly toward the east, where the mountains fell away and I could see the light green haze of the plains, the Llanos Orientales, stretching away into infinity. I felt something tear inside me, and for a moment I believed that I would have to go back, but then I realized that if I stayed this land would break my heart, and I realized also that I had never really been a part of it.

Once again, I had simply been passing through.